THE
STONEHENGE
MURDERS

THE
STONEHENGE
MURDERS

A DINO ROSELLI NOVEL

Herb Hemenway &
LindaSue Johnson

The Stonehenge Murders

Contact info:
hemenwayandjohnsonbooks.com
herbhemenway.com
lindasuejohnson.com

ISBN: 979-8-9877071-0-4 (paperback)
979-8-9877071-1-1 (ebook)

Acknowledgments

First of all, special thanks to Alice for her detailed editing and comments, and to Greg for his consistent support and encouragement along the way.

We would like to thank Sergeant Shawna Curtis of the West Saint Paul Police Department for her review and critique of police procedures. We especially enjoyed our personal tour of the police station.

And we would also like to thank Detective Chief Inspector Eric Fegan of the Greater Manchester Police (retired), for his help with numerous questions. We owe you several pints the next time we are in England.

We need to thank Jill French, our editor, for keeping us on the straight and narrow, and for her numerous suggestions for making our book better.

Jonathan Sainsbury brought our book to life by creating a cover that starts the story before anyone turns a page. Thanks for teaching a couple of newbies how it's done.

Before the first sentence was written, Micah Whetstone helped us brainstorm the book concept with his always creative ideas. Thanks too for your work on our websites.

We feel obliged to recognize Sir Arthur Conan Doyle for his creative genius, expressed in the entire Sherlock Holmes canon. Here from Silver Blaze, in the Memoirs of Sherlock Holmes:

"Is there any point to which you would wish to draw my attention?"

"To the curious incident of the dog in the night-time."

"The dog did nothing in the night-time."

"*That* was the curious incident," remarked Sherlock Holmes.

And finally, we would like to thank you for purchasing and reading our book. It was great fun to write. We hope you enjoy it!

—Herb & LindaSue

Chapter 1

Saint Paul, Minnesota, USA
Present Day

E rik sat alone at a large table in a dark room lit only by a single white candle. He wore a black robe, with the hood pulled over his head. His body was motionless, but behind his closed eyelids his eyes moved rapidly, jerking left to right, up and down. The muscles of his body twitched randomly. His chest heaved and his arms came up. He raised his head, opened his eyes, and cried out, "They murdered her! They took my beloved Rayla and murdered her. The bastards! But this is not the end. I will get my revenge."

Erik Foster lived alone in a two-bedroom duplex apartment carved out of an old 1930s frame house in northwest St. Paul. All the rooms of the apartment were sparsely furnished, except for the second bedroom. That room was unique. It was a secret room that Erik kept locked and that no one ever entered, except Erik. He called it the Stonehenge Room. Erik Foster was more than just interested in Stonehenge—he was obsessed with Stonehenge.

His secret room had two small windows, both covered with full shades which were always drawn. There were shelves on one wall, and a personal computer with a monitor and printer against another wall. The center of attention however, was a wooden table holding a large-scale, detailed model of Stonehenge. It had taken Erik more than a year to construct the model. He had installed lighting in the ceiling, including a movable spot light, that could be dimmed to simulate scenes of bright daylight or nighttime twilight. The table top could rotate to duplicate the alignment of the sun at both the winter and summer solstice events. Nearly all his non-working hours were spent in his Stonehenge Room.

Erik was a loner. Always had been. He wore ragged jeans, old Jack Purcell bumpers, and a black T-shirt. As a little boy, he never seemed to fit in. He had few friends, and always ended up alone. His worried parents took him to the family doctor, who recommended a psychiatrist. With a combination of therapy and medications he survived high school. But he never had many friends. He seldom talked to women, much less dated them. He did not care about sports, music, cars, or anything else.

In his freshman year of college, Erik took a class on ancient civilizations and prehistoric monuments. It started out with the pyramids of Egypt, and continued on with the Great Wall of China, the Moai statues of Easter Island, and the Mayan ruins of Chichen Itza on the Yucatan Peninsula of Mexico. But when they got to Stonehenge, Erik's world stopped. He was home.

He gobbled up anything he could find on Stonehenge. He read books and magazine articles. He watched videos, documentaries, and movies. He was fascinated by the size and grandeur of the stones, their perfect positioning for the solar solstice and equinox alignments, and their alignment to celestial constellations. He thought about how the monument was built and why. At night, he dreamt about how it would have been to work on the stones. To belong to a group working toward a common goal. To be part of a team. To fit in. Everything about Stonehenge appealed to him immensely. He couldn't get enough of it.

One evening while studying, he stumbled upon the idea that there must have been some outside intelligence or force that provided the design and guidance to build the monument. *What else could explain it?* These were people with no written word, no system of mathematics, not even the wheel. *There must have been some outside influence.*

Then Erik discovered the book *Chariots of the Gods*, by Erich von Däniken. There it was—all laid out. How else could they have transported giant twenty-ton stones more than twenty miles over the countryside, worked them to a smooth finish with mortise and tenons to fit them together, and then placed them upright to align perfectly with the solar equinox and solstice? Totally convinced, he became a believer.

Bored with the rest of school, Erik started skipping classes. He stopped going to therapy and eventually stopped taking his medications as well. Soon after that, he proclaimed himself cured. He dropped out of college and instead enrolled in a computer programming course at a local vo-tech school. There he discovered he was a natural at programming, and flew through his classes.

On his drive home from school one day, he was listening to a rock music station and heard an ad for the Stonehenge Interest Group, which was meeting that night in Saint Paul. The ad said that anyone interested in Stonehenge was welcome to attend. Although Erik was an acute introvert, and reluctant to meet new people, he decided to give it a try.

The President of SIG was Tom Morris, who founded the group nearly twenty years ago and was still its enthusiastic leader. Tom had studied abroad during college, at the University of Sheffield, and fell in love with Stonehenge and English pale ales, not necessarily in that order. SIG had grown through the years from just a handful of guys sitting around drinking warm British beer and speculating about Stonehenge, to a pretty serious group of nearly a hundred.

"Welcome to the monthly meeting of the Stonehenge Interest Group, or as we affectionately refer to it, SIG! I would especially like to welcome all the newcomers here this evening. We're glad to have you with us.

"Stonehenge has been called the most mysterious place in the world. It's a place that begs endless questions: Why was it built? How was it built? When was it built? Why are there no markings or inscriptions on the stones? And on and on. The purpose of SIG is to explore these mysteries together as a group. Each month we examine, study, and even critique the work of archaeologists, historians, scientists, and laymen who attempt to answer these questions. You might think that there's nothing more to be learned from the old pile of rocks, but the exact opposite is true. New research is being conducted continually and new archaeological evidence is being uncovered all the time. New tools and tests are being developed to analyze not only recent evidence, but to reanalyze the evidence of the past."

Tom went on, "Each month, we select one topic and discuss it at length. We try to maintain an academic approach to our discussions. Everyone is entitled to their own opinions and interpretations, and we give all members a chance to express those opinions, no matter their perspective. Though we give preference to evidence and theories that are grounded in solid scientific research, we nearly always have some differing views, which result in, trust me, very lively discussions. And don't worry, there are no quizzes or tests.

"We like to get any items of club business and activities out of the way before we start our discussions. At the end of the meeting, we have a brief social time, where we enjoy a few good English ales together. Tonight, Fred Stanton has lined up some Marston's Pedigree, one of my favorites!

"So, there you have it . . . the method to our madness!

"Our sole item of business this month is a reminder that applications for our annual trip to Stonehenge are due this Friday. This year, as you know, we have arranged attendance for a limited number of members at the summer solstice activities on June 21st. This is a first for the club, and a once in a lifetime opportunity. There are only two slots left. We previously announced the costs and details for the trip. Please see me after the meeting if you're interested in going.

"So now, we're ready for our discussion topic for the evening, which is: Why are the stones laid out as they are? Where did this design come from? For reference, on the screen behind me, I have a diagram of Stonehenge as it would have existed at about 2,500 BC. There is, of course, the sarsen circle, with the bluestones . . .."

Erik found the discussion irresistible and had not missed a single meeting since. His involvement reinforced his total fascination with Stonehenge.

At the first few SIG meetings, Erik always sat at the back of the room by himself. When the main meeting ended, he left immediately, to avoid talking with people he did not know. After a few meetings, Erik noticed that there were several other guys who always sat in the back. Together, they looked like people who sit in the same pew week after week in church. They were much like him—interested, but quiet. He eventually struck up a conversation with one of them, then later with the others. They became a clique of like-minded friends that talked only among themselves.

Over time, Erik developed an interest in some of the fringe viewpoints of Stonehenge. He would discuss these viewpoints with his buddies in the group, and they typically agreed with him. However, these ideas often clashed with those put forth in the monthly meetings.

At this month's meeting, Tom was presenting the generally accepted archaeological explanation for the layout of Stonehenge. In the ensuing discussion, several members chimed in with agreement on the current popular explanation.

For the first time, Erik felt compelled to express his viewpoint publicly. As the unofficial spokesperson of their little group, Erik mustered his courage, stood up, and expressed a contrary opinion that the builders of Stonehenge had to have had some outside help with its design. He argued, "The builders were people who had no form of written word. With the work spanning a thousand years, how was the design communicated from generation to generation? Also, how could the design have incorporated not only the solar solstice events, but more abstract celestial alignments? I know many of you have heard of the book *Chariots of the*

Gods, by Erich von Däniken. He lays out a pretty convincing argument for the influence of advanced alien beings at Stonehenge, as well as at many other ancient monuments." As he spoke, his buddies nodded and muttered sympathetic support.

Tom responded, "I agree Chariots makes for interesting reading, and that von Däniken has a large following, but to me, it seems there is little actual evidence or demonstrable proof for his ideas." Tom felt he was being careful to keep things academic, but Erik felt Tom's tone was condescending, if not demeaning.

Erik backed off a bit, saying, "I grant you that there is safety in accepting the current archaeological explanation for the layout, but I think it ignores several real objections."

The discussion continued on for a time, ending with both sides agreeing to disagree.

Normally, Erik and the other members of their small group would leave as soon as the main meeting ended. However, this time, as they were getting up to leave, Tom came over and asked if they would like to hang around and have some English beer. Erik was still smarting from Tom's rebuke but glanced over at his buddies, shrugged his shoulders, and said, "Sure." His buddies looked surprised, but Tom made a point of extending the offer to them as well, and they decided to stay too.

As they stood drinking their beers, Tom emphasized that his earlier comments were "Nothing personal, there's just no proof."

Erik responded, "The very existence of Stonehenge, standing there today, is proof all on its own. No further proof is needed."

Just then, Tom's wife, Jennifer, joined them. Tom introduced her to Erik and his group and explained they were discussing some points brought up in the meeting. They continued on for a few minutes, but Erik was losing patience with the whole thing. Finally, he said he had to leave, as did the others. He thanked Tom for the beer, then turned to go. As he walked away, he smiled to himself. *I, of all people, ought to know about Stonehenge . . . I helped build it!*

Chapter 2

Dino Roselli was afraid it was another one. He got the call from Saint Paul Dispatch at 2:04 a.m., and when he heard the location was Frogtown, Dino knew it had to be another gang murder. *God, I hate those. No real clues, no real motive—nothing but another dead body. Just senseless violence that I get to write up in a 25-page report for the chief.*

From his house in the Cathedral Hill neighborhood Dino drove north on Dale Street, then east onto University Avenue, and immediately saw the flashing lights of squad cars and emergency vehicles several blocks up ahead. As he approached the scene, he did some quick math in his head. *Let's see, what will this make it?* Fifteen homicides so far this year, now sixteen, and it's only early May. At this rate, we'll hit over forty for the year. *Ouch! The mayor is going to be pissed.* Just last November, the newly elected mayor made crime reduction his major campaign issue. *There's going to be hell to pay.*

With the Light Rail Trains (LRT) still running in the center median of University Avenue, Dino pulled in behind one of the squads, got out, and walked over to the cop holding the perimeter of the crime scene with the familiar yellow tape.

"Hi Don, lucky you."

Having spent over sixteen years in the Police Department, Dino knew most of the patrol officers, at least the older ones.

"Yeah, I get all the good ones. George is right over there if you're looking for him."

"Thanks."

George Erickson was with the Gang/Gun Unit. He had a reputation as a good guy, who knew his stuff. George was standing next to a rusty old Honda Prelude that had crashed up onto the right-hand sidewalk and was wedged up against the building. The driver was still behind the wheel, slumped over, dead.

"Hey George, what've we got?"

"Hello Dino. I'll tell you what we've got . . . we've got to quit meeting like this—and especially at this time of night."

"Oh, come on, it's been almost a week, hasn't it?" Looking past George to the crashed car, he asked, "Just the one victim?"

"Yup. Young male, shot twice. Once in the upper chest from some distance, and once in the head at close range. Dead when the first patrol car got here."

There were three obvious slug holes in the driver's side door. The windows were down.

"We ran the plates, but records said they were reported stolen almost a month ago. Ran the VIN and it came up as stolen two weeks ago over in Minneapolis."

"So, what do you think, ambush?"

"Could be."

"Gang?"

"Almost certainly."

"Any idea which? The Downtown Dogz?"

"Maybe, but my guess would be the Midway Boys. They've been busy picking fights with everybody lately. There's a gun in the victim's car. Maybe he was looking for trouble."

After a pause, Dino commented, "God, I hate these cases. You get shit for evidence and no leads. Any shell casings?"

"Three so far. Look like .38 caliber to me. They're bagged up over in my car if you care to take a look."

"That's fine. You know them better than I do."

Dino continued, "Any security cameras around?"

"I've got two patrols going out four blocks in either direction along University, but they probably won't find many folks around until morning."

"You never know, once in a while we get lucky."

"Not often enough. The Medical Examiner should be here shortly. Crime scene guys will start processing the vehicle as soon as the ME gives the OK."

They talked a bit about the few details they had, a bit about office gossip that was going around, and the score of last night's Twins game. "What was the final score?" George asked.

Dino was about to reply when he heard a loud pop, followed by the heavy thud of a slug hitting the nearest squad car. Both Dino and George dove behind the squad. The shot appeared to have come from across the Light Rail median to the north. The shooter had to be at least thirty yards away. Dino pulled his gun and peered over the front hood of the car when he saw a muzzle flash, and heard another thud on the far side of the squad car. "Thank God this guy can't shoot!" he shouted to George as he pulled his head down behind the front hood of the squad.

George replied, "Damn it. I left my gun in the car!" He was unarmed.

Just then, they heard the rapid footsteps of someone running on the pavement behind them toward the victim's car. They both turned, Dino with his weapon up, and saw a masked man throw a glass bottle into the front seat of the car, then run back toward an alley on the side of a nearby building. Just before entering the alley, he swung his right arm around and fired two quick shots toward Dino and George, one whistled right by Dino and shattered the driver's side window of the squad car behind him.

A second later, there was a whoosh of wind and flames coming out of both windows of the crashed Honda, followed by an explosion that lifted the car several inches in the air, and shook Dino, George, and the squad car.

"What the hell was that?" George shouted, followed by, "You OK?"

"Yeah, I'm fine," said Dino, brushing some dust and sand from his shirt. He looked at the shattered window on the squad car and told George, "Damn, that last one was close." He thought for a moment, then added, "I think Mr. Lousy Shot was just a diversion for our buddy with the bottle."

"I think you're right," said George. "There was obviously

something in the car they didn't want us to find."

Both men stood and watched as the blaze grew in intensity, quickly consuming the victim and his car.

"Well, I think we can assume they won't be back," offered Dino. He holstered his sidearm, then called Dispatch for support with the fire.

"The ME is going to love this," said George.

"Me too," said Dino. "Gun shots and a fire? My 25-page report just went to a hundred pages."

It took less than five minutes for two fire trucks to arrive, and within just a couple of minutes, the fire was out. By then, however, the car was completely burned out, and any evidence that may have been in the vehicle was either burned up or flooded.

When the ME and his team showed up, they reviewed the sequence of events with Dino and George, and then started to process the scene. Despite the early morning hour, a group of onlookers had formed, and the uniformed cops were now dispersing them. Light Rail Trains had been halted earlier but were now allowed to resume. TV news teams from both Channel 7 and Channel 12 had appeared, eager to get a story for the early morning news.

Dino told George, "Time to let forensics do their thing. Why don't you take off George?"

"What about the TV guys?"

"I'll chat with the vultures this time, but I'll mostly just refer them to the Public Information Office in the morning. We'll release details to the press through regular channels."

"Sounds good to me. Thanks Dino."

"It's been a pleasure George, like always. Can I get a copy of your prelim first thing in the morning?"

"Sure."

"Oh, and let's not do this again for a while, OK?"

"We can only hope. See ya."

Dino spent ten minutes with the TV and other media reporters, then started to wrap up his own work. He left the scene sometime after 5 a.m.

As he headed back home, he thought how tragic these murders were. This victim appeared to be just seventeen or eighteen years old. Even though Dino had seen dozens of dead bodies in his seven years in homicide, he could still never really numb his feelings about them. *Hell, they're all frickin' tragic, and it can get to you after a while.*

His head finally hit the pillow just before six o'clock in the morning. It was a short night.

Dino was single, lived alone, and was never much for breakfast, preferring to just get up and get going. He showered, shaved, pulled a comb through his jet-black hair, and was headed to work by eight.

The St. Paul Police Department Headquarters is located on the northern edge of downtown, within a mile of the Minnesota State Capitol. The Homicide Unit keeps a low profile in the back of the nondescript, hundred-year-old building.

Dino found a parking spot at the far end of the lot, got out, and started walking toward the building. Fine spring days are rare in Minnesota, and you have to savor them whenever they come. Somehow, on this fine day, walking an extra 300 feet qualified as savoring.

He passed a cop heading out for patrol duty who said, "Hey big guy! You had some excitement last night."

Dino replied, "Yeah, I've been having a bit too much excitement lately. Have a good one, John."

Dino walked past the rows of squad cars and into the front entrance. He went down the hall, and just as he had done nearly every day for the last sixteen years, he looked up at the Wall of Honor—and the framed picture and plaque of his dad, Luca.

Dino was a second-generation Italian immigrant. Both his dad Luca, and his mother Sophia, had emigrated from Italy in 1975. Not long after arriving, Luca managed to join the St. Paul Police Department as a rookie beat cop, while his mother started an Italian restaurant in downtown St. Paul—Roselli's Ristorante. Luca loved being a cop. He always said he took the job because his family needed a steady income while Mom and the older kids were working to build the restaurant, but Dino knew his dad just plain loved being a cop. He loved the unpredictability of each day. And he loved the recognition he got in the community—an immigrant who had become a genuine part of their new home. He had a place.

Until the day that Jim MacGregor shot him dead.

There was a botched robbery of a corner convenience store on the East side. Dino was seventeen the day it happened. There was a big cop funeral for Luca, who died a hero. Dino would never forget the funeral—all the men in uniform, the loud rifle salutes, the hundreds of cop cars in the parade to the cemetery, and his entire family crying. He decided that very day that he would become a cop, just like his dad, in St. Paul, just like his dad.

Dino finished high school and went on to the University of Minnesota in Minneapolis to get a degree in criminology. Upon graduation, he applied for a job back in St. Paul, and started out as a patrol officer. He had a spotless record of service, and earned a promotion to the Homicide Unit after just nine years. To this day, he carries a worn photo of his dad in his wallet.

Dino continued on into the office, greeting everyone as he entered. "Good morning, one and all." He asked the unit admin, Carol Sullivan, if a prelim report about last night's case had come in from George Erickson.

She said, "Just got it fifteen minutes ago. New suit?"

"Nope, just a new tie, but thanks." Dino was just over 6-feet tall and slender, with brown eyes and a dark complexion that complemented his black hair. He was easily the best-dressed detective on the force. Dino liked the way expensive clothes felt, and how he felt in them.

He wandered over to Suzette Hawkins' desk. Suzette was a junior detective in the unit and often worked as support with Dino. "Good morning again, how was your evening?"

"Nothing special," she replied. "Went for a run, then vegged out on a movie. What's up?"

"I wanted to make sure you got a copy of the prelim report from George on last night's case. We need to start the workup ASAP. I know you have the Williams and Gonzales cases still in the works."

"Those are pretty much taken care of for the moment, they could sit for a day or two. I'll get started on this one right away."

"Thanks. Did we get a confirmed name yet?"

"Yup—Campbell."

"Great! Thanks Suzie. I appreciate it."

Suzette only allowed Dino to call her Suzie. It was sort of a mutual admiration thing they had, with a bit of history added on.

Dino continued on to Paula Dunn's office. Paula was the head of the unit. She had more than twenty years in homicide, was still sane, and very sharp. Dino enjoyed working for her. "Good morning. Got a few minutes for some details on the case from last night?"

"I do. Come on in." Dino filled her in with what they had, and did not have. They discussed details for release to the media, and Paula said she would get it all started up the chain.

"Suzette is helping on this one. I assume that's OK?"

"Sure."

"Perfect. We'll keep you updated."

"Thanks Dino."

Back at his desk, Dino mumbled quietly, "I hate gang murders." He hated that there were seldom any significant clues, never even one reliable witness, and never any motive, other than just gang members shooting other gang members. *For what, bragging rights? Just frickin' tragic. Just once in a while, it would be nice to play Sherlock Holmes, and do some real detecting.* In these cases, the best you could do was chase. He sometimes thought that maybe he had seen enough dead bodies and done enough chasing. Whatever, the case had to be processed, and promptly. Mayor Bennett would have to face the news media today and was no doubt going to be grilled brutally. Afterwards, he would, of course, take it out on his own staff. *Because that just makes sense, and will somehow motivate us to solve the case instantly. Really?*

Dino spent most of the morning on his own report. He checked with George a couple of times to see if he had any updates. No security video tapes, at least so far. No match on the shell casings either. *Crap.*

By mid-afternoon, he was dragging from the short night. By five, he had had enough for the day, and decided to head over to Roselli's to see his mom and have dinner. Mom had always told him, "Pasta makes great brain food."

Along with a good bottle of Chianti Classico.

Dino closed down for the day and headed out of the building. As he walked toward his car, thinking about the total futility and frustration of cases like this one, he admitted to himself, for the first time really, something that had been nagging him. A blasphemous something. An unthinkable something. *Oh my God, what if I don't want to be a cop anymore?*

Chapter 3

E rik was now totally consumed by Stonehenge. At the end of each day, he would rush home, often skip dinner, then go straight into his Stonehenge Room. After closing and locking the door, he would put on a black robe, sit down at the table, light a candle, and think about the ancient times, 4,500 years ago, when Stonehenge was being built. In his mind, he saw himself as one of the workers—moving, dressing, and placing the large stones. Over the past few months, he had started experiencing what felt like real life to him, with details that were colorful, vivid, and alive. He was beginning to believe that he had actually lived back then, and was simply being transported back and forth in time to . . . the year 2,500 BC, Stonehenge, Salisbury Plain, Wiltshire, England.

Every day's work involved moving the large stones, dressing them to a smooth finish, or lifting them into position. It took us many days to move the stones from where they lay, far away over the plains. A single stone could take more than two seasons. Many men were needed to pull the vine and leather ropes, and to continually reposition the rolling logs. Once we got the stones to the monument site, we used hammer stones to pound the large stones into shape by hand. It was bone-jarring work. We dug holes for the stones, using antlers and other animal bones. Lifting the giant stones was dangerous. We used braces that often broke or gave way. Just this season, a man was crushed under a stone, and several others were injured. I myself injured my left leg this season.

At the end of each day, my muscles burned from all the work. My whole body ached. At night, I slept like a dead man.

Yet, it was work that bound us together spiritually. Men came from far away, even beyond the shores of the great waters, to work on the stones. The work made us a community. It bound our souls together, with those of our ancestors. We became one with the mighty stones.

And it had to be done. We had to finish what was started before us. And we were getting close.

The elders directed our work according to the sacred tablets that were passed down through the years from the very beginning—the beginning when the Gods in the fiery ships came from the sky. At night, we built campfires, and sat around sharing stories of the early times.

I had worked on the stones for three seasons now, coming each season from the hills of my family's homeland. Besides the men who came to work, women came to prepare food, care for the children and livestock, and keep the huts where we slept. This season, I came to know a woman who was my age, named Rayla. She belonged to a family that had traveled from far north. I saw her nearly every day working near the huts, and at night, I would look at her across the campfire. When she saw me watching her, she would smile, then sheepishly look away. I could tell she was attracted to me, and I was attracted to her.

One evening, I gathered my courage and asked if she wanted to go with me to gather firewood, and she agreed. She smiled the entire time and was so beautiful. She brought out strange new feelings in me. I began to make excuses to talk with her. One night, I asked to sit with her at the campfire. Rayla smiled and nodded agreement. We talked, trying not to raise too many suspicions among the elders. After the campfire, in the shadows of a hut, we kissed. I could feel my heart beating in my chest. That night, though I was bone-tired from working the stones, I could hardly get to sleep. After several days, I asked Rayla's father if she could become my wife, and he said yes. We are to be married at the end of the season, and Rayla will return with me to my homeland.

Erik was developing an alternate personality—a Stonehenge personality. It was becoming entirely real to him, and the lines between his two personalities were starting to blur. It was taking him longer to recover, both mentally and physically, when returning to his real self. He would fall asleep in the room, and when he awoke in the early morning hours, he would go to bed feeling physically exhausted, just as if he had worked on the stones all day.

At the same time, stark conflicts were developing between his two personalities. In his Stonehenge life, he was part of a community—building something important, something permanent, that would last for the ages. He liked that feeling. In real life, he was not a part of anything, except his small group of SIG members that sat together at the monthly meetings.

But what surprised him most were his feelings of affection for Rayla. In his real world, Erik barely had the courage to say hello to a girl. Just last year, at a local bar, he tried to chat with a girl two stools down from him. The girl quickly blew him off, and he retreated like a turtle pulling back into its shell. But in his Stonehenge world, he cared deeply about a woman and was to be married. He was having difficulty living with the two personalities and felt conflicted. More importantly, he was starting to prefer his Stonehenge personality far more than his other personality. His Stonehenge personality was like a drug, and he was becoming addicted.

After so many seasons of brutally hard work, by so many people, the monument was nearing completion. It was already a spectacle to behold—truly magnificent. There could be nothing like it in all the world. And I was proud of my contributions.

The elders had decided that they would hold the inaugural consecration ceremony and sanctification of the monument at the end of this season, just twenty days from now. There would be a procession, a consecration of the stones, offerings to the gods, and finally a feast for all. During the feast, Rayla and I would be married.

There was great excitement. And I couldn't help but wonder— would the gods themselves appear in their fiery ships from the sky?

Chapter 4

After graduating from vo-tech school, Erik quickly got a job as a systems programmer for Superior Technical Services, Inc. The company provided technical support to businesses nationwide, but was headquartered in St. Paul. After only a short time with the company, Erik was considered the best technical expert in the firm. Contrarily, Erik had a rather low opinion of the technical skills of his coworkers, but he kept those sentiments to himself. He could at least tolerate them. On the other hand, he was quite sure that his direct supervisor was the inspiration for the pointy-haired manager in the Dilbert cartoons. Dumb as a brick. Erik just ignored him.

At the moment, Erik was working on a mainframe operating system upgrade. It was important work, but very routine—boring actually. His mind was far away from his job, his little cubicle, and the silly-ass file server. When the work day mercifully ended, he rushed home, went straight to his Stonehenge Room, hit the lights, and closed the door behind him. It took only moments for him to assume his alternate personality, his Stonehenge personality, and to travel back . . .

Now 2,500 BC, Stonehenge, on the Salisbury Plain, in Wiltshire, England.

The monument was finished, and the work of untold generations was finally complete. Surely the gods must be pleased.

There were now just three days until the grand ceremony and sanctification of the monument. More people were arriving from all over the countryside, as well as from far-away lands. I was still hopeful that the gods themselves would appear. None of the current people had ever seen the gods or their fiery ships, but everyone knew the stories told by the elders, who assured us that the gods would see the work we had completed and be pleased.

To ensure their appeasement, the elders declared we must make sacrifices to the gods. Pottery and tools were to be offered, as well as some of our food. We were told there was also to be a supreme sacrifice made, which would be revealed at the ceremony itself. There was much anticipation.

The day before the ceremony was rainy. I walked among the tall stones, and could hear their voices in my mind. I could feel the spiritual presence of all those souls who had worked so hard, and for so long, to make the monument great. Looking out from the stones toward our nearby village. I thought of the wooden and grass huts in which we lived, and how, in time, they would perish and be gone. But the great stones would never perish—they would last for all eternity.

After our evening meal, Rayla and I talked of the life we would have together. We were surely in love, and tomorrow we would be married.

The new day broke clear with full sunshine. As prescribed by the elders, at high sun, we began to assemble by the river for the procession to the monument above. At the sound of the drums, the procession started up the long avenue. We could see the magnificent monument sitting atop the distant ridge, with nothing but blue sky behind it. It was majestic. Rayla and I walked together hand in hand until we joined everyone around the great stone circle.

Wood for a huge fire had been laid out, and upon the command of the High Priest, the fire was lit. The High Priest then proclaimed the consecration of the monument. The many sacrifices which had been prepared were heaped on the fire, one by one, and it soon became a terrific blaze.

When the sacrifices had all been offered, the High Priest declared it was time for the ultimate sacrifice. We must offer our dearest, and most holy of all sacrifices—a precious human life. A life in its prime, and yet unspoiled. Holding the sacred staff high, he lifted his arm and, to my utter horror, he pointed it at Rayla. There were cries of anguish from the people. The High Priest commanded it must be done. Everyone knew the High Priest could not be questioned. To do so was punishable by death.

My body convulsed as they took my beloved Rayla from me, and placed her on the slaughter stone. She had fainted, and her body was limp. Several of the elders stood guard by her, with their heads bowed. The High Priest then raised an ornamental stone knife above his head, and after crying out at the top of his voice, beseeching the gods to be appeased, he plunged the knife through Rayla's heart. It was done.

I felt the fatal wound in my own heart. With the full effect of the agony upon me, a tremendous fury rose up in my mind. A single, profound emotion consumed my entire being, and became the sole purpose of my life thenceforth. **REVENGE!**

Chapter 5

The next morning, Dino was up and on his way to the office early. The warm spring weather was continuing. Two consecutive days of good weather in Minnesota at this time of year causes an epidemic of spring fever. Sudden and suspicious mass absences from offices, guys dressed in shorts and flip-flops—happens every year.

He had hoped to beat Suzie in this morning, but she was already on her second cup of coffee when he arrived. "Good morning Sunshine! Any updates on the Campbell case since yesterday?" he asked.

"Indeed, there are," she replied. "I've got some good news and some bad news. Which do you want first?"

"I'm in terrible need of some good news. Hit me!"

"First of all, we were finally able to track down the 911 caller. Turns out the guy was riding the LRT home from his late-night shift over in east Minneapolis, and just happened to be looking out the window of the train when he saw two cars jockeying with each other, side by side, heading east. He said he saw several flashes of what he thought was gunfire between the cars, and then the car on the right swerved hard off the road, up onto the sidewalk, and crashed into the building. The car on the left screeched to a stop, and a guy got out of the passenger side and ran over to the crashed car. He pointed a gun into the driver's window and there was another flash. The train continued down the street away from the scene, but our witness looked back and saw the guy run back to the other car. That was it. He called it in on his cell right away, but then got nervous and hung up on the operator. The call center tried repeatedly to call him back, but he wouldn't answer."

Suzie continued, "It took a while, but we were able to track him down through the phone company. We sent a patrol car over to find him, and he admitted immediately that he had made the call, but had then started worrying about retaliation. He said he takes the LRT to and from his work each evening, and has seen some threatening gang-member types on the train, especially on his trip home, and he wanted nothing to do with any of them. However, after talking with the officer, he's agreed to make a statement. I called him and he's coming in at two this afternoon."

Dino said, "Great! I don't suppose he saw what kind of car it was, or could we be so lucky . . . a license plate number?"

"Well, yes and no," she said. "He said it all happened so quickly, and the train was moving right along, so he didn't get any real details, but he did say he was pretty sure the vehicle was a *blue one*."

Dino said rhetorically, with a smirk, "Really, a *blue one*?" then, "Oh well, better than nothing. We'll see if we can get something more out of him this afternoon."

Suzie added, "There's actually some more good news. The patrol cars found two businesses with video security cameras rolling at the time of the shooting. Both were east of the scene on University. We'll hopefully be able to review the tapes later this afternoon."

"Maybe we'll get lucky and find us a *blue one*." Dino then asked, "OK, so what's the bad news?"

Suzie smiled and said, "The mayor is major league pissed, and wants action. He called the chief, who called Paula about a half hour ago, and right after she hung up on the call, she came looking for your ass. She asked me to let you know she needs to see you ASAP. So there, now you know, and I'm off the hook."

"I figured it was coming. Well, speaking of the devil." Paula was coming around the door, headed straight for Dino.

Still walking, she said, "Good morning. I need to see you

right now."

Dino said, "Of course."

They went into Paula's office and, as she shut the door, she started in. "The mayor is on the warpath. The media have latched onto this case, and are playing it, and I quote, 'as yet another example of the violent gang warfare that has the citizens of St. Paul worried for their safety,' unquote. Bastards!"

Dino knew that last night Channel 7 had run a full three-minute piece on gang violence in the city at both the six and ten o'clock newscasts.

Paula continued, "The mayor wants to know right now what we've got so far, and he wants to form a task force to look into this particular case, and the gang thing in general."

Dino rolled his eyes. *Oh no, here it comes. Task forces are as popular as a sharp stick in the eye. They take mountains of time and never get jack shit done.* To Paula, "You know, of course, the mayor is just covering his ass."

"Oh stop whining, I already put Larry on it."

"Good idea! I think Larry is the perfect guy for the task force. Just please don't tell him I said so."

"Not to worry, you'll get your turn," she assured him. "So, what do we have so far?"

Dino gave Paula the latest information from Suzie about the 911 caller and the two security tapes.

"Put it altogether and get Larry up to speed. Let me know what more you find out at your meeting with the caller. And if anything else comes up, let me know immediately."

"Will do."

Dino found Larry, expressed his condolences, and gave him everything they had so far. He then went to Suzie and gave her an update about the exchange with Paula. He looked at his watch and asked. "Are you interested in lunch? We can come up with our plan for the two o'clock interview."

"Sure, where to?"

"How about the Sunshine Cafe? It's close by, and the food's pretty good."

"I love that little place. Good idea!"

"I'll pick you up out in the lot at eleven thirty."

Always punctual, Dino pulled his Alfa Romeo SUV around the lot right at eleven thirty. Dino was proud of his Italian heritage, and a few years back, when Alfa Romeo started selling cars in the US again, he was first in line to buy one.

Suzie was right ready and jumped in. "Gotta say, you look great in this thing. Love the red."

"Thanks. It's great fun."

It took less than three minutes to get to the cafe. They got in line to order, and both decided on the daily tuna sandwich special. They found a table and sat down.

Dino took one bite of his sandwich, then said, "I wanted to thank you for tracking down that 911 caller. It gives us at least something to go on. Hopefully, he shows up, and doesn't forget to bring his memory."

Suzie replied, "It sounds like he'll cooperate. I assume you've got a list of things to go over with him?"

"I do. Hopefully, we can get something more on the second vehicle, as well as descriptions of the driver and passenger. He said he saw flashes of what he thought was gunfire between the cars. I'd like to know if it appeared to be coming only from the getaway car, or did it appear to come from the crashed car as well?"

Dino listed a few other points, and the conversation continued, back and forth, while they ate their sandwiches. Within a few minutes, they had a pretty good agenda of items for their meeting.

Dino and Suzie had a bit of history together. A couple of years back, they had dated for a short time. Suzie was divorced almost four years ago, and was raising a three-year-old son pretty much on her own. They had a good time together, but after a few dates, Dino seemed to drift away from the relationship. Suzie was disappointed, but never let her feelings be known to Dino. Still, they continued to have a cordial personal relationship, and a productive professional one.

Through the years, Suzie had learned to read Dino quite easily. "I don't mean to pry, but is something bothering you, Dino?" she asked. She then added, "Something you'd like to talk about?"

"You know me too well, Suzie." He paused for a few moments, then said, "Do you ever think about your career as a cop?"

"You mean, do I want to stay in homicide, or try management, or what?"

Dino was obviously struggling with a response, but finally he leaned forward, looked side to side as though someone might be listening, and said quietly, "I mean, do you ever wonder about being a cop period? Do you ever think about quitting and doing something else?"

Suzie was stunned. This, from a guy who had decided on the day of his dad's funeral, that he would be a cop, just like his dad. "Wow, didn't see that coming. What brought that on?"

"I don't know. Maybe it's the whole homicide thing. I've been at it for seven years now. Early on, it was challenging, and very rewarding, but lately it seems nearly all the cases are frustrating, like this gang one. Once in a while, it would be nice to play 'Colonel Mustard, in the library, with the candlestick,' you know what I mean? Some real detecting."

"I think I do." After a couple of moments to let it sink in, she asked, "Have you thought about what you would do instead?"

"A bit. I don't know—Marketing? Accounting? I was always pretty good with numbers."

"Um, I don't mean to make light of your dilemma, but it's hard for me to imagine the Great Dino Roselli, the pride of St. Paul's finest, as an accountant. By the way, I'm pretty sure they forbid accountants from driving Alfa Romeos."

"Very funny. I don't know, I've been thinking about it quite a lot lately."

"Well, I'm sure you'll sort it all out. If you did actually resign, I can tell you it would be the shocker of the decade in the department."

"Oh, I'm sure. Anyway, thanks for chatting. And please don't mention it to anyone. You're the only one I've talked to about it at all."

"No worries, your secret is safe with me. Thanks for lunch, but we better get back."

"You're right."

It was now 2:10 p.m. and Mr. Jonathan Powell, the 911 caller, was nowhere to be found.

"Crap, maybe he got cold feet?" asked Dino. He and Suzie were waiting for him in an interview room.

"I don't know. When I talked with him on the phone yesterday, he told me he would come in," said Suzie. "He said he was scared about becoming involved. Those damn TV guys have been hitting the whole gang violence thing pretty hard lately, on nearly every newscast. Maybe they scared him off?"

"I hope not. I need this guy. He's all we have."

At 2:17 p.m. there was a chirp from the intercom. The receptionist announced that Mr. Powell was in the lobby.

"Whew, better late than never. I'll go get him," said Suzie.

Jonathan Powell turned out to be a thin, middle-aged Black man, who was obviously very nervous. Dino stood as Suzie brought him into the interview room. "Thank you, Mr. Powell. We appreciate your taking the time to come in and make a statement."

"I said I'd come, so I did, but I gotta tell ya, I'm awful frickin' nervous about the whole thing. I don't wanna get popped by one of those damn kids myself."

"I can understand that Mr. Powell, but believe me, you're doing the right thing. These recent murders have people starting to worry about their safety on the streets, and we appreciate any help you can give us."

"OK." Then after a pause. "I guess."

"Based on what you've told us so far, Mr. Powell, we'll not be asking you to identify any specific person. Given the time of night, the poor street lighting at the location, the speed of the train, and the distance from which you were viewing, we don't think accurate identification of any person is possible. However, we would like to get a statement about any details you can remember about the vehicles, shots fired, that sort of thing."

"I didn't see much. The train was going right along, and I just happen to look over and see the shots. I couldn't hear anything, 'cause of the train. I really just saw them flashes."

"OK, Mr. Powell. That's fine." Dino was trying to put Mr. Powell at ease, but it did not seem to be working. He was still very jittery. "We just need to get down in your own words what you did see. We're going to make an audio recording of our questions and your statement. Understand?"

"Yeah, I figured."

"I will start by stating several details for the record." Dino reached over and punched the start button on the recorder. "This is Detective Dino Roselli, of the St. Paul Police Department. It is May 6th, 2:35 p.m. We are in Interview Room 4B. Detective Suzette Hawkins is also present, along with Mr. Jonathan Powell. Mr. Powell was a witness to the May 5th homicide of Paul Campbell, on University Avenue in St. Paul . . ."

Dino finished the introductory stuff, confirming Powell's address, employer, and the details of his trip on the LRT that night. Dino then asked Powell to describe what he saw, in as great a detail as possible.

Powell was right—he had not seen much. They were hoping to get some details on the vehicle the killers were in—make, model, color, but all Powell could recall was that it was a "*blue one*," and "probably one of those small Japanese things. Oh, and I think it had one of those fart pipes out the back. Oops, sorry Miss Hawkins. You know . . . fart pipe?" Dino nodded that he knew what Powell was referring to.

Powell did have a couple of details on the guy who got out and ran over to the other car and fired his weapon, but they were not much. He was sure he had a baseball cap on, and that he had it on backwards. The guy was short, wearing white sneakers, and he guessed he was eighteen to twenty years old.

Dino asked, "Did you see shots fired from both cars, or just the one?" Powell responded there were one or two shots fired from the victim's car as well, just before the car swerved to the right and into the building.

And that was it.

Dino and Suzette thanked him for his time and concluded the interview. They mentioned they may need to get in touch with him again later and asked him to please respond to any calls. He said he would, and was gone.

"Oh well," said Dino. "Better than nothing, I guess. Are we still expecting those security video tapes yet this afternoon?"

"As far as I know. I'll let you know when they get here."

"Thanks Suzie."

The tapes came in about an hour later. They were a bust.

Suzie called Dino. "The tech guys converted both tapes to MPGs. I've got the first one up on my screen if you want to come take a look."

"On my way."

Like most security videos, the tapes were of poor quality, and the images often jumped on the screen. The first video was from a business just four blocks east of the crime scene. Suzie positioned the time-stamped video to the time of the shooting, and they walked it forward in slow motion, through the next five minutes. They saw only six vehicles, which would have been about right for the time of night. There was no blue one, and no fart pipe. There was nothing even close to Powell's vague description.

"Damn. They must've turned off right after the shooting. OK, how about the next one?" said Dino.

Suzie brought up the second video, which was from a parking lot entrance three blocks further east on University Avenue. She again positioned it to the time of the shooting and started it forward slowly. Same as the first. Nothing.

Even allowing for "*blue*" not always being blue in the late-night sodium streetlights, and that many cars look "Japanese" nowadays, there was nothing even close.

"Bummer," said Suzie. "But we did get one more tidbit. We got confirmation that the gun found on the floor of the victim's car had been fired recently, and the only prints on it were those of the victim."

"No surprises there," said Dino. "Crap, we're striking out

here. Well, it is what it is. I'll go update Paula."

After that, Dino decided to call it a day, feeling like they had next to nothing to go on with the case. *Damn gang murders.*

He left the office and walked through the parking lot toward the Alfa. *When all else fails—pasta and wine.* Dino had a dinner date for the evening, and after the day's events, was looking forward to a distraction. He was quite sure that the lovely Amy Williams would provide that, and maybe a little more.

Chapter 6

Dino enjoyed the company of women and dated two or three times a month. He especially enjoyed conversation with women. But he never allowed himself to become involved in a long-term relationship. He did not know why. At least, that is what he told himself. But actually, he knew exactly why.

Just after he graduated from the University of Minnesota, he had gotten close to someone—Sarah Davidson. After a few months, Sarah decided she wanted to move on. Dino was hurt. Deeply. Since then, he never allowed women to get too close. Friends yes, but that was it. Until Amy Williams. Dino liked Amy. She was attractive for sure, but more important, Dino enjoyed her company. Conversation with Amy was easy. The topic really did not matter, it was fun. She made him laugh.

They had gone out four or five times in the past couple of months. Early on, Dino learned Amy was a widow. Her husband had been killed in a traffic accident during a heavy winter storm three years ago. They had been married for only a couple of years and had no children. She had started dating again only recently.

No matter, Dino liked Amy. Surprisingly, he was even allowing himself to consider—just maybe—Amy was worth taking a chance again. *Is she the one?* That idea scared him and thrilled him at the same time. A while back, he had started to tire of playing the games that came with dating. Maybe it was time to stop running every time a woman got close. If ever he wanted to have a wife and family, the clock was ticking. He was not sure what to do, but he decided he would continue to see her, at least for now.

For tonight, rather than going out again, he had invited Amy to his place for dinner. And he was very much looking forward to it.

Dino was a foodie, no doubt derived from his growing up working in the family restaurant. He and his siblings had helped out since they were old enough to wash dishes and push a broom. His other siblings were still active in the restaurant. Dino's direct involvement had tapered off quickly when he started full time on the force, but he still loved to cook, and was famous for his Italian dinners.

Tonight's menu was *Cavati e Ravioli Alla Ragusana* with pork sauce. It was a favorite, but he was looking forward to the wine even more. A lovely Nebbiolo from the Piedmont region of northern Italy. The only sad part was that the bottle was the last of a case he had been enjoying over the past year.

Still, Amy was worth it. She was great fun and great looking. On top of that, she appreciated good food and fine wine. She showed up at his front door and knocked promptly at seven o'clock.

Dino opened the door and greeted her, "Hello! Come on in. Very good to see you. You found the place OK?"

"I did. Just like you said, right across the street from the old brownstone birthplace of F. Scott Fitzgerald. Charming neighborhood."

"Well, it's not Summit Avenue, but there are lots of great old houses, and I love the feel of the whole area. This house was originally built in the early 1900s, and is still in pretty good shape." Dino escorted her into the kitchen, which he had renovated to include a larger space for working, and for guests to sit and help or just watch dinner preparations. "Glass of wine?"

"Of course," said Amy, and Dino poured her a glass of the Nebbiolo, which he had decanted forty-five minutes before.

"See what you think of this one," he said.

She swirled the wine in her glass, smelled it, took a sip, swishing the wine in her mouth for a few moments, then swallowed. "My goodness, it's fabulous."

"It's one of my favorites. I thought you might like it. Have a seat on the stool there. I just have a few minutes of food prep left." Dino described the meal he was preparing.

"It smells wonderful."

"So how was your day?" he asked.

"It was good." Amy worked for a realtor in downtown St. Paul that sold business properties in the Twin Cities. "I have a high-end property that looks like it may close next week. I could use the commission."

"I bet you get it," Dino reassured her. They continued chatting, and after a few minutes, sat down for a candlelit dinner in the adjacent dining room. Amy tried the *Cavati e Ravioli*, and could not stop ooh'ing and aah'ing.

"This is truly delicious. Where'd you learn to cook like this?"

"Just like Mom used to make," replied Dino with a smile. "Actually, just like Mom still makes."

"Well, she obviously taught her little boy very well."

They finished the bottle of Nebbiolo, and Dino asked her if she would like another wine. She quickly agreed.

"Let's go pick one out," he said. They got up from the table, and he led her down into the basement. Amy seemed puzzled, but he waved her along, coaxing her. "Come on."

He opened the door to his small wine cellar and flipped on the light. Amy was amazed by the number and variety of bottles stored in wood racks against each wall.

"Very impressive!"

"Let's see, maybe something more from Piedmont?"

"Sounds great."

After looking at several different bottles, he picked one out and said, "This Barbaresco is quite good. Let's see what you think." They took the bottle and headed back upstairs to the dining table. He uncorked the bottle, poured the wine into a decanter, gave it several vigorous swirls, then poured her some in a fresh glass.

She tried it. It's just lovely. Really. I must say, if you're trying to impress me with all this food and wine, it's working. Thank you so much."

"Definitely my pleasure."

They continued their meal, chatting comfortably back and forth. When they had finished eating, they took the rest of the bottle and their glasses and went into what Dino described as his sitting room. There was a fireplace against the wall. Dino went over to it, flipped a switch, and flames popped up in the hearth. "I always feel like a cheat doing that, but I am too lazy to do all the work of a real fireplace."

"No worries, it's very pleasant," said Amy.

They sat on the couch and continued their conversation. Amy asked Dino about the murder case he was working on, and all the attention it was getting on the local TV news programs.

Dino cried, "Out of bounds—no work talk."

"Sorry," she replied. She looked around the room and spotted a picture on the wall of a red sports car. "What's that?" she asked.

"That," he replied, "is my Ferrari Dino."

"Really, you own a Ferrari?"

"Not just a Ferrari, a Ferrari *Dino*."

"You named the car after yourself?" she asked.

"Actually, the other way around. I'm named after the car. Or more accurately, the man who designed and developed the car."

"OK, I'm confused."

"It's a bit of a story?"

"I would love to hear it," said Amy.

"Well, my dad was a great admirer of Enzo Ferrari, the founder of Ferrari automobiles. In Italy, my dad was one of what people there call the *tifosi*—super passionate fans of Ferrari, and in particular, the Ferrari Formula One racing team. Enzo had a son named Dino, who worked with his father when he was quite young. Dino helped develop a new mid-engine sports car that was smaller than traditional Ferrari sports cars, but still had the trademark Ferrari performance. Unfortunately, Dino, who Enzo loved dearly, died when he was only twenty-four from muscular dystrophy. In his honor, Enzo decided to name the new car the *Dino*. My dad bought one early on, though I am not sure where he found the money. When I came along, he decided to name me after Dino Ferrari, and the *Dino* sports car. When my dad died, I inherited the car."

"So there you have it . . . I'm actually named after the car."

"I have to confess, you are quite the guy, Mr. Roselli. Chef extraordinaire, wine sommelier, exotic sports car owner, gun-toting cop, and a sharp dresser to boot."

"Oh, you're only just beginning to learn of my many talents," he replied. He leaned forward and kissed her softly.

"Please tell me more," she cooed, as they embraced and fell together onto the sofa.

Dino proceeded to show her some of his other talents, which lasted late into the evening.

Chapter 7

E rik awoke a little after five in the morning, still in his Stonehenge Room. His shirt was drenched in sweat from the physical and mental agony of reliving the sacrifice of Rayla. The shirt was cold, and he was shivering. He got up from his chair, stumbled into the bathroom, and took a hot shower to warm himself up. Afterwards, he lay down in his bed and tried to sleep, but it would not come.

Until this point, Erik had managed to keep his personalities distinct and to appear normal to others, at least most of the time. But now, his two personalities had effectively merged into one, driven by the horrific murder of Rayla and his all-consuming vow for revenge.

More by osmosis than rational thought, his utter hatred and contempt for the High Priest authority figure of ancient Stonehenge had been transferred to the present-day authority figure of SIG. They were the leaders, and they were responsible. The focal point of his hatred and the object of his revenge was now Tom Morris.

By seven thirty, he knew there was no way he could go to work. He called in sick and went back to bed. His mind worked on how he would carry out his revenge. *An eye for an eye.* That seemed entirely fair. *You took my love, so I will take yours.* He would kill Tom's wife, Jennifer. *Yes, it seems entirely fair.*

He concluded it would only be fitting that the method should also be exactly the same. He would murder her with a knife, plunged into her heart as viciously and cruelly as the High Priest had done to his Rayla. *Yes, it seems entirely fair.*

There was a strange comfort in now having a plan for how he would extract his revenge. Now he could sleep, and he slept for several hours.

He awoke just after 1 p.m., and his mind turned to specifics. *What options were there for the when and where?* He thought about going to Tom's house, breaking in during the night, and murdering his wife as they lay in their bed. But how could he avoid getting caught? It seemed like there was a lot that could go wrong with that option. *What if Tom keeps a gun in his nightstand? What if they have a dog?* At the very least, Tom would try to fight him off. And he would almost certainly end up covered in blood. How could he make an escape and not be noticed? He wanted to carry out justice. He did not want to end up in jail for the rest of his life.

Maybe I could follow Jennifer in her car and simply walk up to her as she gets out? That seemed very crude, and again, there was a lot that could go wrong. He would have no control over the location or time. What if she noticed him following her and called the police?

This was all much more complicated than he first thought. He was going to have to think about it more.

He returned to his Stonehenge room to ground his thoughts. As he sat looking at his replica of the stones, it came to him—he would kill her exactly where they had murdered his woman, on the Slaughter Stone at Stonehenge.

He remembered the upcoming SIG trip to Stonehenge for the summer solstice. He knew that Tom's wife always accompanied him on his trips. Were there any slots left? Could he be so lucky? He looked up Tom's number and called.

"Hello, this is Tom."

"Hello Tom, this is Erik Foster from SIG. Sorry to bother you if you're working."

"It's no problem. What's up?"

"Are there any slots left for the summer solstice trip?"

"Funny you should ask. We were full, but yesterday, Patrick

Taylor called and had to cancel, so there is one open as of now. Are you interested?"

"I am! I didn't think I would be able to get off work, but now I think I can swing it. I'd like to take that slot."

"And we'd love to have you! I'm sure you will love England, Stonehenge, and the summer solstice event. Our pre-trip meeting is next Tuesday evening at seven o'clock. We can get you setup then. I'll email the details."

"Thanks! This is just great," he said. "I'd kill to go on this trip!" Smirking, he hung up the phone.

Chapter 8

"We're all here, so let's get started."

Tom Morris hosted a final trip planning meeting at his home in Sun Fish Lake for the twelve people going to Stonehenge for the summer solstice.

"First of all, I want to make sure everyone here knows Erik Foster, who's now going in place of Patrick Taylor. Patrick had a situation come up at work and couldn't make the trip. We're thrilled to have Erik joining us."

Erik replied, "Thanks. I'm really looking forward to this trip. This will be a first for me, since I've never been out of the US, I'm all excited to finally see Stonehenge. Having read about it and studied it for so long, I feel like I've been there before."

Tom continued, "OK. We leave in just three weeks. Although I've been to England and London many times, I'm always excited to go back. You've probably heard the quote from Samuel Johnson, 'When a man is tired of London, he is tired of life.' Well, it's true, London is one of the world's great cities. And my personal favorite!

"I tried to include all the information you'll need for the trip in the packets I gave you earlier, so tonight we just want to confirm key details and answer any questions you may have. Before we get to the itinerary and details, there's an all-important thing. Do you all have your passport? No passport—no trip. Period. You don't even get on the plane." They all affirmed they had their passports, except for Erik. He had applied for an expedited passport and had been told he would have it in time for the trip.

"OK, our flight with Delta is a non-stop into Heathrow Airport. We should all be at the airport no later than three hours before the flight. After going through security, we'll meet at the Fox & Hound pub on the B Concourse. We can practice drinking pints."

"Once we're in London, we'll take the Tube to our hotel, The Bayworth, in the West End. It's reasonably priced, at least for London, and is centrally located. The British Museum is only a few blocks away. The hotel serves Full English Breakfast in the morning, included in the room charge. It's a great way for tourists to start the day."

"I've arranged for an early check-in, so we can drop our luggage at the hotel, and then do some sightseeing. Even if you feel really jet lagged when we get there, I don't recommend going to bed, or trying to nap. It's better to just stay up."

As Tom went on about the trip, Erik tuned out, and instead he thought about *his* plan for the trip. He had researched knife regulations for the flight, as well as for England. He could pack a three inch or less assisted opening knife in his checked baggage, as long as it was sheathed. It would also be legal in England. He found one that was perfect at Cabela's. As soon as he bought it, he carried it around, feeling it in his pocket. He practiced opening it, and imagined over and over, using it for its sole purpose. As he sat listening to Tom, he moved his hand to his pocket and felt the knife. Felt its power. It made his heart race.

"If you pull the itinerary out of your packet, you'll see that on the second day, in the late afternoon, we'll be taking a private minibus out to Stonehenge. I've arranged for it to pick us up at the hotel and drop us off right at Stonehenge when access begins at seven. We need to be there early to ensure we get in, but don't worry about being too early, there's lots to do throughout the night. Be prepared to see and talk with some of the most interesting people you'll ever meet. Nothing spookier than a devout Druid in summer solstice garb. It'll be great fun. The minibus will pick us up in the morning and bring us back to our hotel."

"The itinerary has the rest of the daily schedules, including our flight back on Day Four. Any questions?"

Erik barely heard the others talking. Still caressing the knife in his pocket, he glanced over several times at Jennifer, Tom's wife. He imagined how he would carry out his mission. He imagined her soft body, and the exact way he would use the knife to fulfill his pledge of revenge. Startled to realized Tom was looking at him, he quickly pulled his hand from his pocket.

"Are you OK Erik?" Tom asked.

"Oh yes! Just daydreaming about the trip. Sorry."

Tom shrugged and resumed following the meeting. There were numerous other touristy questions from the first-time travelers, such as currency conversion and credit card pre-authorizations, but most everyone seemed comfortable with Tom's preparations and excited about the trip.

Tom concluded the meeting saying, "OK, if we're satisfied with our plans, we can now practice our British beer-drinking skills by having a pint or two. I've got some Fuller's London Pride, and some Black Sheep Best Bitter. We need to be in prime shape come three weeks from now, and practice makes perfect. Cheers!"

Chapter 9

Dino pushed open the doors of his garage, and the bright warm sunlight beamed into the shop. Finally, he had a full Saturday to get the Ferrari out of winter hibernation and back on the road. He was late in getting the car out this year, the homicide biz had been way too active for the last few months.

He pulled the cloth cover off the car, took one look, and blurted out "Hello Gorgeous!" Though he had seen the car a zillion times since he was a boy, it took his breath away to see it again. The Ferrari Dino is one of the most breathtakingly beautiful cars in all the world. Viewed from any angle, the lines are timeless, the curves graceful and sexy at the same time. The car looks fast just standing still. The *rosso corsa* or red racing paint color, screams Ferrari. People who know sports cars get weak-kneed looking at it, but even people who do not know or care about any kind of car know immediately that it is something special.

Dino reached into the cockpit and shifted the transmission into neutral, then pushed the car out into the driveway. *Time for a bath!* He gathered all his cleaning paraphernalia together, ran the hose out to the driveway, and started in. Dino enjoyed washing and cleaning the Ferrari. As a small boy, he would help his father with the car. Luca showed him the proper techniques for washing, rinsing, polishing, and waxing—two buckets, proper sequence, his favorite products, and most importantly, how to steal Mom's best rags without getting caught. At least once every session, Dad would somehow lose control of the hose and sprinkle him, causing him to squeal with delight. Dino, of course, had to finagle the hose away from Dad, and squirt him in return. When they finished cleaning, they would test drive it together to make absolutely sure everything was running properly. Dino could never forget his dad shifting through the gears—the wonderful sound of the powerful engine behind you, the high-pitched whine of the transmission, and the glorious noise from the exhaust—a full symphony of sounds. Thinking back, it all seemed a bit simple and childish, but they were the best of memories, and now, the worst of heartaches. He so missed his dad and their car time together.

Dino finished up the cleaning, put in the freshly charged battery, checked tire pressures and all fluid levels, and then finally started it up. The engine sputtered a bit, but then came to life, the whole car throbbing with energy, begging to go. After it was warmed up, he shut it off and went inside to change into some comfortable driving clothes and his favorite driving shoes. Twenty minutes later, he was back out, with a couple of bottles of water, ready for an afternoon of serious driving.

He headed out but had to first stop at a nearby gas station that sold high-octane gas to fill up the tank. Perish the thought of ever running the Dino on anything but the best premium gas. Actually, gassing up was often a bit of a pain, since he invariably caused a commotion with the car. People just could not resist coming over to ask questions. "Is this a real Ferrari?" or "How fast will it go?" He was generally polite, and would chat a bit while fueling, unless someone asked something unforgivable, such as "Is this a Lamborghini?" This, he considered, deserved only the curt reply, "No!"

He was soon on the road, headed south from St. Paul along the Mississippi River on US Highway 61. Past the small town of Miesville he turned off onto the Welch Village Road, which has some of the best corners and elevation changes of any road in southeastern Minnesota. The perfect place to practice hitting a late apex in corners. Great fun.

Dino literally lost himself when driving the Ferrari. The

Dino is a car that demands your full attention. Unlike a modern-day vehicle with high tech "nanny" aids to do everything for you, it must be actively driven. There is no traction control, no ABS braking system. Just you and your skill. The gated manual transmission can be unforgiving if not treated properly but is exceedingly rewarding when you match the engine revs and clutch with a perfect heel and toe downshift.

Dino always drove alone. He considered the interior of the car hallowed space, where he could remember his dad, and think things out. No one else would appreciate its significance. If anyone ever pressured him for a ride, he would deflect them with, "The cabin is really cramped, the ride is bone jarringly harsh, and the noise is so loud, I'm afraid you wouldn't enjoy it at all."

Once in Red Wing he decided to stay on the Minnesota side of Lake Pepin. The road follows along the river bluffs, with scenic views of the lake itself, as well as sailboats, cruisers, and the occasional canoe. At Wabasha, he crossed the bridge over the river into Wisconsin and headed back north along US Highway 35. On the east side of the river, the afternoon sun sparkled on the waves. As he drove along, he thought about his dad, and he wondered what his dad would think of him even considering quitting the force. It made him nervous to think about what he would say if he were alive. Would he call me a traitor, or would he understand my doubts? What advice would he give me? Or would he give me a swift kick in the rear end instead? *I no doubt deserve it.*

At Hager City, he crossed back to the Minnesota side. Back in Red Wing, he had passed Barn Bluff, and was waiting at a traffic light, when a young family of four crossed in front of him. His thoughts hit him with the other dilemma that had been nagging him. *Well, are you ever going to have a family?* The quiet voice speaking to him now was that of his mom. She had gently nudged him on the topic about a month ago, which started the guilt flowing. He pushed it aside, as he had done many times before, but it had been creeping back into his consciousness every so often. And here, right in front of him, was this idyllic young family, with two little kids skipping along happily, while the watchful parents held hands and walked through the cross-walk. His mind wandered to Amy and their wonderful evening together just a few days ago. *Is she the one? Can I take a chance again? A family with Amy?* Hmmm.

Dino started to wonder if his whole life was off track. What the hell are you doing? *Heading straight to hell!* was the answer that came as the light changed and the car behind him beeped. He revved the engine, let out the clutch, and took off. *I know. I have some thinking and deciding to do.*

He continued on home to St. Paul. Though troubled by the issues facing him, the drive was the best mental health fix he had had in months. The Ferrari ran beautifully, the scenery was great on a warm sunny day, and he at least had time to ponder things. Important things. He resolved to decide them soon. *The clock is ticking.*

At home, he put the car away in the garage, headed into the house, and went straight to the wine cellar. He pulled out a 2009 Barolo he had been saving. Just the thing to cap off a great day. He dug out a couple of delicious cheeses, some bread with plenty of butter, and sat down to enjoy a movie. Dino was a Humphrey Bogart fan and decided to watch *The Big Sleep* for the umpteenth time. He loved the scene where Bogie describes his occupation to a female bookstore clerk as a "private dick." Dino had actually thought several times about becoming a private detective, but he was not sure he could handle the risks of going into business for himself. More to the point, he wondered why nobody ever called themselves a private dick anymore, but then after a brief moment, he was pretty sure why not. The movie ended just as Dino finished the Barolo, with Bacall saying, "You've forgotten one thing—me." Bogie then asks her, "What's wrong with you?" and Bacall replies, "Nothing you can't fix." *Gotta love old movies. And Barolo.*

It had been quite the day.

On Sunday, after a light breakfast, he headed over to the gym and started in on his usual weight training circuit. He finished that, and was about to head out for a run, when he bumped into

Amy. He had first met Amy at the gym.

"I thought I might find you here. Thanks again for the wonderful evening," she said.

"Oh, thank you for coming. It was great fun," he replied. "Interested in a run?"

"Sure. How far are you going?"

"Oh, a couple miles. I need to burn off last night's Barolo and baguette. Does that work for you?"

"It does. Just let me grab a light hoody. I'll meet you at the front door."

"Sounds good."

They took off together at a leisurely pace. Dino could crank out a six-minute mile when he wanted to, but today they were doing about an eight-minute pace, which allowed for some light conversation along the way.

"So how's your weekend been?" he asked.

"OK," she replied. "Yesterday I puttered around the apartment and then went out with a couple girl friends for drinks last night. Nothing special. How about you?"

"I took advantage of the great weather to get the Ferrari out of winter storage, and back on the road. I went for a drive down along Lake Pepin on the Minnesota side, then back up along the Wisconsin side. It's one of my favorite things to do."

"Sounds great. You'll have to give me a ride sometime."

Dino very much enjoyed Amy's company, but he instinctively replied with his, "Actually, the cabin is really cramped . . ." spiel, and she seemed to accept it. *Maybe one day.*

When they finished their run, Dino suggested they meet up for dinner one night this week.

"I thought you'd never ask. I'd love to."

"How about Wednesday?" he offered. "I'm pretty sure that works, and I can confirm by Tuesday, if that works for you."

"I'll keep it open—just for you. Let me know."

They said goodbye, and Dino headed for the showers. When he was done, he started dressing. He reached into his locker for his wallet, and as he did most every day, he looked at the photo of his dad that he always carried. He hesitated a bit before putting it away. A thought came to him, and after considering it for a few moments, *Yup, it's time.*

After he finished dressing, he walked out through the parking lot to the Alfa. He got in, fired it up, and started driving to Our Lady of Hope Cemetery. He wound his way through the gravesites and stopped near his dad's plot. Dino came to be with his dad every so often. Sometimes, he would "talk" with him aloud. Sometimes he would just think quietly. He was sure his dad would hear him either way and would always reply. Other times, he just stood for a while, not thinking anything specific. He was just hanging out with his dad.

Today, he said nothing aloud. He was not quite ready for that. *Dad, did you ever think of doing anything but being a cop?* He listened for a reply but heard nothing. Not a word. *First time for that!* He stood for several minutes, hoping to hear something. The silence was worse than any reply his dad could have given. Then out loud, "Talk to me Dad. Something. Please." His heart had sunken below his stomach. *He won't even talk to me.* Finally, Dino turned and walked back to the Alfa. He drove away slowly, looking over at the gravesite, still listening, but there was nothing.

Dino did not feel like going home. Too much on this mind. The weather was still pleasant, so he decided to drive around for a while. He headed northeast toward Stillwater, on the St. Croix River. There was the usual heavy tourist traffic in town, crawling along the main drag. He found a spot to park and walked over to a bar with a patio overlooking the river. He ordered a Peroni and sat looking out at the boats cruising up and down the river. A couple of young ladies threw some inviting glances his way, but he just smiled back politely and looked back out over the river. After nearly an hour of wrestling with his thoughts, he decided. *Time to go see Mom.*

He drove back to St. Paul, and headed downtown to Roselli's, where he was sure his mom, Sophia, would be. He walked in the front door of the restaurant and there she was—as reliable as gravity itself.

"How's it going Momma?" he asked.

"Just fine Dino, nice to see you," she replied.

"Got a few minutes to chat?"

"Always for you."

They sat down at one of the back tables. Sophia signaled a waiter to bring a bottle of the house Sangiovese and a basket of bread.

"What have you been up to?" she asked.

"Yesterday, I finally got the Ferrari out and went for a drive down to Lake Pepin."

"Is that old rattle trap still running?"

"Mom!"

"Just kidding. You must have needed a good think."

"You know me too well."

"That's a momma's job."

"And I went out to the cemetery this afternoon."

"Gracious, this must be serious."

"Ah, maybe. I'm kinda thinking it all through."

"What is it, girl problems?"

"No, not that."

"Darn, I was hoping maybe . . ."

"Mom!"

"Well, a momma can dream you know. You need a nice girl and some babies. And I need some grand babies!"

"I know, I know."

"Then what is it, Dino? Spit it out."

"It's hard to even say out loud."

"Come on, out with it."

"Well, sometimes . . . sometimes I wonder if I want to be a cop anymore. Damn. There, I said it."

"Is that it?"

"I tried to talk with Dad this afternoon, but he wouldn't even talk with me. Crap, he always talks to me."

"Hmm. Your dad just loved being a cop. Maybe he doubted himself in other ways, but not about that. It was the one constant in his life."

"Really?"

"I'm sure he would have been so proud of you and your fine

record. I can imagine it would be hard for him to hear you want to leave."

"Momma, I don't know if I can keep doing this. Sometimes, the homicide thing can get you down. And lately, it's been getting worse."

"I've read in the papers about the mayor clamoring for progress."

"No shit."

"Dino!"

"Sorry Momma. Yes, I'm very much aware of the mayor's sentiments on the subject."

They sipped wine for a time, then Dino said, "I'm sure I can figure it out."

"I'm sure your dad would want you to do what makes you happy. I know that."

"I think he's sure I'm a traitor for even thinking about leaving."

"That's just silly."

"Easy for you to say."

"And even easier for you to accept and believe. I know you won't do anything rash, but be honest with yourself. When you've decided what you want to do, move forward and don't look back. That's what your dad would have said. I'm sure of it."

"Thanks Momma."

"And besides, you should be thinking about more important things, such as . . . ahem."

"Yes Momma, I know."

They shared some more wine, and after a bit, Dino thanked her again, kissed her on the cheek, and headed home.

Chapter 10

The day for their trip and flight arrived, and to Tom's great relief, everyone showed up at the airport on time, with their passports, and made it through security. *Whew.*

They convened at the Fox & Hound pub in the Concourse. As they sat and sampled Bass Ale, Boddingtons Cream Ale, and Guinness, Tom commented, "These beers taste OK here, but you'll be amazed at how much better they all taste in England, especially the cask beers."

Noah Miller from Minneapolis confessed, "I'm not sure I can get used to drinking warm beer."

"It's not warm," scolded Tom mildly. "It's actually *cellar* temperature, around 55 degrees. You'll see. Besides, 'When in Rome, do as the Romans do.'"

When it was time to board, they packed up and headed for their gate. Everyone found their seats without any issues, and the flight took off right on time.

The flight was uneventful. Some people were able to sleep, others just rested. Near the end of their long flight, as they approached Heathrow, it started to get light on the eastern horizon and sure enough, with the aid of hot towels to wash their faces, some strong coffee, and a bit of something that was apparently made with eggs, it felt just like morning, and the start of another day.

They landed, deplaned, and luckily, everyone's checked baggage showed up. Tour director Tom congratulated himself again.

So far, so good.

Everyone queued up to buy Oyster Smartcard passes for the Tube. Erik joined at the end of the line, and after making sure no one was watching, he discreetly went into a side compartment of his checked suitcase, retrieved his knife, and slipped it into his pocket. He felt better now that he could touch it.

With tickets in hand, they all jumped on the Piccadilly Line for the West End of London. The London first timers were astonished that the first part of the trip from Heathrow into London was actually above ground. They could see houses along the way, as well as cars traveling on the wrong side of the road. *Weird.*

When they first boarded the train, Erik hung back a bit, and after Jennifer had selected a seat, he sat down several seats away from her, where he could watch her without staring. He slowly slid his hand into his pocket and onto the cold metal of his knife. The fire burning in him for revenge was growing. As the train rattled along, he started to drift in and out of his Stonehenge personality. He imagined himself at Stonehenge luring Jennifer from their group, and at the supreme moment surprising her with the knife, thrusting it as hard as he could into her abdomen. He dwelled on that vision for a moment, then snapped back to himself, looking around to see if anyone had noticed, but everyone was occupied with themselves.

As they approached each stop, they heard the famous British Tube announcer say, "Mind the gap!" a reassuring sign that they were indeed in London. Several of the people found the names of the stops along the way interesting—Hounslow, Hammersmith, Piccadilly Circus, and Cockfosters. They got off at Holborn and walked the short distance to the Hotel Bayworth. Karen Halvorsen from St. Cloud said, "I had no idea the Tube was so easy and convenient to use. And, at least for me, it's downright fun!" Others in the group chimed in their agreement.

They checked in at their hotel and took the "lift" up to their rooms. They dropped off their bags, freshened up a bit, and then reconvened in the lobby before heading out to be tourists.

Since it was so close, Tom suggested they first walk to the British Museum. As they approached the grand entrance, he told them, "This is one of the world's greatest museums." They were surprised that the Museum was free to enter, but Tom said that it was appropriate to make a freewill donation, even if it was only a pound or two. They walked around and viewed the impressive Egyptian and Grecian exhibits, as well as the Rosetta Stone. Like the Wright brothers' plane at the Smithsonian in the US, and the Mona Lisa at the Louvre in Paris, it's always fascinating to see genuine articles of history. And here was the Rosetta Stone—the one and only—which had had such a profound impact on the translation and interpretation of ancient history.

With the time short, Tom told them, "You could easily spend a couple of days here, but we only have a few minutes. We need to move on to all the other things we'd like to see today."

So off they went, back on the Tube, with a change from the Piccadilly Line to the Northern Line, getting off at the Embankment station. It was stunning to come up from the Underground in central London, and see the Thames River, Big Ben, the London Eye, Westminster Abbey, and more.

Tom recommended they all buy two-day Hop-On Hop-Off double-decker tour bus tickets, as he felt it was the best way to tour around Inner London. They passed by the Tower of London, St. Paul's Cathedral, Piccadilly Circus, Trafalgar Square, and Tower Bridge.

Just as he had done on the Tube, when they boarded the tour bus, Erik hung back and picked a seat where he could watch Jennifer unobtrusively. He rehearsed the supreme moment over and over in his mind. Each time, it made his heart race and sent a thrill through his entire body. Yet he feared others would notice him, and he had to work harder each time to force himself back down, and to look normal.

Near four o'clock, they were dragging a bit, so Tom suggested it was time to hit the pubs. Their first one was a Fuller's pub, where they had pints of London Pride, ESB, and Chiswick Bitter, all cask beers. Tom explained that cask beer may seem flat to Americans at first, but it has wonderful mouthfeel, is very pleasant to drink, and is great with food.

As they sat chatting and enjoying their pints, Tom commented that many pubs were like this iconic one. Unlike American bars, which can be harsh, with flashing neon signs and big screen TVs in your face, pubs are traditionally comfortable, with warm wood interiors, and often fireplaces. There are lots of modern-day exceptions, but most pubs are very cozy.

After a couple of pints, Tom told them it was time to move on to another pub. He suggested the Museum Tavern, back by the British Museum, since it was close to their hotel. Tom pointed out that many pubs do not serve food, but the Museum Tavern offered very good food, including British staples of Fish & Chips, Steak & Ale Pie, Bangers & Mash, and heaven forbid, even burgers. Most of the group tried one of the British plates and enjoyed them, along with more cask beers.

The pub was too intimate a place for Erik to watch Jennifer, so in an effort to build some trust with her, he worked to get a seat right next to her at the table. He resolved to be cordial, and make conversation with her, as well as the others nearby. He would need her trust at Stonehenge, to get her away from the group. She seemed reserved at first, but the beer seemed to relax everyone and make the conversation easier. She started to chat more freely with him, and they became more comfortable with each other. Erik was entirely pleased with his efforts. *This will work.*

By this point however, it had been an extremely long day that had started out back in Minnesota. "Time for some sleep. We have another big day tomorrow," said Tom.

They strolled back to the hotel and turned in for the night, all of them falling asleep quickly, except for Erik, who lay awake for nearly an hour, rehearsing. Finally, just before he fell asleep, he swore out loud, "I will get my revenge!"

Chapter 11

Dino was working on several follow-up reports at his desk Monday morning when his cell phone chirped. He looked to see the caller, *Johnny Jump Up.*

John R. Johansen was known to nearly everyone as Johnny Jump Up. Dino and Johnny were lifelong friends who had attended grade school, junior high, and senior high together. They had played on sports teams together, and there was one thing that Johnny was especially good at—better than anyone else—he could *jump.* On the track and field team, he came within one half inch of the all-time state record for the high jump. He set a new state record for the long jump. In basketball, he had a jump shot no one could defend. As a senior, Johnny led his team to the State Tournament, but early in the Championship game, he sprained his ankle and had to sit out. Without him, his team lost badly. But for sure, Johnny could jump. And the name stuck.

"What's up Johnny?" said Dino.

"Interested in lunch today? I'm buying."

"Sure. What sounds good?"

"Is that Roselli's place still in business?"

Dino could sense Johnny grinning through the phone. "It is indeed. What time?"

"Does twelve thirty work?"

"I'll make it work."

"Great. See you there!"

After high school, Johnny had enlisted in the Army. He

started out as a regular infantryman, but soon found his way into the Military Police. After he got out of the service, he went to work for a series of security-related companies. About eight years ago, he formed his own company, "Johansen Security." He was successful from the start and now employed twenty-eight people.

Dino drove to the restaurant and found Johnny waiting for him near the front door.

"Hey Dino, how's it going?"

"Great! Good to see you. Thanks for the invitation."

They headed into the restaurant and were greeted by Dino's mom. "Hi Johnny, it's been a while. How are you?"

"Great Momma! You look lovely as ever!" Johnny had called Dino's mom Momma ever since his days as a grade schooler, running through the Roselli household with Dino.

"You're too kind. Pick any spot you want Dino."

"Thanks Mom."

They picked a spot near the back of the dining room so they could talk with some privacy.

"How's Anna," asked Dino.

"She's doing fine, busy raising the boys. Todd is six now, and Peter is four. They can be a handful. So when are you going to get married and have some kids of your own?"

"Have you been talking to Momma? She's dying for some grandkids." After an awkward pause, he added, "I'm working on it."

When the waitress came, they both ordered a salad with a small side of pasta.

"Glass of wine?" asked Johnny.

"Not while I'm on duty, but you go ahead."

"I'd better not either. A couple of Pellegrinos?"

"Sure. So, how's business?"

"Funny you should ask," said Johnny. "That's actually what I wanted to talk to you about."

"Really?"

"The last four to five years, much of our growth has come from corporate security contracts. The customers are primarily medium-sized companies, predominantly local. We contract with them to provide a fixed schedule of security services. Mostly we do physical and event security. It's been good business for us."

"Good for you."

"Thanks. I have a team of great employees."

Johnny continued, "I want to expand into larger companies, but many of them want investigation services as well as security from a single provider. They're looking for services such as employment checks, criminal history, credit history, and executive search. I haven't felt comfortable getting into those areas. We really don't have the expertise necessary to do a good job. But I think I know somebody who does."

"And who might that be?"

"You!"

"Me?"

"Yes you. Your background would be perfect for the services these larger companies are looking for. Don't be so modest. All that stuff is right up your alley."

"So what are you proposing?"

"I'm proposing that you join me, as a full partner, and head up our new Investigations Group. Simple as that." After a quick sip of Pellegrino, he asked, "We would change the name of the firm from Johansen Security to Johansen & Roselli, Security and Investigations. What do you think?"

"Well, I am flattered."

"Dino, I know friends don't always make good business partners, but we've known each other our entire lives, and I feel sure we would work well together—complement each other. And quite frankly, I think it'd be fun!"

"Boy, I have to think here. You've caught me off guard. I guess my first thought is that I've never done anything but police work."

"I'm well aware of that, but your experience applies directly to private investigations, especially those of this type. Beyond that, I can imagine the St. Paul Police Department would be horrified at losing you. But just think, no more calls in the middle of the night or on weekends. No more hours spent filling out tedious report forms, we'll get you a personal assistant for whatever admin work is required. No more being at the mercy of the mayor's whims."

"Right now, it sounds too good to be true."

"Oh, it gets better," said Johnny. "I'm sure you have tons of contacts, and I know for a fact you have an excellent reputation here locally. I believe we can translate your experience and network into a ton of new business. And this new business is lucrative, with excellent profit margins. There's money in this for both of us. In fact, I'll add a $50,000 signing bonus, payable on your first day of work, for agreeing to join me. That's fifty big ones for you Dino!" He paused for dramatic effect, and then asked, "So what do you say?"

"Well, you've certainly piqued my interest," replied Dino, "but I would have to think long and hard before leaving the force." After a pause, he continued, "I certainly get frustrated at times, but it's been my everything since leaving school." After another pause, "Boy, I'm not sure what to think. What sort of time frame are you thinking?"

"The sooner the better. I have opportunities on the table right now."

"Well, again, I have to think about it."

"I understand. Take a few days, and we'll talk again."

Just then, their food came, and they turned their attention to enjoying their lunch.

Afterwards, Dino asked a few more questions, but then finished with, "I'll definitely think about it. Thanks."

Johnny paid the bill, and they left together, stopping to say goodbye to Momma on the way out.

Dino pulled out his keys as he walked toward the Alfa, but when he got there, he decided to keep walking. His mind was reeling. He did not want to show it in front of Johnny, but the offer had hit him like a punch in the gut.

From out of the blue, here was a solution to all his frustrations and aggravations. No more senseless gang murders, no more dead bodies to look at, no more of those endless silly reports. And a chance to make some real money—starting with $50,000 on Day 1! He did not know what to think, but he knew this was big, no—huge. A once in a lifetime opportunity, with a friend he knew well.

There was only one problem—and it trumped everything else. His promise to his dad, to be a cop, just like him. *What would he think of me?* He could barely bring himself to consider it. His stomach was in knots.

He walked back to the Alfa and drove to the office. In the hallway, he barely glanced at the picture of his dad on his way by. At his desk, he went through the motions of completing some reports, but everything around him had changed. The walls looked different somehow, the voices and chatter of the office sounded different. What would it be like to leave these people I have worked with for sixteen years? But there would be new people, new surroundings. *That would be a good thing, wouldn't it?*

The thought of actually leaving the force was scary. If he left, there would be no coming back. If it was a big mistake, what would he do?

The rest of the afternoon, he struggled to concentrate on his work. He completed a few reports and worked his way through conversations with Paula and Suzie. By quitting time, he was ready to get out of there.

He drove home and went straight to the wine cellar. He needed something to help him sort it all out. Something inspirational. *A Dolcetto should do nicely.* Once back upstairs, he got out a couple of good cheeses and some crackers. Plopping down in front of the fireplace, he grabbed the remote and flicked it on. *Maybe I'm nothing but a fake, just like this fireplace?*

His mind could not stop whirling, and it kept coming back to one thought. *What will Dad think of me if I walk away?*

Chapter 12

"You really should try it," urged Tom Morris, to the members of his Stonehenge traveling group. "A Full English Breakfast is the perfect start to a day in London."

Everyone slept well following their very long first day. They met at eight o'clock for breakfast. Tom was a big fan of the Full English Breakfast. "It's a tradition that dates back to the 1300s," he told them. "Most every English cafe, restaurant, or bed & breakfast will offer it. Traditionally, it consists of back bacon, eggs, British-style sausages, baked beans, fried tomatoes, fried mushrooms, and toast. Sometimes, it may include black pudding. If you don't already know what that is, and what it's made of, don't ask. And whatever you do, don't eat it!" he exclaimed. Most of the group ordered the Full English Breakfast and liked it. Others had something a bit lighter, but Tom urged them all to eat a solid breakfast. "You'll need the energy. It's going to be a very long day."

After breakfast, they went back to their rooms to grab light jackets and umbrellas. They reconvened in the hotel's lobby, and Tom went over the itinerary for the day. When they headed out the door, they found that there was a light fog, which Tom said was common for London, but he assured them it would burn off quickly, as the forecast was for a mostly sunny day. "Sunny days can be rare in London," he said, "but it does happen, and today, we're lucky to have great weather."

They walked to Holborn tube station and took first the Central Line, and then the Circle Line to the Tower Hill station. From there, it was a brief five-minute walk to get to their first attraction of the day, the Tower of London. They "queued up" to buy tickets for the next available tour, then queued up again for the tour itself. Within a few minutes they met their Beefeater tour guide, Charles.

"They're actually know as Yeoman Warders," explained Tom, "and they're usually very entertaining, as well as informative." Charles turned out to be just that. Interjecting typical dry British humor as he spoke, he described the Tower's history as a fortress, a palace, and a prison. They toured the grounds, as well as the White Tower, where Sir Isaac Newton carried out some of his research on gravity. And, of course, they gawked at the famous Crown Jewels in the Jewel House, while standing on a slow-moving walkway.

After the Tower of London, they headed to St. Paul's Cathedral, which was just a short tube trip on the Central Line. "I am deeply humbled, each and every time I go into St. Paul's," Tom told them. "It's Sir Christopher Wren's 300-year-old masterpiece. To this day, its dome is one of the largest in the world. That it survived World War II is a genuine miracle." Once inside, everyone was simply awestruck. As they walked the main floor listening to an audio guided tour with headsets, Erik positioned himself close to Jennifer, trying to gain some trust. They walked up a long staircase to the Whispering Gallery and looked down—an eerie view. Continuing on, they climbed to the Golden Gallery, which circles the outside of the dome. As they took in the breathtaking, panoramic views of London, Erik made small talk with Jennifer about how happy he was to have made the trip. When everyone had seen enough, they climbed back down the stairs and outside to the plaza in front of the church.

It was time for lunch, and Tom directed them to the Sherlock Holmes pub. The pub was only a twenty-minute walk from the Cathedral down Fleet Street and the Strand. Several members of the group said a brief walk would be good exercise, and so off they went. Along the way, Tom had to warn them about crossing

British streets. "In the US we're used to looking to the left for oncoming traffic. But here, you need to look to the right for traffic. Also, the traffic can pass quite close to the curb, so you must always be careful." Duly warned, they all made it to the pub just fine.

"This pub is a bit touristy, but the Sherlock Holmes is still a proper pub, and it serves food. They serve beer from the Greene King Brewery, including Old Speckled Hen and Abbott Ale." Tom recommended Abbot Ale as a pleasant, easy drinking real ale. The pub served a good selection of traditional pub fare, including Shepherd's Pie, Bangers & Mash, and Toad in the Hole. Everyone found something to their liking, and after a second round of pints, they were back on the street.

They walked just a couple of short blocks to get to the west bank of the River Thames, then south along the river to Big Ben, the world-famous icon of London. The bell tolled as they stood and looked at it, which gave them shivers. From there, they crossed Parliament Square to Westminster Abbey, where they saw the tombs of Charles Dickens, Sir Isaac Newton, and King Henry V.

For their next stop, they crossed over the Thames and went north along the river to the London Eye. The London Eye is like a giant Ferris wheel, with large glass capsules that hold up to twenty-five people each. Everyone is free to walk around inside the capsule as it slowly turns so they can look out over London in all directions. It takes about thirty minutes for one rotation, and then the ride ends.

When they got off the Eye, Tom told them they needed to head back to the hotel to get ready for the trip out to Stonehenge for the big summer solstice event. "We have to be at the Stonehenge Car Park by seven. They will let in about twenty thousand people, but to ensure we get in, we need to be there promptly. Everyone, please meet in the lobby, at four. We'll grab some fish and chips down the street for dinner. Our minibus will pick us up right there."

Walking from the hotel, they approached a shop with a neon "CHIPPY" sign in the front window. They went in, and several members of the group where surprised to find there were choices of fish—cod, haddock, or plaice in this shop. Everyone chose quickly and they were soon fed and ready for the bus. When the bus arrived, they climbed on immediately and were on their way.

Everyone was looking forward to the big event—the main reason they had come to England—the summer solstice at Stonehenge. But no one was more excited than Erik.

Chapter 13

Dino walked into the office Tuesday morning to find his boss, Paula Davis, waiting for him at his desk.

This can't be good. He took a deep breath and walked toward her. *Could she have found out about Johnny Jump Up's offer that quickly?* He offered a "Good morning," as he put his briefcase in his chair and took off his suit coat.

"Think again," she replied.

"That bad?" asked Dino.

"Worse," she said. "The mayor has called an emergency meeting for nine o'clock, and he wants you and Larry there, as well as George Erickson from the Gang Unit, and of course, the chief and unit heads."

"And the topic?" he asked, as if he did not already know. Besides Dino's Campbell case, there had been another fatal shooting late Friday night, just outside a nightclub in the Midway district. Paula had assigned the case to Larry Potter.

"Channel 7 ran a special last night about the most recent, and I quote, 'St. Paul crime wave,' and the mayor's lack of progress in curbing street violence. The press is all over him about it." She continued, "The mayor has gone flat out berserk, and I'm concerned the next case of violence might be here in our own department."

"I'll be there. Wouldn't want to miss that," Dino said.

"Better get your shit together, this one could get ugly." And she walked off toward her office.

Dino hated this part of the job—the political crap. He could handle long days, and the odd hours of nights and weekends, but politics was just not his thing. Though he understood it was a necessary evil, it was one more aggravation he would not have to put up with if he signed on with Johnny Jump Up.

The meeting started poorly and went downhill from there. Newly elected Mayor Richard Bennett was livid. "Can you believe it? A frickin *crime wave*. The nerve of these guys, calling it a *crime wave*? And the bastards make it sound like we're pulling the trigger!" The mayor's face was red and getting redder. The mayor had run on this very issue in the most recent election, and the press was now making him eat it.

"OK, so what've we got so far on these cases? Dino?" the mayor asked.

"Well, it's the typical gang case. We don't get many leads, there's no real motive, and few witnesses. This case is unique with the subsequent fire, but otherwise there's been little to go on. However, just this morning, the lab got back to us on the shell casings from the second murder. They match those of the first murder! That's a break for us. It means we're looking for one suspect rather than two."

"Good! That's something!" the mayor said, sounding a bit relieved. "Paula, can we release a statement on that this morning?"

"Sure. I'll get at it right after this," Paula replied.

"Great. Make sure those bastards at Channel 7 get it first."

"OK. How about the Task Force? What've we got going there?" the mayor asked.

"We were just getting things going on Friday when the second case came up. We'll resume our work on that today," Paula replied.

"We need to make some hay there," the mayor emphasized. "How about adding some civilian members—some guys from the community? It might help us deflect some of this heat."

"We can do that. Do you have anyone in mind?"

"I don't know. Find somebody that makes sense. Clergy maybe? Youth leaders? Somebody good with the press."

The mayor added, "Dino, Larry—I need you guys to come through on these cases. I know you usually work separately, but with this fresh evidence, maybe you should work together."

"We can do that," said Dino, with Larry nodding his agreement.

"OK. We need action here, and more importantly, results. Let's get busy! I want an update tomorrow morning at nine sharp."

"That went well," Dino said jokingly to Paula as they left the meeting and walked back to their area. Mayor Bennett was a bit more refined in public situations, but in internal affairs, he could be quite crass and often profane. Chief Kingston resented that the mayor often bypassed him and went directly to department heads and even individual employees, including detectives. But the chief had resolved that there was little he could do about the mayor's meddling, and that it was pointless to fight him on it.

"I'll grab us a conference room," Larry said. "See you in five?"

"Works for me," Dino replied.

Larry Potter was a fifteen-year veteran of the Homicide Unit. He was undoubtedly the most well-known detective to the public, having solved an intricate double murder case eight years ago, which had dominated the local news for months. Known as the Schafer Murders after its unfortunate victims, the case involved a prominent local businessman and his wife, who were gunned down late one Saturday night in downtown St. Paul. Larry was able to piece together a solid string of evidence against the victim's longtime business partner. The partner, along with a paid accomplice, were both sentenced to thirty years without parole at the State Penitentiary in Stillwater. Larry became a bit of a celebrity.

However, as competent as Larry was in his professional life, he was thoroughly incompetent in his personal life. He had divorced twice in six years and was working on his third. Still, he was respected as a skillful detective.

Dino started by reviewing the file on his case, then Larry did the same. They quickly agreed there was little to be gained from the forensic evidence available. Larry had three witnesses, but knew it was going to be difficult to get any real information from them. The night club where the murder took place, was a popular hangout for gang members, and no one wanted to go on record with anything against them. Jonathan Powell, the Light Rail Train witness in Dino's case, was not much better.

Both Dino and Larry had talked extensively with George in the Gang Unit, but George was not hopeful that direct interviews would be helpful at this point. The fear of retaliation both inside and outside of the gang community was strong and very real. People quite literally feared for their lives.

Larry felt the next best place to look for leads was the security tapes available. Both murders were committed on major downtown streets, and it was now common for businesses to have 24-7 surveillance cameras. Dino had a couple of tapes, but both were busts. Larry had been able to find four tapes from surrounding businesses, one of which was a business almost directly across the street from the night club crime scene. Larry pulled up the tapes on his laptop and started walking through them with Dino. The prime tape showed two cars entering the camera's view from the east at a high speed just moments before the shots were fired. Both cars slowed as they passed in front of the club, where a group of young people were standing. The windows were open on both cars, with multiple occupants in each car, who were gesturing out the windows at the group of people. Just after the cars passed out of view to the west, shots were fired and the people in the group hit the ground or ran for cover behind other parked cars.

"It's hard to see clearly in these grainy images," said Larry, "but we're quite sure that the car closest to the camera is a 2008 Honda Civic. The other is a 2012 Audi A4. With this side view, you won't see the plates but from another camera a block west of the scene, we got a clear plate number on the A4. However, when we ran it, records showed it was reported stolen in Minnetonka two months ago."

Larry had also worked to zoom in on the images of the people on the street at the front of the club. "I had George take a look but he doesn't recognize any of them. His people are out asking around, but no one's talking."

After lunch Dino and Larry continued to cross check details of their cases for a couple more hours, and then they called it a day.

"Can I get copies of your security tapes?" asked Dino.

"Sure. I'll send them now," replied Larry.

"I'll send mine to you as well, for what they're worth," said Dino. "I'll see if I can work the tapes a bit more tonight."

"I'll try to do the same but I have an issue with the wife tonight, so it doesn't look promising."

"No worries. Talk with you in the morning. Thanks."

They broke up and headed back to their desks. Dino cleared up a few admin things and then headed home.

Dino was actually grateful to get assigned to these two hot cases, as it helped get his mind off Johnny's offer for a while. The details of the two cases were whirling in Dino's head as he pulled into his garage and headed into the house. Once inside, he dumped his stuff and pulled out a bottle of Chianti Classico. He plopped down at the dining room table and fired up his laptop. While it was powering up, he opened the bottle of wine and poured a glass. The first sip was the most pleasant thing he had experienced all day. It was so good, he finished that glass and poured himself another.

Occasionally, Dino would feel some pangs of guilt over his wine drinking. *Is it possible I drink too much?* is how it usually started. It seemed most cops drank beer, or maybe whiskey. *But I'm Italian! And Italians drink wine every day. And besides, cops drink—it's what we do. No use fretting over it.* This is where his rationalization typically ended, as it did tonight.

For a couple of hours, he sat reviewing the tapes and drinking the Chianti. By nine o'clock the bottle was gone, and he decided to give it up for the day and try to get some sleep. Once in bed, he fell asleep quickly, but kept waking up with the details of the two cases still whirling in his head.

Just after four a.m., after perhaps the twelfth time of waking up, he was trying to get back to sleep, when he paused, sat bolt upright, and exclaimed, *that's it!* He jumped out of bed, ran downstairs and fired up the laptop. Since going to bed, he had been plagued with the idea that he was missing something on the tapes. His subconscious had apparently been chewing on it all night, and now he thought he might have something. He called up one of Larry's tapes first, and scrolled slowly forward through it, then the next tape, then the next. *There!* He pointed to one of the cars rolling past the scene, just a couple of minutes after the shots were fired. *Those wheels! How could I have missed them?* As a car guy, Dino just naturally noticed the smallest of details about the cars he saw each day. It was almost a subconscious thing. Non-car guys would not understand it, but car guys cannot help but notice paint colors, trim, exhaust pipes, tires, and yes, wheels! Many guys replace their stock wheels with custom wheels. This car was a Subaru WRX STI, with very distinctive wheels. Definitely custom. He paused that video, then called up the first of his own tapes. *Damn it.* Nothing there. He called up the second tape and started scrolling through it. *There it is.* The same car, with those distinctive wheels. He paused the video and noted the date timestamp. Same for Larry's video. *Gotcha!*

Dino knew he would never get back to sleep. He showered, got dressed, ate some yogurt with a piece of toast, and headed out the door to the office. When he got there, it was still dark. Flipping on the lights, he went straight to his desk and brought up the tapes. Using the best of the two, he prepared a still image that showed the wheels, both front and back. He then prepared an enlargement of the front wheel, saving both images as email-friendly JPEGs. Next, he went to Google to find out about the Minnesota Subaru Car Club, knowing there had to be one. He found not only that, but even better, he found a national Subaru WRX Forum. He quickly created a login, and then posted his two images in the forum questions section, with "Anybody know where I can get a set of these wheels for my 07 STI? Urgent. Thanks!"

It was nearly five thirty when he hit send on his forum post. He figured it would take a few hours to get any response but was pleasantly surprised to get one a few minutes after seven. *Don't these guys sleep?* A guy from Spencer Performance Parts in New York replied. "I was having my first Dunkin Donuts Espresso of the morning and saw the post. A place called Altbody Tuners in Jersey makes them. They specialize in Subaru parts. I don't see those wheels all that often, but a few guys around here run them. Nice wheels—light as a feather, but really pricey. Good Luck!" He included a link to the Altbody website. Dino looked at the website, and sure enough, there were the wheels, model XB-STI-KH-17. *The Internet can be a wonderful thing!" Let's see, if it is 7:25 a.m. here, it's 8:25 a.m. on the East Coast. Gotta be worth a try.*

He dialed the number on the website, and a guy named Kevin answered after just a couple of rings. "Altbody Performance."

Dino introduced himself and his reason for calling. The guy seemed a bit flustered at first but said he would try to help. "We only sell direct," he said.

"Can you tell me if you have sold any of the XB-STI-KH-17 wheels to anybody in Minnesota within, say, the last two years?" Dino asked.

"I can look, but it will take a few minutes. Can you hold?"

"Gladly, I really appreciate your help!" replied Dino.

Kevin came back a few minutes later. "We've sold three. One set to a guy in Minnetonka, about five months ago. Another set to a guy in Minneapolis, about ten months ago, and the last set went to a guy in St. Paul, about two months ago."

"Bingo! Can you give me the contact info for the one in St. Paul?" Dino asked.

Kevin hesitated for a few moments, but then said, "I don't see why not," and he gave him the information. Dino thanked him profusely, and before hanging up, asked for an email with the information for all three buyers, which Kevin agreed to do.

It was nearly eight and Dino checked to see if Larry was in yet. He was, but he did not look like a guy looking forward to the nine o'clock update meeting.

"You won't believe this!" exclaimed Dino. "I got a name!" He explained his chain of investigation.

"Are you kidding me?" asked Larry. "What a break!"

Dino said, "I've always said, 'If you ever have a choice between being good and being lucky, pick lucky!'"

They quickly verified the contact information and indeed, the contact was eighteen years old, and lived on the East Side.

They went to Paula's office and explained what they had put together. She could barely believe it.

"Great job guys!"

"It was Dino," said Larry.

"Just lucky," said Dino. "And thank goodness a criminal always returns to the scene of the crime," he added.

"I think we're ready for the mayor now!" said Paula. "I'll update the chief."

The meeting was like eating candy for Dino. The mayor was ecstatic. He followed with, "Nobody breathes a word of this outside this room, understand? If I find out anybody leaked this, that person is going to lose an appendage. I'm serious."

Dino and Larry left the meeting immediately and headed straight for the Alfa. A squad car with two officers was ready to follow them for backup. Dino was familiar with the general area of the address, but not the exact address. They kept under the speed limit but were still in the area in less than seven minutes. Dino was expecting an apartment building, or perhaps a single-family house, but instead found a small automotive tuner shop called Phalen Auto Sport. Dino called in their location and status, then sent the squad car around to the back of the building to cover any possible escape. When he was sure the squad was in place, he got out of the car and headed to the front door, followed by Larry.

They entered and found a small desk at the front of the space, and two maintenance bays at the back. A younger male was seated at the desk doing some paperwork. He looked up, and said pleasantly enough, "Can I help you?"

They flashed their badges and Dino said, "We're police officers looking for Samuel Cruz."

"That's me!" he said with a smile that was disarming. "What

can I help you with?"

"Did you purchase a set of custom wheels from Altbody Tuners in New Jersey a couple of months ago?"

"I sure did. What's up?" he asked, still pleasant.

"Do you own a Subaru WRX STI?"

"I wish! That's a little out of my league, at least right now. I have a 95 Honda Civic. It's parked out back if you want to see it."

A bit deflated, Dino replied, "Not right now. We've talked with Altbody Tuners and they only sell direct. Why did you buy wheels made for an STI?"

"I bought them for a customer of ours, and you're right, Altbody only sells direct. In order to get them for my customer, I had to say they were for me, and I had to use my personal credit card. OK, so I fibbed a bit, but gee, I didn't think it was actually illegal. My customer didn't have a credit card to pay for them directly, so I bought them for him. He paid me cash when they showed up, so I didn't even mark them up."

Dino paused, then asked, "Can you give us the name of your customer?"

"Sure, one sec." He got up and went to a file cabinet behind him. He searched one of the drawers and pulled out what appeared to be a service order. "Tony Martinez," he said.

"How about an address?"

"Let's see . . . 9336 McGill. It's over by Harding High School."

"Phone number?"

"Doesn't look like he gave one."

"OK, well thank you for your cooperation. We're interested in talking to Mr. Martinez. Please don't attempt to contact or otherwise alert him."

"I understand. No problem."

"Thanks again for your help."

Dino and Larry went back out the door and alerted the officers in the squad car. "New address is 9336 McGill, near Harding High School. Let's go."

They got back in the Alfa and headed straight for the new address. In less than five minutes, they pulled up to an apartment building with about twenty units. There was no Subaru

WRX STI in the attached parking lot. On the first floor they saw the manager's office. They left the squad in the lot, went to the door of the office, and pressed the buzzer. An elderly man answered.

Dino flashed his badge, saying, "I'm Detective Roselli, and this is Detective Potter, of the St. Paul Police Department. Do you have a tenant here named Tony Martinez?"

"No, I don't. Sorry."

"Are you sure? Drives a Subaru WRX STI?"

"Ah, that might be the guy that's been hanging out with the Petersons in 25A. I'm not real good with cars, especially foreign ones. Subaru is foreign, right? But I think that's what that guy had. Had it all fixed up fancy. To be honest, it was too damn loud."

"Are the Petersons in? We need to speak with them. Can you show us to their apartment?"

"Sure thing. It's on the second floor. I'll just grab my keys." The manager escorted them to the apartment and knocked on the door.

A woman inside asked, "Who is it?"

"It's Tom Bailey, Mrs. Peterson, the manager. There are a couple of police officers here that would like to talk with you."

"OK, one sec." They heard a security chain slide, and then the door opened. She saw Dino's badge, and instinctively stepped back a couple of steps, and asked, "What's this about?"

"Mrs. Peterson, I'm Detective Dino Roselli with the Police Department, and this is Detective Potter. We'd like to ask you a few questions. May we come in?"

"I guess so. I'm afraid it's a bit of a mess."

Tom Bailey interjected, "I need to get back to the office, and you don't need me."

"That's fine. Thanks Mr. Bailey."

She let them into the apartment and offered them chairs at the kitchen table.

"Mrs. Peterson, do you or your husband drive a Subaru WRX STI?"

"No, we don't, but we did have a friend living with us recently who had one. At least I think that's what it was. It was a Subaru something."

"Did have?"

"Yeah. He moved out two days ago."

"What was his name?"

"Tony Martinez."

"Do you know where he went?"

"I'm pretty sure he went back to Chicago. He's from there."

Crap, thought Dino.

"Do you know where in Chicago?" asked Larry.

"No. Tony was always a bit secretive. To be honest, he's my husband's friend. I don't know him that well. He stayed here a few weeks, but he really wasn't here all that often. He would stay out late at night and not come back until the next morning. One time, we didn't see him for a couple of days. Then two days ago he came back to the apartment, packed up his things, and said he had to leave. He was gone within thirty minutes. Never did give us any help with the rent. He did give us a little cash for meals. He must be in trouble?"

"We're not sure Mrs. Petersen. We just need to talk to him. Did he have a cell phone?"

"He had one, because I saw him use it, but I don't know what his number was. I think my husband knows."

"If you could ask him, that would be helpful. Could you call your husband now?"

"I can try." She went and got her own phone and called. "Hi, honey. There are two policemen here looking for Tony." She paused and they could hear her husband speaking on the other end, then she said, "I don't know. Do you know his cell number?" She jotted it on a piece of paper said, "Thanks. See you soon," and hung up. She handed the paper to Dino.

"Thank you, Mrs. Petersen. You've been very helpful. If Tony happens to call, could you please get in touch with us immediately?" Dino handed her his card.

"I will."

"Thanks again."

As soon as they were out of the building, Dino let out a "Shit!

So much for being lucky."

Larry added, "Yup. I'm sure the mayor is going to be ah . . . disappointed?"

"I was thinking more along the lines of . . . *pissed*!"

"I'm afraid you're right."

Many of the major crime characters in Minneapolis and St. Paul came from Chicago, where there was an overabundance of heavy-duty crime. Unfortunately, there was a well-known short-age of police resources there to deal with it all. Though Dino and Larry would immediately ask for assistance from the Chicago PD, both of them knew it was unlikely they would receive any real help—too low on their list of priorities. They dismissed the squad car standing by and headed back to the office.

While Dino drove, Larry called Suzette to have her contact the phone companies and ask for the latest cell phone tower usage for the number they had. After he hung up, he remarked, "That phone is probably lying in a ditch somewhere between here and the great state of Illinois."

Dino then said to Larry jokingly, "You know, on our way to the Phalen Auto Sport, we passed right by the State Bureau of Criminal Apprehension building. Maybe we could drop in and ask them for help with some *apprehension*. What do you think?"

"Nah, they're too slick for us. Just ask them," Larry smirked. "I'm afraid we're stuck with it. Might as well go back and face the music."

"Crap."

"Agreed."

Chapter 14

Erik Foster had gone along with all the touristy stuff up to this point in the day. He tried to appear cheerful, but his insides were starting to churn. He kept touching the knife in his pocket and rehearsing his plan mentally, over and over. His heartbeat was accelerating, and yet, at the same time, he was strangely calm and entirely confident that he would finally get his revenge. Throughout the day, he had made it a point to mingle and chit-chat with the other members of the group. Several times he chatted with Jennifer, trying to make her comfortable with him, without being obvious.

For the trip to the monument, Erik had packed a small backpack for himself. Backpacks were restricted in size for the solstice event. He brought along some paper towels, a small container of liquid hand soap, and a light throwaway jacket. He figured he would need to cleanup afterward.

Of the members of the group, three had been to Stonehenge before, besides Tom and Jennifer. All the rest were excited about experiencing the monument for the first time. As they rode along in the minibus, they all talked about their expectations.

Except for Erik.

Erik was gradually leaving reality behind and transforming into his Stonehenge personality. In reality, he was about to experience Stonehenge for the first time, but in his Stonehenge personality, he was merely returning to a place he had been many times. He thought about the countless hours he had spent in his secret room, seeing himself at Stonehenge. But now, he was actually going to be there. He noticed that the terrain was beginning to look like the Salisbury Plain in all the pictures he had studied so carefully. He felt his emotions swelling up, but he knew he had to control them until the supreme moment of revenge.

"Are you alright Erik?" The voice startled him. It was Karen Halvorsen, who was seated across the aisle from him, and was now looking directly at him. "Do you feel OK?"

"Oh yes, I'm fine." He paused, then added, "Thanks."

"You looked a little pale a while ago, but now you look flushed."

"I think it might be the strange food we've had here," he said, trying to smile. "My stomach is a bit queasy, but I'm sure I'll be fine."

"I know what you mean. I've enjoyed the food, but the fish and chips we had for dinner is sitting like a lump in my stomach. Too much grease for me. I have some antacids in my purse. Would you like a few?" she offered.

"That's very kind of you. Sure, I'll take a couple." Erik's stomach was fine, but he thought the best way out of this awkward moment was to just accept them. "Thanks."

"Oh, no problem. Just let me know if you'd like anymore."

"Thanks. Really."

Karen finally relented.

Erik scolded himself for allowing his emotions to become apparent to those around him. He knew he had to play along with the group for several more hours and did not want to jeopardize his plan. He had only one opportunity for this, and he was not going to screw it up.

Traffic along the M3 and A303 highways was not too bad, and they arrived at the Stonehenge Car Park just before seven. Tom had made prior arrangements with the driver for pickup early the next morning, which he now quickly confirmed. Everyone then got off, and the minibus pulled away.

Tom led the way to the queue leading into the monument. They had just started letting people in, and it appeared they were early enough to ensure getting in. Everyone in the queue was in high spirits, anticipating a unique experience.

Erik had worried about how tight security would be. He had paid strict attention to the security rules—no large packs, no alcohol, no fireworks, no glass bottles, and, of course, no weapons. As a precaution, he had fashioned a small pouch, on the inside of his wide leather belt, to conceal his knife. He felt confident that even a pat-down search would not find it, but he was concerned there might be metal detectors. He was relieved to see there were none, and he passed along inside the grounds with everyone else.

As their group approached the stones, they were overcome with awe—finally here at the sacred site. The stones were so impressive, standing there just as they have for thousands of years. For most people, a hundred years back in history is hard to imagine. That the Stonehenge site originated nearly 5,000 years ago is just too difficult to comprehend.

The crowd was growing quickly, with a large number of people already milling around. There were Druids in full regalia, and all types of revelers in the oddest of costumes. It looked as if there were people from all corners of the globe—people of all shapes, sizes, ages, colors, and dress. Amongst them all were plenty of everyday people as well. But what they all had in common was that they had traveled here to experience this singular event. It would be truly unforgettable.

Tom managed to find a small patch of open grass on the western edge of the grounds, which the group promptly staked out as their base camp. "By all means, wander around, check out the sights, watch the festivities, and talk with anyone you want, but eventually, make your way back here. This looks like the best place we can get to watch the sunrise, so we should all plan to watch it here together. Jennifer and I squeezed several thin tarps into our packs, and we'll spread them out here on the ground. Feel free to take a turn lying down for a rest as needed through the night. Remember, sunrise is at 4:52 a.m."

Erik was working to control himself and his emotions. He thought the people milling about looked comical and silly. *They have no idea what this place is truly about.* His reverence for the stones was based upon the immense work, sweat, toil, and yes, sacrifice, made by untold thousands of people through the ages, including himself. Of all the people here, *his* was a singular understanding of, and appreciation for, the stones and this site. Still, he knew now he had to work at controlling his emotions. He had to appear normal to the other members of the group. He made a point of chatting with Jennifer: "How many times have you been here? Do you think there will be fog in the morning? Have you been to Woodhenge?" *Blah, blah, blah,* he thought, barely listening to her replies. "When was the last time you were here?"

This last question, Erik silently answered for her. *If you only knew, this will be the last time you'll be here.*

He left her and wandered around by himself for several hours. Amplified music was prohibited, but many people were playing acoustic guitars and drums. There was even a Samba band. Erik ignored it all, working to keep his emotions in check. He had calculated that three thirty would be best time for the supreme moment. He had it all planned out. It would still be dark, which would afford him some cover. By then, the revelers would have quieted down, at least a bit, but there would still be more than an hour before sunrise, when everyone would be up. He forced himself to continue chatting with the other members of the group, but as the time neared, he became impatient, and his emotions began to swell.

Finally, it was time. He put on the light disposable jacket from his pack and felt the knife in his pocket one last time, for reassurance. He found Jennifer near the base camp and, trying to appear calm, strolled up to her and said, "I've always understood that there were no markings on any of the stones. But a few months back, I read something that said there are a few markings on a couple of them. I was just looking at them on Sarsen Stones 4 and 53. Are you interested in taking a look?"

He hoped it would pique her curiosity, and initially she hesitated, but then she said, "Sure, why not?"

A light fog had started to roll in within the last hour. *Perfect. It will provide some cover.* To Jennifer, he said, "I sure hope this fog doesn't interfere with the sunrise. It would be a pity to come all this way and miss out on the solstice event because of fog."

"The weather forecast didn't mention any fog. Seems pretty light right now. I bet we'll be OK."

As they started walking toward the stones, Erik told her, "There are supposedly some markings on the Slaughter Stone as well. We could look for those too." They stopped at the sarsen stones and, using the flashlight of his phone, he pointed at the supposed markings.

"They're somewhat difficult to see," she remarked, bending down. "And of course, it's quite possible the markings were added more recently, perhaps just a few hundred years ago," she said.

"Very true," he replied. "Let's check out the Slaughter Stone."

The Slaughter Stone is located roughly twenty yards away from the main group of stones. The stone had fallen long ago and now lay flat on its side in the grass. Erik was afraid Jennifer would balk at walking over to it, but he stepped confidently in the direction of the stone, and she followed along. Luckily, there was no one nearby. *Perfect.*

Erik's heart was pounding. As they walked toward the stone, with Jennifer on his left, he reached in his pocket and pulled out the knife, keeping that side of his body shielded from her. He had practiced opening the knife with one hand a thousand times, and he now sprang the blade open and it locked into position with a click.

"It's just right here," he told her. He stopped a few steps short of the stone and pointed toward it. He turned on his phone light again and shined it downward. "I guess those must be the markings there. What do you think?"

Jennifer stepped forward and leaned down to look. Erik suddenly turned the light off, and as Jennifer turned to ask him why, he stepped toward her, rage now filling him, and with his right hand, plunged the knife into her abdomen. He felt it go in, and he turned it with all the force he could muster.

Even in the darkness, he could see Jennifer's eyes look at him with total disbelief. She began to move her mouth, attempting a scream, but Erik plunged the knife in again, harder this time, taking her breath away. Erik was completely focused on the deed, thinking all the while of the moment so many years ago, when the elder had plunged the stone knife into his wife-to-be. "I avenge you, my beloved Rayla!"

Jennifer's eyes rolled back, and her body went limp. She fell forward into Erik's arms, and he held her for a moment, then pulled out the knife. He guided her body backward, down onto the stone, leaning her torso forward, to make it look as though she was sitting on the stone, just slumped over. Raising himself up, he stood over her in the darkness, exhausted. He started to regain consciousness and looked about. Quickly, he closed the blade of the knife and wiped the handle clean. There was a small group of people about twenty feet away, but they paid no attention to him. The fog was providing at least some cover. He leaned down to make it look as though he was trying to reassure her, and then stood up, and said, in a voice loud enough for anyone within earshot to hear, "Just rest here for a bit. I'll go get someone to help you. Just sit tight, I'll be right back." And he walked away.

Erik headed back in the general direction of the base camp, trying to act as though nothing had happened. As he walked, he looked down at himself, and there was only a small amount of blood on his jacket. Still walking, he peeled off the thin jacket, and as he passed one of the large garbage barrels on the grounds, dropped the jacket and the knife in. He continued walking to one of the distant toilets and stood in a short queue. Once inside, he used his paper towels and liquid soap to clean his hand. Satisfied with the job, he continued on back to the base camp.

As he approached the camp, he saw Tom and asked if he could take a quick snooze on one of the tarps. He was really just making a point of being seen. Tom said, "Sure, but since sunrise is only an hour away, you'll want to make it a short one." Tom was about to turn away, but he looked back at Erik and asked, "By the way, have you seen Jennifer lately?"

The question threw Erik off balance, but he managed to reply with, "Let's see, I think the last time I saw her she was over by the stones, talking with a couple Druids. Maybe an hour ago?"

"OK, thanks."

Erik laid down on the tarp and collapsed. As he laid there, he smiled and allowed himself a sweet thought. *I have avenged you, my beloved.*

Chapter 15

The morning after the fiasco of the Subaru WRX case, as it had now been dubbed, Dino was at his desk, licking his wounds. Though there was a chance that the Chicago PD would turn up something on their suspect, it was unlikely. There was little that Dino and Larry could do with their guy four hundred miles away, lost in the urban jungle of Chicago.

The mayor was more than disappointed that Dino and Larry had ". . . let the suspect get away." Dino resented the comment but was equally disappointed. He understood the mayor's sentiments, but sometimes wished he was not quite such a loose cannon with his mouth. Boorish comments do nothing to help the situation. The mayor often uttered things he later regretted, but no matter, Dino had learned to just ignore him.

Just after ten thirty Paula Dunn came out of her office into the Homicide Unit's bullpen area to announce that a St. Paul cop had just been killed by gunfire after having responded to a disturbance involving two local gangs in the McKenzie East High School parking lot. There was a collective sigh of "oh no," then the room went quiet. Everyone's face reflected disbelief. Adam Baker was a twelve-year veteran of the force and a four-year veteran of the Gang Unit. There had been an altercation yesterday at the same location, same time, with the same two gangs. Ironically, Adam had gone to prevent one from happening again today. Maybe today's incident was intentional, a trap set for an unsuspecting police officer. No matter now, it was done. Adam was competent and well-liked. Most everyone knew he was married, with a three-year-old daughter.

Dino's own thoughts went from deep sympathy for the family, to anger, to recollections of the day he found out his own father had been killed in the line of duty. After the announcement, Dino went to Paula and offered to help with the search for the killers.

"I'll pass that along to George Dino. Of course, you more than most, understand the futility of these gang confrontations. No one will have seen anything or anyone. No weapon will be recovered. These cases are always frustrating. But I'll let you know Dino."

"Thanks."

Back at his desk, Dino's mind wandered to Johnny Jump Up's offer. *I would finally be done with this gang crap.* It was an appealing thought.

The atmosphere in the office thereafter was somber in the extreme. By mid-afternoon, a rumor was circulating that Adam's wife was pregnant with their second child, which only added to everyone's grief. Late in the afternoon, Paula announced that there would be a police funeral with full honors, on Sunday, three days from now. The service would be held in the Lincoln Senior High Auditorium at two o'clock.

The day of the service, the auditorium was packed full of people thirty minutes before the service was even supposed to start. Additional people were directed first to two overflow rooms with video of the service, then to an outside area where loudspeakers had been hastily set up.

With the flag-draped coffin on full display at the front of the large room, the service started with an opening prayer by the pastor of the Bakers' church. Mayor Bennett then spoke, and for a change, did a credible job. Chief Kingston spoke next, though he had to stop twice to collect himself. A female vocalist sang, then all the attendees sang two hymns. Several eulogies were delivered, and then finally, the pallbearers, all in uniform and wearing white gloves, moved forward and took their positions on either side of the casket. To the sound of the final organ hymn, the pallbearers then carried the casket out to the waiting hearse. The service was incredibly sad—all of it. Many people wept throughout.

A procession formed to go to the cemetery. The train of vehicles had well over two hundred police cars, coming from all over Minnesota, as well as from Wisconsin. At the cemetery, there were final prayers. A color guard of seven uniformed officers fired a three-volley salute. The two most senior officers solemnly removed the flag, ceremoniously folded it into the familiar triangle, and presented it to the chief, who in turn presented it to Adam's wife Andrea. Finally, a lone bugler played taps.

Throughout it all, Dino could not help but compare this funeral with that of his dad. Yet his feelings could not have been more opposite. His dad's funeral had inspired him to become a cop and honor his dad's legacy. But this funeral was having the opposite effect—he was angry, and was again questioning whether he still wanted to be a cop. *What if it happened to me?* Fear of death was something that hung over all cops, but most thought of it only in abstract terms. It was something that *will never happen to me.* But this death was tragic. This death was real. He thought back to the incident just a few days ago on University Avenue, in the middle of the night. Shots had been fired at him, with one of the bullets whistling by just inches from his head. At the time, he did not think that much about it, but now he thought, *My God, I could have been killed, right then and there. Hell of a way to make a living.*

Chapter 16

"**E**rik, wake up! It's nearly sunrise!"

Erik had fallen into a deep sleep just seconds after lying down on the tarp. Tom was nudging him, trying to get him awake. "You don't want to miss it!"

"Whew. Boy, I guess I was tired. Thanks."

Tom added, "Jennifer hasn't come back yet. Did you say you'd seen her with some Druids?"

Still groggy, Erik replied, "Ah, yeah. She was by the sarsen stones with a few of them when I last saw her. Would you like me to go look for her?"

"It's almost sunrise. We'll stay here for now. If she doesn't turn up soon, we'll split up and go look for her." Tom was worried, and glanced around to see if maybe she would show up at the last minute, but not seeing her, he had to get started. "OK, it's time everybody!"

The Druids were chanting and the crowd was coming alive. Two guys at opposite ends of the site blew trumpets, holding their final notes, when a bright speck of light became the tip of the new day's sun, peaking over the horizon. It rose quickly, and then just as it has for thousands of years, it aligned with the Heel Stone, and sunlight streamed into the center of the stones—an amazing sight. There was clapping, singing, and celebration.

After just a few moments of revelry, Tom's demeanor changed to one of deep worry. He turned to the group and said, "I need help to look for Jennifer. She would never miss seeing the solstice here with us."

Bob Anderson replied, "No problem Tom, we can all help. We'll find her."

They were about to split up and start looking, when one of the event's security personnel came running. He slowed as he approached, then stopped and asked, out of breath, "Are you the group of Americans from Minnesota?"

Tom responded, "Yes we are, we're . . ."

The security guard cut him off with, "I need your group to come right now." He turned and started running back, followed by Tom and the rest of the group, except for Tammy Anderson, who said she would stay with the base camp. Tom knew something was wrong, and he was right on the heels of the security guard.

Erik knew exactly what the trouble was. He stayed near the back of the group, but played along with things, trying to wear a troubled look to match those of the others. It was difficult trying to get through the thick crowd, which was still celebrating. They headed straight for the center of the sarsen stones, but once there, they continued right on through and headed for the Slaughter and Heel Stones on the far side.

Erik's heart started pounding again. In the preparations for his revenge, he had not thought much about the aftermath. Now, however, the stark fear of capture was starting to come over him. Preoccupied, he stumbled on something and fell to the ground, but he got right back up. Bob Anderson was right behind him, and asked, "You OK Erik?"

"I'm OK, let's go."

As they approached the Slaughter Stone, they saw a ring of security personnel surrounding it, with flashlights pointed to the ground. Tom tried to force his way between two of them, but the man who had led them there shouted, "Please sir, please wait . . ." But it was too late. Tom saw Jennifer slumped on the ground, motionless.

"Oh God, no! Is she?"

"I'm sorry, sir."

Tom fell to his knees and leaned forward toward Jennifer's body, but a security person grabbed his shoulder and said, "Please don't touch her, sir. What's your name?"

"Tom. Tom Morris. Jennifer's my wife! Oh God, what happened?"

"She was stabbed, sir."

"What?" Tom stood up. "What the hell? Who did this? Why would anyone kill Jennifer?"

"We're not sure, we're securing the area now."

In the distance, there was the sound of approaching British police cars, with their distinctive "nee ner nee ner" sirens. People started gathering around, but the security personnel were pushing them back, establishing a perimeter around the scene.

As word of an incident spread through the crowd, the sounds of celebration had all but disappeared. The lead security person told Tom, "Sir, we need to gather all the members of your group for questioning."

"My group? What about those damn Druids? She was last seen talking with several of them by the large stones. The bastards! I assume you're asking all of them what the hell happened here?"

"We will indeed, sir. Please stay calm."

"That's going to be difficult. Damn it!"

Police personnel were arriving, and they quickly established security over the scene. They had bullhorns and were instructing the people in the crowd to stay back. They made an appeal for anyone who had seen anything suspicious to come forward.

"How about the damn Druids?" Tom yelled. "They're the ones you need to check out, before they all run away, if they haven't already! Perfect time and place for a religious sacrifice, isn't it? Jesus, don't let them get away. Bastards!"

"We're securing the area now, sir. Everyone will be checked."

Though the security personnel were trying to secure the event, with a crowd of over twenty thousand people, and only a handful of security and police personnel, complete security was impossible. People were starting to leave. Many had already left.

Overhead came the *"whup whup whup"* of a police helicopter approaching. It landed about three hundred yards away from the monument, in an area cleared by security personnel.

Erik stood with the other members of the group, watching what looked more like a circus than a crime scene. *There's no way they can conduct any real investigation here.* It relieved his fear of capture. He knew they would all be questioned, but he was growing confident that he was safe. He continued with his outward expression of disbelief. "How can something like this happen?" he asked, with an appropriate level of outrage. But inwardly, he was congratulating himself. *I'm home free.*

It was nearly four hours later that the group was allowed to return to their hotel. Each member of the group had been questioned about what they had been doing and what they had seen. Erik played up the Druid story, and the police seemed eager to hear it. Tom had been taken to a nearby police station for further counseling and processing.

As Vice President of SIG, Bob Anderson had taken over leadership of the group, with everyone's approval. He managed to contact the driver of their minibus, and they finally got back to the hotel around two in the afternoon. Everyone was exhausted at the end of their long and horrific day. They had been told they must stay at the hotel until contacted by the police, and that they were not to talk to any news reporters. They all had dinner in the hotel restaurant before retiring to their rooms.

The next morning, after an early breakfast, the police called them to a small hotel meeting room.

"Hello, I'm Detective Superintendent Jack Wright, of the Wiltshire Constabulary, and I've been assigned as the Senior Investigating Officer on this case. I assure you my team and I will do everything possible to find out who did this.

"It's important to act quickly here. I can tell you we're looking into all possibilities. As Tom here has suggested, it is indeed possible that one of the Druids is responsible, although they don't have a history of violence, much less murder. It's also possible this was a random act of violence by someone in the crowd. There were people from all over the world at the solstice. In any crowd, there are good guys, and unfortunately, there can be bad guys. However, quite bluntly, there's also the possibility that a member of your own group is responsible."

Several members of the group reacted immediately with, "That's not possible!" and "You're on the wrong track there Detective!"

"Please, I'm not accusing anyone. I'm simply saying it's a possibility, and we must look at all possibilities. I will add that this murder appears to have been premeditated, and even staged."

"For what purpose?" replied Bob Anderson, with several others in the group nodding in agreement.

"I can't tell you. I'm just saying, it appears that way."

"Jesus, if any of us wanted to kill Jennifer, they wouldn't have had to come all the way to England to do it. That just doesn't make sense."

"I agree with you, and yet she was murdered by someone. For now, I must ask that you all stay in the hotel."

"But we have flights home today," several responded indignantly.

"No one can leave until we've completed our questioning. It will be at least a day."

Several members of the group complained they had jobs and families they had to return to.

"We're sorry for the inconvenience, but this is a murder investigation. I think you can understand our need to complete at least our initial questioning. We'll get you on your way home as soon as possible. We appreciate your cooperation."

Luckily, the hotel had rooms enough for them to stay several days if need be. They ended up staying two more days before they were allowed to fly back to Minnesota. Tom would be staying an additional day to make arrangements to bring Jennifer home.

Over the two days of waiting, the police had questioned Erik twice. Each time, he pressed the Druid explanation, and since she was supposedly last seen with several of the Druids, the police seemed to be buying it. No one mentioned anything about a knife or jacket. Erik was feeling increasingly confident, almost smug, that he was in the clear.

It took a while for everyone to re-book flights home, but they were all able to get seats, though they had to split up onto different flights.

Erik boarded his flight, and as he sat awaiting takeoff, he congratulated himself. *They have no idea.*

Chapter 17

Dino was working at his desk just after eight thirty the next morning when Paula came to him, "I have an assignment for you."

"Oh oh, that sounds ominous."

"It's nothing like that. Let's go into my office."

They started walking toward her office.

"This isn't another task force for the mayor is it?"

"Nope. Come on."

When they were both in her office, she closed the door, sat down, then asked: "Have you heard of the Stonehenge Murder Case?"

"Sure, it's all over the media. What about it?"

"The British police believe the murderer is a member of the St. Paul group that traveled to Stonehenge for the summer solstice."

"Really? Wow."

"Do you know much about Stonehenge? And the summer solstice thing?"

"I've always been interested in Stonehenge, but really don't know that much about it."

"Ever hear of the Druids?"

"Didn't they build Stonehenge?"

"This case is about a *murder* at Stonehenge, not about Stonehenge itself. But you may want to bone up on it at least a bit."

"OK."

"The British police considered that the Druids may have been involved, but Stonehenge is a sacred place for Druids. It's like religion. They have no history of violence, much less murder. The police also considered that it may have been a random act, but they now think that's unlikely. They feel the murder was definitely premeditated. And then there's the old 'the victim knew the murderer' thing, that points to some member, or members, of the group.

"Since the Stonehenge Interest Group, or SIG as they call themselves, is located here in St. Paul, the British police have asked for our help in finding the murderer, or murderers, and I'm assigning the case to you."

"It all sounds interesting. Really."

"I'll reassign the two active cases you have now. You should be able to work pretty much full time on this case. Suzette can support you."

"Perfect."

"We're scheduled for a video call with Detective Superintendent Jack Wright, their lead on the case, at ten this morning. They're six hours ahead of us, so that will be four o'clock their time. We'll take it in Conference Room B."

"I'm really ready for a case like this. Something different."

"I kinda thought you'd like this one."

Dino started to leave, when Paula added, "Wait a sec, before you go. I've noticed that you've been pretty quiet lately, anything bothering you?"

"Ah . . . no, I'm fine."

"You're sure?"

"Yup. I'm fine. Really."

As Dino walked away, he worried. *Geez, is it showing that my mind has been elsewhere lately? I need to be more careful. I'm glad to have this new case.*

Detective Jack Wright started the call by introducing himself. Paula, Dino, and Suzette reciprocated.

He then continued, "As you may know, the UK and US have a long-standing extradition agreement, the most recent being the

Treaty of 2003. But extradition only comes into play once we've got a probable suspect and some evidence. With all the members of the group located in Minnesota, we're asking for your help with the case."

"We're happy to help," Paula replied.

"Of course, this must officially be run through your Justice Department, but I'm told that's pretty much a formality."

"Sure. How do you want to proceed?"

"I think I need to come to St. Paul. It would be difficult to try and work back and forth, and it's compounded by the time difference. You're just getting to work there in Minnesota, when it's time to start hitting the pubs here. Hoping for your cooperation, I booked a flight out of Heathrow early tomorrow. It's a direct flight to MSP, and gets there just after five p.m."

"I can easily pick you up," replied Dino. "Do you have a hotel booked?"

"I do not. I thought I'd get a recommendation from you for something convenient."

"There's a Hilton nearby that's comfortable, right in downtown. I can get you a room there. I think we may even get a bit of a discount."

"Cheers for that."

"Sorry?"

"Ah . . . thanks."

"Easy to do. How long are you planning to stay?"

"Good question! Let's make it a week, and I can adjust it one way or the other as needed. Hopefully we can catch our guy, or guys, quickly."

"I'll send summaries of our work thus far for your review. I'll include a list of the group members with what background we have on them." He continued, "OK, that's about it for now. We certainly appreciate your help."

Dino concluded with, "No problem. We're looking forward to meeting you in person. I'll pick you up at the airport tomorrow." They signed off.

"Well, this will be something different," said Paula.

"Sounds very interesting to me!" said Suzette.

Dino chimed in with, "I'll dive into the summaries as soon as I get them. And I guess it wouldn't hurt to bone up on Stonehenge a bit." He continued, "I've always been fascinated by Stonehenge. Never thought it would become personal!"

Dino received the summaries just after noon and started on them immediately. There were surprisingly few specifics gained from the initial questioning of the group members. The fact that the murder took place in the middle of a crowd of twenty thousand people, celebrating the solstice, in predawn twilight, made things difficult. The confusion that followed the initial discovery of the body only made things worse. He spent the afternoon studying what Detective Wright had sent and then decided to head home to do some general Stonehenge research.

At home, he headed down to his cellar, and pulled a bottle of Chianti Colli Senesi. Dino felt Colli Senesi was every bit as good as Classico, but at a better price. They were both Chiantis, the only difference being that the vineyards were separated by a 3-foot goat path running along a ridge line. *Pays to know your wines.*

He made a light dinner, then afterward sat down with the rest of the Colli Senesi to do some research on Stonehenge. He reminded himself that the case was not about Stonehenge itself, but about a murder committed there. Still, it was clear that the setting, and even the Druids, were fundamental to the case.

He started with some general Google searches for 'Stonehenge.' Thinking, *5,000 years old. Heck, that's almost as old as Margie in the Accounting Department.* Wine tended to make Dino a comedic genius, with the formula being 'more wine equals more genius.'

'Druids' was his next search. There are references to the Druids going back to as early as 400 BC, but they certainly did not build Stonehenge. The ancient Druids were philosophers and teachers. Modern-day Druids generally promote harmony, connection, and reverence for the natural world. They claim to respect all beings, as well as the environment.

He then Googled 'images of Druids at Stonehenge.' From

the results, he could see why someone might point a finger their way. Some of them looked as though they were attending a zombie convention. Add in some possible ancient legends of human sacrifice, and the whole thing did seem plausible. Yet Detective Wright said modern-day Druids had no history of violence.

Interesting.

"OK, I guess I have a feel for it." He polished off the Chianti and headed for bed.

For the first time in a long while, Dino was looking forward to his next day as a cop. *Maybe I need to reconsider my thoughts on Johnny's offer.*

Chapter 18

E rik awoke with a start. He had jerked his left arm up, and nearly upset the tray in front of him. He looked around and realized he was still in his seat on the long flight home from England.

The passengers on either side of him seemed a bit annoyed but said nothing.

"Sorry," he said quietly.

Though still confident he was in the clear, he had been dreaming he was being pursued by the police and was running as fast as he could to avoid capture. Awake now, he dismissed the dream and started thinking about returning home. He was looking forward to things getting back to normal.

The ten-hour flight home seemed to go on forever, but eventually they landed at MSP. Off the plane he headed for customs. He grabbed his bag off the carousel and suffered through the long line, but eventually made it through, and headed for the exit.

As the doors out of the passenger security area opened to the area for the general public, Erik was hit with a slew of bright lights and news reporters staring at him. They had been waiting for him, and they now pressed forward. Two TV reporters stuck microphones in his face and shouted questions at him. He was stunned and confused. *Why do they want to talk to me?*

"What can you tell us about the Stonehenge Murder Case, Mr. Foster? Who do you think did it? Did you see the body?"

Erik was reeling from the barrage and stepped backward just as the security door closed behind him. He was pinned against it. Then it opened again, as other passengers were trying to exit. They were working their way around, trying to get through the crowd.

Erik tried to collect his thoughts. "Why do you want to talk to me?" he said aloud.

"You were part of the Stonehenge group, weren't you?"

"Yes, but . . ."

"What details can you give us?"

Erik remembered Detective Wright telling all of them to not talk to reporters. "I'm not supposed to talk to reporters."

"That's for the UK, Mr. Foster, you're back on US soil now. Surely you can talk to us. What progress have the British authorities made in finding the killer?" They continued to press him.

"I'm sorry. I have nothing to say." He pushed his way to one side and headed for a men's room across the hall. He dove in, and thankfully, they did not follow him. Inside an open stall, he sat down and tried to make sense of it all. *The Stonehenge Murder Case*? What the hell is going on?

While the group was still in England, the incident had captured the interest of the local Minneapolis/St. Paul news outlets and the general public. International intrigue, woman murdered on the Slaughter Stone at Stonehenge on the summer solstice—what more could people want? The TV stations were playing it up, and people could not seem to get enough of it.

Erik pulled out his cell and found a number for airport security. He called it and asked if they could escort him to his car. They said they could, and after about 15 minutes, they led him out of the men's room, past the reporters still waiting, and got him to his car in the airport ramp. As soon as he got in, he locked the doors. *I can't believe it.* He was not expecting anything other than to collect his luggage and head home.

At least they had not followed him to his car. He started it up and headed out of the ramp and straight to his apartment in St. Paul. Afraid reporters were following him, he parked his car, hurried inside, closed and bolted the door. *Home!*

He put his luggage in the bedroom and found something in the kitchen to eat. Turning the TV on to Channel 7's 10 p.m. news, he stared in disbelief as he saw himself coming out of the security area doors, into the rush of reporters. He looked dumbfounded and nervous. His responses sounded like he was mumbling.

Then he panicked. *Did I look guilty? Oh my God!* He shut it off. He didn't want to deal with it anymore, and went to bed. He slept fitfully, but luckily, there were no dreams.

With their stay in England extended by the police, he had missed more days of work than he had planned on, so in the morning, he needed to go to work. He got ready, drove to work, and walked into the building, not knowing what to expect. No one was near the entrance to the building, or in the hallway, but as he entered his department, everyone stared at him. Someone spoke up and asked, "How're you doing, Erik?" He ignored them and quickly made it to his desk.

After a couple of minutes, his pointy-haired manager, right out of the Dilbert carton strip, came to his desk. He welcomed him back and asked how he was doing. Erik said he was fine. His manager told him to collect himself, get caught up on emails, and let him know when he was ready to review the status of current projects. Erik agreed, and his manager left.

He worked straight through the morning without leaving his desk. People were leaving him alone, but he could feel the stares. For lunch, he grabbed a sandwich and a Coke from the vending machine and ate at his desk. In the afternoon, he met with his manager, who never brought up the incident. He decided to stay late, letting the other people leave for the day, and then he headed home.

Not wanting to shop for groceries, fearing that people would recognize him, he stopped at a McDonald's drive thru for a Big Mac, fries, and a large Coke. He took it all home and sat down to eat. He was exhausted. While he ate, he started wading through personal emails on his phone. Most were junk, but he saw one with a subject of "*I saw you at Stonehenge,*" and a sender of "*eyewitness0621@gmail.com.*" He opened it and almost choked on his food.

"I saw you murder Jennifer, and I saw you throw the knife and your jacket in the trash barrel. We need to talk."

Chapter 19

Dino was at the airport a little before five. The Delta website was reporting Jack's flight as on time. While he was waiting in the arrivals area, Dino watched the overhead TVs. One of them had Channel 12 reporting that the St. Paul Police were coordinating with the British police on the investigation. Dino was pleased that apparently no specifics had gotten out of the department about Jack's arrival. Police stations can leak secrets like a sieve sometimes.

The arrival screens were finally reporting the flight as "Arrived," and a few minutes later, passengers started streaming out of the international arrivals doors. Dino held up his "Jack Wright" sign and within a couple of minutes a man matching Jack's description, dressed in a conservative, English-looking suit, walked up and offered Dino his hand and said, "I'm Jack Wright. You must be Dino."

"Indeed, I am." They shook hands. "How was your flight? You look reasonably refreshed for such a long flight."

"It wasn't too bad. I managed to nap a little. Still, I was happy to finally get off the plane and walk a bit. Thanks for picking me up."

"No problem at all. Happy to do it. You got all your bags?"

"Yes. I had to claim them before going through customs. I'm ready to go."

As they headed toward the parking ramp, Dino asked, "First time in the States?"

"It is. Everyone told me it's cold in Minnesota. I half expected to see snow on the ground."

"Quite honestly, you don't want to come here in January or February. But we do enjoy all four seasons, and it can actually get pretty hot in the summer. They're forecasting nineties for next week."

"Let's see, that would be roughly, ah, 30 degrees Celsius. Gee, I had no idea."

As they got near Dino's SUV, he popped the rear door.

Jack was surprised. "Wow, an Alfa Romeo! Cops must be paid pretty well here."

"Hardly. I have a bit of my own money and I love cars. An Alfa Stelvio seemed like a good way to get around, especially in the winter. Here, give me your bags."

"Thanks." Jack walked around to the front of the car to get in and said, "Wait a minute, it looks like they put the steering wheel on the wrong side of the car! Oh, that's right, you Yanks drive on the wrong side of the road."

"Funny. We call it the right side of the road—get it? Right side?" After a brief pause, he added, "Touché! Just kidding. Couldn't help it."

Dino left the airport and drove along the Mississippi River toward downtown St. Paul. They chatted about the case.

As they neared downtown, Jack remarked, "The cathedral up there on the hill is certainly impressive."

"That's the Cathedral of Saint Paul. It's over a hundred years old, and the third largest Catholic cathedral in the US, though it's not quite the St. Paul's Cathedral you have in London."

Dino added, "I live less than a mile west of the Cathedral."

"What's that building with the red tile roof and green copper capped turrets? It looks like a castle."

"It's called the Landmark Center. It's also more than a hundred years old."

"Well, I'm impressed. St. Paul is certainly a charming city."

"I don't really think much about it—I've lived here my whole life. But yes, it is charming. Much more so than our twin of Minneapolis."

"Oh?"

"Minneapolis is much more modern looking, with straight streets and rectangular blocks. Over there, they're known for tearing things down and building new ones that are bigger, better, and shinier. In St. Paul, we just clean it up and call it 'historic' and put it on the National Register of Historic Places. The two cities together are known as the 'Twin Cities' and there's a friendly rivalry about things, but I confess I prefer St. Paul."

"Hungry?" asked Dino.

"Yes!"

"Like Italian?"

"Sure."

"Then I've got just the place. My family has a restaurant in downtown St. Paul. The food's pretty good, and I can personally guarantee the wine list is the best in town. You a wine drinker?"

"Absolutely. My wife and I went on holiday to Tuscany a few years back. Loved the food and especially the wine. Anything from there, as well as most anything north of there, from Piedmont."

"Well, now I'm jealous! And I'm the Italian guy here. My mom and dad emigrated from Italy."

"Really? I guess I should have guessed with a name like Roselli. Have you been to Italy?"

"Only once, as a kid. Dad took the whole family back to his hometown, Ponticelli, in Umbria. It's a small town, just east of Tuscany. We still have family there."

"Interesting."

"Where is the restaurant?"

"It's a couple of blocks from the hotel where you're staying."

"That's perfect."

They arrived at the Hilton, and Dino parked the Alfa while Jack checked into his room. In just a couple of minutes, Jack came down and they started walking toward Roselli's. As they approached the restaurant, Jack saw the entrance with its two wood-framed doors with large glass panes, decorated with "Roselli's Ristorante" in ornate gold leaf. To the left of the doors was a glass window into the bar area. On the right was an even larger glass window into the dining room. Both windows had the impressive gold-leaf lettering and provided an inviting view of the inside of the restaurant.

There were two valets on duty at the front doors, and their faces lit up when they saw Dino. The one closest greeted him, "Hey Dino, how's it going?"

"Just great John. Larry, how're you doing?"

"Fine. Where's the Alfa?"

"Ah, it's so nice out this evening, I thought we would walk. Momma here?"

"Of course. When is she not?"

"Good point."

The valets each opened a door for Dino and Jack to enter.

"Thanks guys," said Dino.

Just inside the door, they were met with the smell of warm bread and marinara sauce. Behind a small hostess stand was an attractive woman who smiled brightly when she saw Dino.

"Hi Momma, I brought someone to meet you. He's a Brit."

"Really?"

"Momma, this is Jack Wright. Jack, my mom, Sophia."

"Welcome Jack. Please come in. I suppose you're here for the Stonehenge Murder thing?"

"I am."

"Tragic. I've been watching it on TV. I don't know how anyone can do something like that."

"It's always hard to understand."

"You must be hungry. Let's get you a table." She motioned to them to follow her, saying, "We're nearly full tonight, but your favorite spot in the back corner is open Dino."

"Thanks Mom."

She led them to the table and got them seated. "Stacy will be over in just a minute. I'll let Dino help you pick a wine and something to eat. It's nice to have you here, Jack. Buon appetito!"

They sat down, and Jack declared, "What a charming lady."

"Yeah, she's special."

Jack looked around the dining room. White tablecloths covered the tables. The floor was all dark wood, as were the chairs. There was a high ceiling, with simple chandeliers casting a delicate light over the dining room. The back wall of the dining room had alternating sections of wine racks, then Italian-themed paintings illuminated with soft museum lights. The waiters and waitresses wore white shirts with black ties, black slacks, and white wraparound aprons. There was a pleasing level of conversation from the surrounding tables.

"This place is lovely. Reminds me of a favorite restaurant of mine in Tuscany."

"It took a few years to build up, but we're now one of the top-rated restaurants in the Twin Cities. See anything that appeals to you on the wine list?"

"Oh please, pick something. I'm quite sure your nose and taste for wine are far more sophisticated than mine."

"It's all about practice! How about a Montefalco? It's unique to Umbria, and something you have probably never had. It's roughly seventy percent Sangiovese, fifteen percent Sagrantino, with the rest usually Cabernet Sauvignon, or even Merlot. Wanna give it a try?"

"It sounds great! Thanks. Honestly, this is a real treat."

Dino beckoned Stacy, their waitress, who greeted them. "Hi Dino, who's your friend here?"

"Stacy, this is Detective Superintendent Jack Wright. He's here from England on a case."

"Ah, the Stonehenge thing, eh?"

"Yes. It seems the case has caused quite a stir here?"

"Oh, it has indeed. It's been all over the TV. Good luck with the case."

Dino ordered the Montefalco.

"Sounds good. I'll be right back."

"Take a look at the menu, Jack. I recommend anything and everything."

The wine came, and Dino did the honors, pouring some into each glass. Jack gave it a couple of quick swirls, then tasted it. "I don't think I've ever had a wine quite like this. There's a lot of complexity for a Sangiovese-based wine."

"Exactly! Well my goodness Jack, it's nice to drink wine with somebody who's knowledgeable about it." Dino raised his glass toward Jack. "Cheers."

"Cheers."

For their meals, Dino recommended a couple of red sauce bolognese pasta dishes to go with the wine. Jack ordered the rigatoni, and Dino ordered the pappardelle.

"This crusty bread is great!"

"It's made fresh in house each day. I ought to know, it was one of my jobs as a kid to help with the baking. Good Lord, I had to get up at four o'clock every morning. I think I'm still sleep deprived. But in a family restaurant, you do what Momma says!"

"Is there a papa Roselli?"

"Not anymore. My dad Luca was a beat cop. He was gunned down in a robbery attempt, twenty-one years ago."

"Sorry to hear that."

Dino then asked, "How long have you been a cop, Jack?"

"Let's see, almost twenty years."

"Good for you. Does twenty years qualify for retirement in England?"

"It's a bit more complicated than just years of service. It's related to your age as well. I probably won't retire right away anyway."

"Really? You must like your job."

"I do actually. I'm a third-generation bobby. Never thought of doing anything else, really."

Dino could not help but compare himself to Jack. They were close in age, with similar service time. But where Jack seemed content, even happy being a cop, Dino was struggling every day with staying or quitting. His subconscious was constantly arguing back and forth over Johnny Jump Up's offer. But Dino didn't think it was appropriate to bring up his personal issues after having just met Jack, so he just continued with, "How long have you been in homicide?"

"Homicide? Let's see, just over thirteen years. But I have to say, I think it's easier to be in homicide in the UK. Our murder rate is a small fraction of what you have here in the US. Violent crime in general is much less in the UK."

"Sometimes I think murder has become a national sport here. A sport where nobody wins."

"True."

"It can wear on you after a while."

"How about you Dino? How long have you been in law enforcement?"

"Sixteen years, seven of it in homicide. Sometimes, it seems like twice that."

"I can imagine. Well, as cases go, this one is certainly interesting."

"Oh, for sure. It's a refreshing change for me. Beats working another gang murder. I'm looking forward to working with you on this case."

"Well again, we appreciate your help."

After a few moments, Jack continued, "I must say, this place is a real gem. I love the atmosphere, and you're right, the food is just excellent. My wife would love it here."

"You'll have to bring her sometime."

They had nearly finished their entrees when Dino offered, "Coffee? We have an espresso machine custom made for us in Italy. We'll stop and look at it in the bar on the way out."

"I'd love a double espresso," said Jack.

"Good choice. We'll make it two."

As they sipped their coffee, Dino said, "We have a fabulous dessert tray, but frankly, I can't afford the calories. But please have something if you'd like."

"Thanks, but I'm pleasantly full enough. I'll pass as well."

They finished their coffee, and Dino asked, "What do you have in mind for tomorrow?"

"I would like to meet Paula and Suzette, as well as anyone else you feel is appropriate. I can review with all of you the case-work to this point. Specifically, I'd like to review what we have on each member of the travel group. We've not eliminated other possible suspects, but the group members are our focal point right now. I have several options in mind for our steps thereafter, but I'd like to hear what you think first."

"Sounds like a plan. Breakfast is served starting at six thirty at the Hilton. How about I pick you up at eight? Will that work?"

"That'll work. Can I get the check?"

"It's on the house tonight. Momma would insist."

"Well, thank you so much for the hospitality. It was a truly fabulous meal, and easily the best wine I've had in a long time." He added, "I'm looking forward to working with you Dino."

"Ditto. I think we're going to make a good team."

Dino split what little was left of the Montefalco wine between their glasses, and offered a toast, "Here's to finding our murderer."

"I'll drink to that!"

Chapter 20

Erik's jaw dropped open in disbelief after reading the email: *I saw you murder Jennifer, and I saw you throw the knife and your jacket in the trash barrel. We need to talk.*

He chewed his bite of Big Mac and quickly washed it down with a gulp of Coke. *What the hell? He read the line again. How can this be?"* His mind whirled with questions. *How could anyone know? Who sent this? Why now?*

Before leaving England, he had congratulated himself on having pulled off the murder so cleanly. He was sure the British police had no idea he committed the murder. But now this. *It just can't be. It's got to be some kind of joke, a prank.* He considered it some more. *If it's real, they're bluffing. Yes, that's it, they're bluffing!* That satisfied him for a few brief moments, but then. *The knife would have been obvious, but how could they have guessed about the jacket, or the trash barrel?* He finally resigned himself. *Somebody knows. Damn it!*

Erik's world had been turned upside down in one short email. *Shit!*

His mind whirled with all the implications. *And what does 'We need to talk' mean? Do they mean actually meet? How would that work? Hell, it couldn't possibly work.*

He needed to get himself together. He looked at the clock. It was almost time for the news. He flipped on the TV and went straight to Channel 7. They led off the newscast with the Stonehenge Murder Case, as it was now being called. And there was a video of Detective Jack Wright of the Wiltshire Constabulary in England. *Shit, he's here in St. Paul!* There was also a video of Detective Dino Roselli of the St. Paul Police Department, "We are cooperating with the British police in an investigation of the Stonehenge Murder Case . . ." He continued on, but Erik did not hear whatever it was he was saying. *Damn it!*

Erik was now feeling squeezed, smack in the middle of the police on one side, and a blackmailer on the other. His mind was reeling. He sat in his chair—his whole body numb. *What to do?* He decided he would go to bed, try to calm down, and let his mind consider it all while he slept. But he could not sleep. He tossed and turned. Several times, he got up and paced back and forth in his apartment, and then returned to bed. But it was no use. By early morning, he had not slept a wink. He was exhausted and called in sick to work.

A long hot shower helped him to relax, until he checked his phone, and saw another email from "*eyewitness0621@gmail. com:*"

You will wire $10,000 to a bank account I will provide within two days. If you don't, I will go straight to the police. Confirm receipt of this email immediately.

Erik was stunned. *What $10,000? I don't have that kind of money!* He figured he better confirm the email right away, so he typed out a reply of: "I got your email, but I do not have that kind of money." And hit send. He got a reply within just a couple of minutes:

That is not my problem. You either send $10,000, or I go to the police.

Erik started to panic. *Where can I get $10,000?* He did not have credit cards with credit lines even close to $10,000. And the interest would be astronomical. He thought a bit more. *There's no way I can go to my parents for it. First thing they'll want to know is what it's for.* Despondent, he continued in panic. *My car isn't worth that much, and I gotta have something to drive.* Then he remembered he had nearly $14,000 in a 401K account at work, and he was pretty sure he could get a loan against it. He quickly logged into his account online, and saw that he could get a loan, but it would take two business days to get the money. He quickly sent another email, "I don't have credit cards with limits high enough, and I don't have anything I can sell. The only option I have is to take out a loan against my 401K at work. But it takes two business days to get the money. Today is Wednesday, so it will be Friday late in the day before I get the cash."

He waited fifteen minutes, then thirty. Finally, a reply came:

Alright. It will have to do. Late Friday, but no longer! After that, I will not hesitate to go to the police. When you have the money ready, I will send instructions for wiring it. Do not be late!

Erik was relieved by the blackmailer's response, but as he thought more about it, he became angry. *It would take me years to repay that loan. And that bastard will surely ask for more later on. It will never end.* Erik was now pissed. He declared, *I'm not gonna pay anything, except maybe a visit. I will explain things, in what will be a very one-sided, and final, conversation.* And then, *I'll kill them!*

But who are they? He had to figure that out. And quickly. He had just two days to find them and get rid of them. He scrolled through a list of the members of the travel group in his mind, ticking them off: Tom Morrison? Can't be him. Or could it be? Nope. Not him. Bob and Tammy Anderson? Bob was supposedly in plain sight of everyone at the base camp. Can't be him. Can't imagine it would be his wife. She was Jennifer's friend and seemed pretty upset over her death. Richard and Isabelle Kelly? Not likely to be a husband/wife thing. Don and Karen Halvorsen? Ditto. Owen Murphy? Young grad student at U of M. Was a student of Richard Kelly. Has written papers on Stonehenge history. Probably dead broke and needs the money for student loans. Mikhail Andropov? The foreigner, talked with a Russian accent. Heard him arguing it had to be the Druids. Maybe he was faking it? Putting on a show? Single, loner kind of guy. Definite possibility! Noah Miller? Buddy of Owen. Runs at the mouth. Saw him wandering around through the night. I talked with him for a while about the markings. It could be him.

Erik concluded it had to be Noah, Mikhail, or Owen. He would have to think it over a bit more. He now had a list of possibilities, but he set it aside to think. How to do it? *Knife?* No way, not this time. *Handgun?* Buying a new one would be instantly traceable, and they were already suspecting him. Same for a rifle or shotgun. Buy one off the street? *What, just walk up and down Hennepin Avenue asking shoddy looking characters if they've got a gun they want to sell? Half those guys are probably undercover cops anyway.*

Then he remembered, *What about that old hunting rifle in Dad's basement? I'm sure no one has touched it in years. And Dad used to keep a box of ammo as well. Yes, that will work nicely.* However, he would need to get the rifle and ammo out of his parent's house without them knowing about it. That would be easy enough, since they both work during the day and he had a key to the house. *I can run over at lunchtime. No problem.*

He felt somewhat relieved. He had the start of a plan, and he was sure he was on the right path to solving his problem.

The bastard's going to regret he ever started this.

Chapter 21

When Dino picked up Jack at the front door of the Hilton the next morning, Jack was dressed in a classic subtle plaid, dark gray, lightweight English wool suit, with a white shirt and blue polka dot tie. *Very sharp.*

Dino was easily the best dressed guy in his office. He typically wore modern Italian suits or sport coats with slacks, but he could certainly appreciate classic English fabrics and styles. Most male detectives and plainclothes cops wore sport coats at best.

"Good morning, Dino. Nice day!"

"It is. Nice suit."

"Thanks. I wasn't sure what people wore here. I figured it's always better to overdress than under dress. You're looking especially Italian today."

"Gotta keep my reputation up you know. Sleep well?"

"I did. Thanks. I got some breakfast too, so I'm ready to get started."

"Sounds good. We have a conference room booked for the day, or as long as we need it. We'll meet Paula and Suzette first, then Chief K. At some point, the mayor would like to meet you. He's supported our full cooperation on the case, but he's worried that if the murderer is indeed from the local area, the whole incident will make St. Paul look bad in the media. In the most recent election, he ran on an anti-crime theme, but quite frankly, it seems crime has gotten worse. He's a little sensitive about it. You know politicians."

"I do. Thanks for the heads up."

"Hopefully, by a little after nine we should be able to get started on some real work in the conference room."

Dino parked the Alfa, and they walked together through the lot. They went in the front door and started down the hall, pausing briefly by the Wall of Honor. Dino pointed out his dad's picture and plaque.

"He was a handsome guy," said Jack. "Looks to me like he is smiling down on you Dino."

"Sometimes I'm not sure if he's smiling or scowling, but today we'll go with smiling. This way."

They entered the Homicide Unit and stopped first at Dino's desk to dump off their stuff. Suzette saw them and came over to introduce herself. "You must be Detective Wright. I'm Suzette. Welcome to St. Paul and Minnesota."

"Thank you, please call me Jack."

They chatted for a few moments, and then headed to Paula's office.

"Welcome Jack, come on in!" she said.

"Thanks. On behalf of the British police, I want to thank you for your help."

"Well, we haven't caught anybody yet, but I'm sure we will."

There was a bit more chatting, then Paula said, "We're meeting with the chief at nine. You'll like him, he's a great guy. Over forty years with SPPD. The mayor is booked this morning but would like to meet with you sometime after lunch."

"That sounds great. I'll look forward to it."

"OK, we're going to be in Conference Room C. Why don't you get your stuff and get set up in there."

It was about eight forty-five and, with the few minutes they had before seeing the chief at nine, they chatted about the news coverage of the case, both in the US and the UK.

"The British media have really picked up on the incident. Brits just love a good murder mystery."

"The coverage here in St. Paul has been sensational. In our little part of the world, the case qualifies as international intrigue. I think they expect James Bond 007 to appear any day now."

"Well, maybe we can solve this thing promptly, and make it all go away."

"The mayor would love that!"

They went in to see Chief Kingston. Jack found him to be very cordial and passed along the appreciation of his own manager and chief back home in England. "We genuinely appreciate your help."

"I'm sure Dino and Paula will take good care of you, but if there is anything you need, just let me know."

"Thanks."

They finally convened in the conference room and got to work.

Jack started with, "As I mentioned to Dino last night, my plan is to first review the casework, then to review what we have on each member of the group, and finally, to lay out our next steps."

"Sounds good," said Paula.

"I went through all the material you sent me," said Dino. "But let's maybe go through the highlights for Paula and Suzette?"

"Of course. You will recall my mentioning on the phone that we feel there are three major suspect groups. First of all, one or more of the Druids. Secondly, someone in the crowd committing a random act of violence. Thirdly, someone in the travel group.

"As far as the Druids are concerned, they do indeed have a quirky reputation, but they do not have a history of violence. In spite of the legends of supposed human sacrifice at Stonehenge, there has never been an actual murder, going back a couple hundred years.

"As far as the random act of violence theory, we feel the murder was premeditated, even staged, which goes against the idea of a random act. Moreover, there was no sign of a struggle, violent or otherwise. That indicates that Jennifer trusted, or at least knew, her assailant. That point discounts the Druids option as well.

"So, we come to the possibility that it was someone in the travel group. When we interviewed the members of the group in London, several asked a valid question, 'If a member of the group wanted to kill Jennifer, why bother going all the way to Stonehenge in England to do it? Why not do it in Minnesota?'

"As I said, the question is valid. The answer is that evidently, the killer attached some significance to killing her at Stonehenge. Hence, we arrive at the idea that the murder was not only premeditated, but it was also staged. But why? Was Jennifer the intended victim, or would any member of the group have served the purpose of the murderer? Was killing Jennifer the sole objective, or was the murder a means to something else? We don't know at this point. But it seems most likely to me that the answer lies with someone in the St. Paul group. Comments?"

"I agree with nearly all of your points," said Dino. "But I've been thinking that there may be some added complexity. The list of members naturally starts with Tom Morris, their leader. And you quickly tell yourself, 'Well, Tom wouldn't kill his own wife.' Or would he? It wouldn't be the first 'husband kills wife' case. And yet, based on the initial testimony of the group members you sent me, Tom was in plain view of everyone the entire time before the discovery of the body, as he was leading and assembling the group for the all-important solstice event. It seems he has a very strong alibi.

"But then I thought, what if he had an accomplice? Sort of a *shadow* accomplice. It could have been another member of the group. Or, it could have been another person from here who traveled alone to London and out to Stonehenge, and he or she, did the actual killing? I suppose it may even have been an *advance* accomplice. Someone from England, that Tom had schemed with beforehand."

"Excellent points Dino."

"Very possible," said Paula, "though they make our work much more difficult."

"Agreed," said Jack. "But maybe we have some additional information that will help. I'm not sure if I mentioned it to you Dino, but yesterday, just before getting on my flight, I emailed

Paula to see if she could find out anything about Tom and his business, his personal finances, that sort of thing. Paula, were you able to find out anything?"

"I thought you'd never ask! Turns out Tom is founder and sole owner of Mercury Robotics in Woodbury, a nearby suburb. He started the company seven years ago. For the first five years or so, the company did very well. Tom made a lot of money. He bought a big house in Sunfish Lake, an exclusive neighborhood. Two years ago, the company lost its biggest customer. Tom had to let several key employees go, which caused further problems and further sales losses. The company has been losing money for the last two years. I'll let Suzette tell you the next part."

"We found out that Jennifer was actually employed by the company, supposedly heading up the marketing department. The kicker is that Tom had a half million dollars of key-man insurance on her, with himself as the sole beneficiary."

"Oh my," said Jack. "You know, I've had difficulty from the start of this case in coming up with a viable motive. I think you just found one."

"I think you're right," said Dino. "Nice work."

Paula added, "Actually, it was Suzette who did most of the legwork, along with a couple of others in the office."

"Excellent work Suzette, and you as well, Paula. And in only a day's time. Just excellent," said Jack.

"Thank you."

Jack continued, "I think that gives us at least one clear path forward, and we should start pursuing it immediately. I would still like to cover the other members of the group here this morn- ing, at least briefly. I think we should classify each one as either part of Group A, to be investigated as a priority, or Group B, for ones we think are less likely and can wait for at least a little bit."

Using his laptop and a portable projector, Jack began his review. "Based on our initial investigations at Stonehenge and in London, as well as some subsequent research, here is a brief summary of each of the other members of the travel group." The projector showed:

Bob Anderson; age 40; SIG Vice President and second in com-

mand; member of SIG from its inception twenty years ago; works as a chemical engineer for 3M in St. Paul. Bob was in plain view of the other group members the entire time prior to discovery of the body; has been to England and Stonehenge twice before. When asked if he could think of anyone who might have committed the murder, he was at a loss to come up with anyone; said he could only think it was the Druids, which became the default explanation of many of the group. For what it's worth, Bob seems to be a "what you see is what you get" kind of guy.

Jack said "My gut tells me Bob is Group B. What do you guys think?"

"I agree," said Dino. Paula and Suzette nodded their agreement.

From the projector:

Tammy Anderson; age 39; wife of Bob; accompanying Bob on the trip/not an actual member of SIG; has been to England and Stonehenge once before; close personal friend of Jennifer Morris; they would meet every two weeks or so for lunch or drinks; she and Bob would go out for dinner with Tom and Jennifer two to three times a year; last saw and talked with Jennifer about an hour before her death at the group's base camp; said Jennifer appeared entirely normal; no idea about a possible suspect; appeared to be stricken with genuine grief and befuddlement over the murder.

"Though the personal friendship is interesting, I think she is Group B, along with Bob." The others agreed.

Mikhail Andropov; age 45; a Russian immigrant who came to the US 18 years ago; US citizen; SIG member for 10 years; works for Tom at Mercury Robotics as a shop floor supervisor; was passed over for a promotion about a year ago, but has remained with the company; still attends SIG meetings as well; if he had any deep resentment, one would expect it to be with Tom himself, not his wife; quite adamant that the Druids should be prime suspects, having seen their "silly and outrageous" antics at Stonehenge; single, and a loner in his personal life, with little social involvement outside of SIG.

Jack said, "Group A?"

"For sure," the others replied.

From the projector:

Richard Kelly; age 34; SIG member for eight years; history professor at Macalester College in St. Paul; no relationship with Tom Morris outside of SIG; encouraged several of his students with an interest in Stonehenge to join SIG; third time to England, first time to Stonehenge; no idea of possible suspects; as a history teacher, he confirmed the Druids do not have a history of violence, at least within the last two hundred years.

Jack said, "Another Group B I think."

The others concurred. Then from the projector:

Isabelle Kelly; age 35; wife of Richard; accompanying Richard on the trip (not an actual member of SIG). First time to England and Stonehenge; no idea of possible suspects; was with Richard the entire night of the murder.

"Group B, along with Richard," said Jack.

They all looked back to the projector:

Owen Murphy; age 26; single; graduate student at the University of Minnesota in Minneapolis, working on history and Stonehenge; was a student of Richard Kelly at Macalester, who introduced him to SIG 4 years ago. Visited England and Stonehenge just a year ago on his own. has written academic articles about Stonehenge; no idea of possible suspects.

"I say Group A," said Jack.

"Me too," said Dino. The others agreed.

Noah Miller; age 25; single; friend of Owen; joined SIG 4 years ago, same time as Owen; works in marketing at Target Corporation HQ in Minneapolis; first time to England and Stonehenge; rather outgoing personality; he recalled chatting with Erik Foster about Stonehenge and possible markings on some of the stones a couple of hours before the murder was committed; says he spent much of the night roaming among the stones, talking with numerous other non-SIG members, including Druids, but has no idea of possible suspects.

"Group A?" said Jack, with no objection from any of the others.

Erik Foster; age 28; SIG member just over 3 years; computer programmer for Superior Technical Services in St. Paul. First time to England and Stonehenge; very knowledgeable about Stonehenge; has read extensively about it in the 3 years since joining SIG; subscribes to some of the fringe Stonehenge theories—how it was made, who made it, etc.—in particular those of Erich von Däniken in the book Chariots of the Gods; *Erik was mildly berated a couple of times over the* Gods *theories at the SIG meetings by Tom; was seen with Jennifer about an hour before she was found dead, which he freely admits. Claims that he left her talking with several Druids near the large sarsen stones and had returned to the base camp about thirty minutes before security came looking for Tom, which was confirmed by several other members of the group, including Tom; seemed quite keen to push the "it was the Druids" explanation.*

"Definitely Group A," said Jack.

Don Halvorsen; age 55; SIG member over 12 years; lives in St. Cloud, about 70 miles from St. Paul; works for the city in the administrative department; travels to the SIG meetings by himself; first trip to England and Stonehenge; no idea of possible suspects.

"Definitely Group B," said Jack.

Karen Halvorsen; age 52; wife of Don; accompanying Don on the trip (not an actual member of SIG). First trip to England and Stonehenge; no idea of possible suspects; spent some time talking with Jennifer on the trip. Seemed especially horrified by the murder.

"Group B. Well, there they are," said Jack. "No one in the group has any criminal record or obvious motive. From here, I think we take our Group A guys, and get started working on them."

"Agreed," said Dino. "Let's see if we can catch ourselves a murderer!"

Chapter 22

Paula had ordered in sandwiches and drinks for lunch. As they ate, they continued to discuss the case. Afterwards, Paula and Suzette went off to work on several items of research, while Dino and Jack plotted out their next steps.

"Given the new information uncovered by Suzette, I think we need to start with Tom Morris," said Dino.

"I think you're right. Can we call him right now?"

"No time like the present. We should probably offer to go see him, either at his home or at his office at Mercury Robotics. He's no doubt under a lot of stress involving arrangements for Jennifer's funeral, as well as returning to his business." Dino looked up Tom's cell phone number, jotted it on a piece of paper, and handed it to Jack. "I think the initial call should come from you, Jack. He won't know me from Adam."

"True," said Jack as he dialed the number. It rang twice and was answered by Tom.

"Tom, this is Detective Superintendent Jack Wright with the British police. Do you have a moment to talk?"

"It must be pretty late there, Detective?"

"I'm actually here in St. Paul. I flew over yesterday, and I'm working with the St. Paul Police Department, following up on several matters concerning your wife's murder. Once again, I offer my sympathies to you on the loss of your wife."

"Thanks. What would you like from me?"

"We have several questions that we need to ask. I know you're busy, but I don't think it will take very long. We could come to you if that makes it easier."

"It would. I'm at work now, about to go to a meeting, but I could make time at three o'clock this afternoon, if that works for you."

"It does. I have the address from the contact information you gave us in London. We'll see you at your office at three o'clock. Thanks."

Dino and Jack drove the Alfa to the Mercury Robotics offices, arriving ten minutes early. Waiting in the car for a few minutes, they admired the factory building and attached office complex, which were impressive. A couple of minutes before three, they went in and announced themselves to the receptionist. She showed them to Tom's office.

Tom's office was modestly furnished. He sat behind a handsome wooden desk, with a wide-screen computer monitor and keyboard to his left. There were several framed photos on the walls. One of Jennifer, one of Jennifer and Tom, and several group photos that appeared to be of his staff. On the wall to his left, were several larger landscape photos of Stonehenge and England. Tom was smartly dressed in dark slacks, with a freshly starched white shirt with thin blue pin stripes. Tom himself, however, looked tired and drawn. Understandable.

Jack introduced Dino. "Tom, this is Detective Dino Roselli with the St. Paul Police, Homicide Unit. Dino, Tom Morris."

"It's nice to meet you, Tom. Very sorry about your wife. It's no doubt a difficult time for you. We're doing everything we can to assist Jack in resolving the case. I've been assigned as the lead investigator here locally. We appreciate your taking a few minutes to talk with us." Dino offered his card.

"You still think the murderer is connected to SIG here in Minnesota?" asked Tom.

"We do," said Jack. "We're still pursuing the possibility that it was one or more of the Druids back in England, but I believe the murderer is indeed connected with your Stonehenge travel group."

"OK. I confess I don't share that opinion but let's proceed. What questions do you have?"

"We understand Jennifer was an employee of your company?"

"Yes. She headed up our marketing department. She started in that role a little over two years ago, just after we lost a major customer. I had to let the previous director go, and she had an applicable background from college and previous employment."

"Is it true that you carried key-person insurance on her?"

"Yes, I carry it on each of my key executives, including my Controller, the VP of Sales, and the VP of Manufacturing. What is it you're driving at Detective?"

"Respectfully sir, we are simply investigating all possibilities surrounding the murder of your wife."

"Well, I'm afraid that you are barking up the wrong tree."

"And why do you say that, Mr. Morris?"

"Because each of the key-person insurance policies on my people only pays a benefit if death is by accident or natural causes. There is an explicit exclusion for death by murder. The exclusion made the premiums more affordable, and I never envisioned that ever happening. So you see gentlemen, I will not receive one red cent from the policy for Jennifer's death. You can verify that with my insurance agent. Quite frankly, I don't care for you insinuating that I had anything to do with my wife's murder. If you came all the way from England just to do that, you're wasting your time, and I'm in the middle of making funeral arrangements for my wife, so you're wasting my time as well. From this point on, I want to have my attorney involved in any conversations with you. You'll forgive me if I am less than cordial from this point forward, and I ask now that you see yourselves out."

"As we said, Mr. Morris, we're simply investigating all possibilities. We'd be remiss in not investigating this one. Thank you for your time."

Dino and Jack stood, walked out of the office, and then left the building.

As they walked to the car, Dino said, "Gee, that went well."

"It certainly became unpleasant quickly, but we did learn that Tom is no longer a priority suspect. Along with his strong alibi, which has been vouched for by all the members of the group, he did not have the means or any financial incentive to kill Jennifer. An accomplice would still be possible, as well as some other motive, but at this point, they both seem remote."

"Time to head back and take a look at our list?"

"I think so Dino."

Chapter 23

E rik had been going over his short list of possibilities, and he was now sure that Mikhail Andropov was the blackmailer. *It's gotta be him. The bastard!*

Next, he had to figure out "Where?" and "When?" He was able to get the rifle at lunch time without a problem. And the box of ammo his dad had was right there with it. Some of the rounds were hollow points. *Perfect.* The ammo was old, but Erik was quite sure it would fire. There was really no place for him to test fire the rifle, but he had fired the rifle lots of times back when he and his dad used to go deer hunting. He never did shoot a deer, but he was at least comfortable with the rifle. He would just have to take his chances. More importantly, the clock was ticking. The money was due in just two days. *This is going to work. Just stay calm.*

It had been easy to find Mikhail's house. He lived in the Highland Park neighborhood of southeastern St. Paul, just a couple of blocks off Cleveland Avenue. It was roughly seven miles from his apartment near Lake Como in northwest St. Paul. Erik had already driven by the house a couple of times. The neighborhood was older, with houses fairly close together. Most had small yards in the front and back. Some houses had fences between them, but Mikhail's did not. There was an alley that ran the length of the block behind the back yards. That might prove useful, though he was not sure how.

He parked his car a couple of blocks away and walked past

the house. No evidence of a dog, which was good. There was a stoop outside the front door, and it gave Erik an idea. He could get a small Fedex box, place it on the front lip of the stoop, press the doorbell, and run to a good-sized oak tree that was to the right of the stoop, about fifteen yards away. He could get back to the tree easily and would have the rifle ready. Mikhail would have to step out onto the stoop to pick up the package, giving him a clear shot. *Can't miss at that range.* It would have to be a bit later in the evening to provide some cover, and Mikhail might question the delivery of a Fedex package at that hour, but it was not uncommon. Erik had seen Fedex delivery guys out well into the night in his own neighborhood. And they usually ran or jogged to the house, dropped off the package, hit the bell, ran back to their truck, and were gone. Erik figured it was all reasonable.

The sight lines from the tree were such that even if Mikhail did not come out onto the stoop, he had a decent shot right through the screen door. At fifteen yards, there would be no stopping the 30-06 round. *And who can resist a Fedex package? He'll think it's Christmas.* Erik laughed to himself. *Yes, the shot will make a loud crack, but city neighborhoods often experience odd noises, and people pretty much ignore them. Most of these city people wouldn't recognize a rifle shot anyway.* There was a strip mall with businesses making noises just two blocks away, and there was always traffic on Cleveland Avenue. He would just have to chance it.

Erik's only regret was that Mikhail would never know who pulled the trigger. Didn't matter. It would be over. *Bastard shouldn't have fucked with me!*

Chapter 24

On the way back from interviewing Tom Morris, Jack confessed to Dino, "I think jet lag has caught up with me."

"I'm not surprised," said Dino.

"When I first arrived, the flurry of activity and meeting everyone kept my adrenaline up, but now, I'm starting to feel quite knackered."

"Knackered?" asked Dino.

"Oops, sorry . . . *exhausted*. I'm tired out."

"Ah, very understandable."

"I confess too, that I'm a bit deflated by our interview with Tom. I thought we were onto something there. If it's OK with you, I think I'd like to head back to the hotel and get a good night's sleep. I can just grab something light from room service for dinner."

"I get it. No problem."

Dino dropped Jack off at the Hilton and headed back to the office. He updated Paula and Suzette on what they had learned from Tom Morris.

"Bummer!" said Paula. "I thought we had a break there. Oh well, back to the list."

"That's the plan," replied Dino. "We'll call and start interviewing first thing in the morning."

"Sounds good. Let us know if you need help with anything."

"Will do."

Dino took care of a couple of admin things, then checked his phone. It was still on silent from just before the Morris interview. But there was a message from Johnny Jump Up.

"Hey guy! Just checking in. Any thoughts or questions about my proposal? Give me a call when you can. Thanks!"

Dino did not want to talk with Johnny from the office, so he decided to call it a day and headed home. When he got there, he changed clothes and went down to the wine cellar. *Nothing too heavy, something contemplative.* He ended up with a Valpolicella from Veneto. He grabbed some crackers and some English cheddar from the Isle of Mull and sat down at the dinner table. He sipped a couple times from his first glass, then called Johnny Jump Up.

"Hey Johnny. Got your call."

"Great. Thanks for calling back. I saw on the TV you're working the Stonehenge Case. Great publicity!"

"Um, great publicity, if we can solve it. Our best lead so far fizzled out this afternoon, but we're just getting started."

"I'm sure you'll get him! Given any thought to my proposal?"

"I have. I'm trying to digest the idea of leaving the force. That would be a huge step for me."

"It's a big deal for me as well. Any questions?"

"Maybe in a couple of days. This case is consuming me right now."

"I understand, but I'm getting pressure from two of my best customers. The timing might not be the best for you, but it never is. Honestly Dino, I don't think you want to miss a once in a lifetime chance like this. The department will get along without you, one way or the other. You need to look out for yourself and your future. Find some time to think it over, and we can talk this weekend."

"OK. Thanks Johnny."

"See ya guy."

Dino hung up. He sat there for a moment, staring at the wine in his glass. He tipped it to one side and rolled the glass by the stem to see the colors of the wine—the deep ruby red shades in the center of the glass, and the thin, pale, translucent pinks at the edge. He then had another one of his pangs of guilt about his wine drinking, but he quickly dismissed it. Still gazing at the glass, he thought, *If only you were a crystal ball, and let me look into the future.* Then waking up a bit, he scolded himself. *That's crazy thinking. I just need to figure out what will make me happy.* He resolved to do that this weekend.

For tonight, he took another small piece of the cheddar and savored its musty flavor. *Wine and cheese. A match made in heaven.*

He flicked on the TV and caught the news on one of the local channels. Nothing new on the Stonehenge case. But he knew the reporters were getting restless. Several had tried to call him during the day, but he just ignored them. Still, the case was big news in the Cities, and people were hungry for any updates about it.

Tomorrow, we'll have to see if we can dig some up! He emptied his glass and headed for bed.

Dino picked up Jack in front of the Hilton at eight. "Catch up on sleep?" Dino asked Jack.

"I did. Yesterday afternoon I just hit a brick wall. But I slept well last night, and I'm ready to go again."

"Great. I briefed Paula and Suzette late yesterday. We should be able to start right in this morning." Dino parked the Alfa, and they walked into the building. As he walked by the photo of his dad on the wall, he was sure he heard him say, "What the hell are you thinking young man?"

Dino replied in his head, "I'm not really sure Dad, but I could use a little help when you get a chance!" Humm, no reply. Dino put it out of his mind, and they headed for the conference room.

Jack called up the Group A list. Next up was Owen Murphy. They called him and he answered on the second ring. "Owen, this is Detective Jack Wright of the British police. I'm here in St. Paul, working on the Stonehenge case. Do you have a couple of minutes to talk?"

Owen replied, "A couple, I guess. I saw you on the TV and thought you might be calling. What do you want?"

"We'd like you to come into the St. Paul station to answer some questions about the case."

"I told you everything I know, several times back in London."

"I know you did, Owen, and we appreciated your cooperation then, but we have additional questions we'd like to ask. Can you come to the station today?"

"Today? I guess so. What time?"

"Does one o'clock work?"

"Let me check, one sec . . . yeah, I can make it."

"Thanks. I have your email address. I'll send contact information right after I hang up here. We'll see you at one o'clock."

"There's one," said Dino. "Who's up next?"

"Let's try Noah Miller." Jack dialed him, and like Owen, he had been expecting a call. He agreed to come at three o'clock that afternoon.

"How about Erik Foster?" said Dino.

"Sounds good." Jack punched in the number, but immediately got Erik's voice mail. He left a message asking Erik to call and hung up.

"Last one—Mikhail Andropov." Jack dialed that number, and Mikhail answered after just one ring. He was not available to come yet today but could get off work and come in at nine in the morning. "That will work. Thanks Mr. Andropov."

"How long will it take?" he asked. "I can't be gone from work more than a couple hours."

"I would think an hour would be enough time. Thanks again. We'll see you tomorrow at nine o'clock."

Mikhail replied with a hesitant "OK," and hung up.

"Would it be possible to meet with Paula and Suzette?" Jack asked Dino.

"I would think so. You mean right now?"

"Right now, would be great."

"I'll go find them."

Within five minutes, they had all gathered in a conference room.

"Thanks for your time on short notice," said Jack. "Back in

England, we've had tech and support staffers working on the case, looking for possible domestic suspects. We managed to get a psychological profiler from Scotland Yard assigned to assist us with the case. His name is Charlie Evans. I've worked with him before, and he's good. He emailed me his initial report a half hour ago and is available now to talk on the phone. It's nearly four o'clock in London, so we have at least a few minutes to talk with him before pub time! I assume you're OK with a call?"

"Sure. Let's do it," replied Paula.

"Great." Jack dialed the number and put the call on speaker.

"Hello, this is Charlie."

"Hey Charlie, this is Jack. I'm here in St. Paul with Detective Dino Roselli, Paula Dunn, Head of Homicide, and Suzette Hawkins, also of Homicide. Thanks for taking our call late in the afternoon."

"Hello everyone. No problem Jack. My mates will hold my stool at the pub."

"Gotta love mates! Thanks for the report you sent. I was hoping you could give us a summary of what you've come up with here on the phone?"

"Sure, happy to. First of all, stabbing a person to death on the Slaughter Stone at Stonehenge on the summer solstice certainly indicates that our murderer attached some special significance to both the time and the place of the murder. But what significance? A sacrifice? An offering? Affirmation? Retribution? Symbolism? Hard to tell.

"One or more of the Druids are obvious suspects here. There's actually extensive documentation available on the Druids. It's important to note that the Druids first appeared in England in about the third century BC, which was more than a thousand years after the building of Stonehenge. It's a common misconception that they built Stonehenge, but they certainly did *not*. Still, in searching, I found that there are ancient references to human sacrifices by the Druids, but there are modern-day scholars that feel they never did any. Regardless, there are no known examples of human sacrifices by the Druids going back several hundred years. Not at Stonehenge, or anywhere else.

"So, I extended my research to the more general categories of Satanists and other black occults. I found that these guys hold eight major celebrations, or *Sabbats*, each year. The top three are: 1) Halloween; 2) May Eve (also known as Beltane); and 3) you guessed it—the summer solstice. And of course, no place in the world is more associated with the summer solstice than Stonehenge.

"But in looking at the crime scene itself, there are none of the typical Satanic or occult indicators. No candles or candle drippings; no branding or burn marks on the body; no mockery of Christian symbols such as inverted crosses; no pentagrams; no ceremonial artifacts, such as animal parts forming signs or symbols on the nearby ground; no missing body parts or mutilation; none of these things. So there's really no physical evidence that someone from one of these groups was involved in the murder. It doesn't prove they weren't, it just doesn't prove they were. No one even attempted to imply occult involvement.

"I was, however, able to put together a profile of the murderer, based on what evidence we do have: Male, fairly intelligent (though probably an underachiever), low self-esteem, difficulty relating to peers, especially females, obsession with role-playing games, collector of objects related to the occult—books, symbols, stones, jewelry, and excessive secrecy.

"I'm reasonably sure about these traits, but I must provide a disclaimer that psychological profiling is far from an exact science. In fact, it occurred to me that the summer solstice event at Stonehenge would provide excellent cover for someone wanting to commit a murder for most any reason—dark of night with a large, loud, often rowdy crowd; and relatively light security."

Charlie could be heard shuffling his papers together on the other end of the line. He continued, "So there it is—an educated guess, with a strong disclaimer, that it could be anyone. How's that for hedging my bet?"

"Gee, were you once an economist?"

"Oh, that hurts! But I've been called worse. I need to run. Hope this helps. I'll let you know if I come up with anything else. Good Luck!"

"Thanks Charlie. Have a pint for me."

Jack hung up the phone, then asked, "Well, guys, what do you think?"

Dino started with, "My first reaction is that his profile fits nearly all members of the SIG group. They're all geeks! It seems like it's one of the qualifications for membership."

"That might be a bit strong, but many of them do seem a little odd. I confess the one thing that has me baffled on this case is the motive. Still, I was glad to get this information before we start our interviews this afternoon. I will forward Charlie's report to each of you, however, the report is confidential, and I must ask that you not share it with anyone else without my permission. Absolutely no part of the report, or this conversation, can be given to the press."

Paula asked, "Can I update the chief and mayor? Mayor Bennett, in particular, is looking for any kind of progress."

"They're OK. But please ask them to keep it confidential, at least for now."

"Will do."

"Unless you have anything further, let's grab an early lunch, so we're ready for our one o'clock with Owen Murphy."

Dino and the others agreed, "Sounds good."

Owen Murphy arrived ten minutes early for his interview. Jack introduced Dino, and then they escorted Owen to a conference room and closed the door.

"Thanks for coming in Mr. Murphy, we appreciate your cooperation." Jack told him.

"Am I a suspect?" asked Owen, obviously nervous.

"Well, technically, everyone is a suspect, but right now, we're simply looking for all the information we can get from members of the travel group. This is a voluntary, informational interview, Mr. Murphy. You're not being arrested, nor are you in police custody. Therefore, there's no need to read you your rights. As I mentioned on the phone, we do have your recorded statement from London. We just want to ask several further questions. Again, we appreciate your help in trying to find Jennifer Morris' killer."

"OK."

"How long have you been a member of the Stonehenge Interest Group?"

"I joined SIG about four years ago."

"You're a graduate student at the University of Minnesota in Minneapolis?"

"Yes."

"And your field of study?"

"I'm working on a Master's Degree in History, with a specialty of Neolithic man in Great Britain, and in particular, Stonehenge."

"Why did you pick that field?"

"I was a student of Richard Kelly at Macalester College in undergrad school. I guess his enthusiasm for the field got me interested. In fact, I joined SIG on his recommendation and encouragement. Last year, I traveled to England and Stonehenge on my own."

"Does your in-depth knowledge of Stonehenge give you any insights into this crime?"

"Well, for one thing, the symbolism of killing someone on the so-called Slaughter Stone is flat out wrong."

"Wrong? Why is that?"

"Because the Slaughter Stone got its name from the red water that appears to seep out of the stone. In fact, the water is red because of the iron in the stone, which combines with algae that grow on its surface. There's no evidence the stone was ever intended or used for human sacrifice. It's a name that appealed to people's perceived mystique of Stonehenge. It got started long ago and it just stuck."

"That's interesting indeed. How well did you know Jennifer Morris?"

"Hardly at all. I would see her at some of the monthly SIG meetings, but not all of them. I don't recall ever actually speaking with her before the trip."

"On the trip, did you see any of the other members of the travel group spending time with Jennifer?"

"Most all the members spent some time with her. Our group

wasn't that big. I guess I saw her quite often with her friend Tammy Anderson. But others as well."

"Do you recall any of them?"

"Let's see, there's Noah, he'll talk with anyone."

"Noah is your friend?"

"He is. We met at Macalester. He wasn't into history; he was more into girls and drinking beer."

"Anyone else you recall spending time with Jennifer?"

"The other two wives, I forget their names. And I recall Jennifer talking with Erik Foster out at Stonehenge. He's a bit of a Stonehenge geek."

"Why do you say that?"

"Erik is really into Stonehenge. Lots of details. In fact, I think he was talking with both Jennifer and Noah about supposed markings on some of the large sarsen stones. He's only been in SIG for a couple of years, but I think he spends a lot of time on it. Not academic type stuff, more layman stuff. He's into 'Chariots of the Gods' and fringe stuff like that."

"Chariots?"

"Yeah, you know, the idea that aliens designed and helped build Stonehenge, and other ancient monuments as well."

"OK. So, of all the people you saw with Jennifer, did any of them appear to have had any disagreements or arguments with her?"

"No. None."

"OK. Tom Morris? How well do you know him?"

"I only know him from SIG. He runs each meeting, so I would see him all the time. I spoke with him a few times during the social hour after the meetings, when we'd drink some Brit beer."

"Do you have a girlfriend, Mr. Murphy?"

"What the hell kind of question is that?"

"Just asking. We really don't care one way or the other, just wondering if you have a girlfriend."

"I do. We're talking about getting married once I finish grad school. But again, I don't see the relevance of that."

"OK. No problem. Just routine questions Mr. Murphy."

Finally, Jack asked Owen, "Who do you think killed Jennifer?"

"I have no idea. Honestly."

"OK, Mr. Murphy. That does it for now. You can take off. Thanks for your cooperation. Detective Roselli will escort you out."

After seeing Owen out, Dino came back to the conference room to compare notes with Jack. "Well, what do you think?"

Jack replied, "At this point, I don't think he's our guy. He fits the 'male' and 'intelligent' traits of our profile, but none of the others really. Let's see what we find out from his friend Noah in our next interview."

Noah Miller was five minutes late for his interview.

"Sorry I'm a bit late, traffic coming from Minneapolis," he offered apologetically.

"That's alright Mr. Miller. Thanks for coming in," said Jack.

"Sure. No problem."

"You work for Target Corporation in Minneapolis?"

"Yes. I'm in Merchandise Acquisitions. It's kind of fun, we get to find new products."

"Sounds like it would be. You're friends with Owen Murphy?"

"Yup. We've been buddies since back at Macalester."

"What did you study there?"

"Business Administration. I'm not the scientific type or anything like that."

"OK. How long have you been a member of SIG?"

"I joined with Owen about four years ago. I'm really not all that active. The meetings are interesting, but I don't make all of them."

"But you decided to go on the trip with the group?"

"I've never been to Europe, or outside the US really. Oh, except Cancun once. Anyway, I thought the trip to Stonehenge would be fun."

"Do you have a girlfriend, Mr. Miller?"

"You mean only one? I usually have several going at one time. Life's short, you know!" said Noah, with a playful smile.

"It sure is. On the trip, did you spend any time with Jennifer

Morris?"

"I suppose I talked with her a few times, but I talked with everyone. I enjoy chatting with people."

"How about Jennifer the night she was killed?"

"I talked with her a bit, and with Erik. He was all excited to show us several faint markings on some of the big stones. I just sort of tagged along for a bit. To be honest, I could hardly see anything that looked like markings. I left them and walked around on my own. I did talk with a few of the Druids, they're quite the characters! And I talked with a couple of girls from Manchester, England. That was fun. I was chatting with them when I heard about Jennifer."

"Do you, by chance, have their names and contact information?"

"By chance I do! Annabelle and Suzie. I can email you."

"We would appreciate that." Then Jack asked, "Do you recall anything unusual about Jennifer that night? Was she nervous? Apprehensive?"

"No. She seemed fine. Hey wait a minute. You don't think I did it do you?"

"We don't know who did it at this point, Mr. Miller. We're simply gathering information. But I have no doubt we'll find whoever did this soon."

As with Owen Murphy, Jack and Dino explained this was a voluntary, informational interview.

"Can you think of anything else that might be pertinent, Mr. Miller?"

"No. Not really. Sorry."

"All right. Well, thank you for your time. If you think of anything else, let us know. You're free to go."

Dino saw Noah out, then returned to discuss the interview with Jack. "Not much there, I'm afraid. What's with the references to the markings? Both these guys mentioned them."

"Not sure. Maybe we could have Suzette do some background research for us?" asked Jack.

"I'll ask Paula. I'm sure it'll be OK."

"Back to Noah, he doesn't really seem to be our guy either.

Doesn't really fit our profile. He's a bit of a rattlebrain, to be honest. Unless he's playing us?"

"I don't think so. But I've been played before," confessed Dino.

With the afternoon interviews concluded, Dino suggested to Jack that they head out for an early dinner. "Do you eat much Mexican food in England?" he asked.

"Some. There are Mexican takeaway places, as well as some restaurants, but it's not as popular as I understand it is here," Jack said.

"Takeaway?"

"Ah, I believe you call it *to go* or *takeout* here," Jack explained.

"I see. Yes, it's quite popular here. Tacos are common even in school cafeterias. Kids love them."

"We do have Spanish restaurants in the UK that are popular, perhaps more so than here."

"I was thinking we could do Mexican for dinner. There's a Hispanic neighborhood just south of the river, and they have a couple of pretty good restaurants. I thought it would be something different for you to try while you're here."

"Sounds good. Let's do it."

They headed out in the Alfa, crossing over the Mississippi River on the Robert Street bridge, stopping at Nueva Cantina. They found a table and sat down.

Dino said, "I enjoy Mexican food, but always have trouble finding a good wine that goes with it. Hard for an Italian guy to get past the urge to drink wine with most every meal. I think of Mexican as more of a beer food."

"I can drink Dos Equis or Corona, but as a Brit, I'm more of an ale drinker."

A waitress brought menus and explained the daily specials, then left to bring them a couple of Coronas.

"I'm afraid we didn't make much progress with our interviews this afternoon," said Jack. "I have confidence in our profile from Charlie Evans, but the two guys this afternoon didn't seem close to the profile at all."

"I think we may learn more from our interviews in the morning." Dino said, "I've got to say, Jack, this case is certainly interesting. For sure more interesting than my typical gang-related murder, although it's a bit frustrating as well. I feel it's sort of like *Murder on the Orient Express*, where all the suspects are on a moving train, and the killer has to be one of them. Most likely, our murderer is one of the travel group members, but so far none of them jumps out as a prime suspect."

The waitress returned with the Coronas, and they ordered their meals.

After a couple of sips of beers, Jack said, "Dino, you've mentioned your frustration with gang-related murders a few times. Tell me if I'm out of line, but it sounds like it's a real issue for you."

"It seems to be all I work on anymore. Gangs are a real problem in St. Paul. They're not as bad as in Chicago or New York, but here locally, they've dominated our case work for the past several years. They're frustrating cases because there are seldom any clues, the motive is typically nonsensical, and witnesses willing to come forward with actual information are few and far between. That's why this case has been a nice change of pace for me."

"I can understand that."

"You know, when I first started out in my career, I wanted to be a cop and nothing else. But lately, it's all been wearing on me. It's forced me to seriously consider doing something else."

"Really?"

"Yes, but I can't help thinking that doing something else would dishonor my father's legacy."

"You have to lead your own life, Dino. I'm sure your dad would've told you that."

"I don't know. He died such a hero, and everyone loved him, looked up to him. I felt obligated to follow in his footsteps, and I did so freely. I still carry a picture of him in my wallet."

"Interesting."

Dino then pulled back his left sleeve. "And I still wear his watch every day."

"Very nice."

Dino laughed, "It looks great, but it keeps lousy time! Thank

God for cell phones." Dino then mused, "Maybe it's just a mid-life crisis?"

"You're too young for a mid-life crisis!" replied Jack. He then added sympathetically, "I've been spared the doubts you are experiencing. I've always wanted to do police work and have never really considered doing anything else. Probably never will."

"That's a real blessing. You're lucky," replied Dino.

"You're right." After a pause, he asked, "So, if you weren't a cop, what would you do?"

"Well, that's just it—I don't know what I'd do. It seems my thoughts dwell mostly on the negative points of what I do now. Recently, I got an offer to do private investigations work. I've thought about it, and certain aspects are appealing, but I just don't know. If you throw in my mom's constant harassment over why she doesn't have any grandchildren yet, my life is pretty challenging right now."

"I'm sure you'll sort it all out for the better."

Their meals came, and the conversation drifted back to their case, and some background on the interviews scheduled for the morning. They each had another Corona and decided to call it an early night.

"I need to check on things back home anyway," said Jack

Dino said, "Thanks for listening, Jack. I think it's something only another cop would understand. Still, I would appreciate you keeping it all to yourself."

"Mum's the word."

"Thanks."

They finished up and left the restaurant. Dino dropped Jack off at the Hilton and headed home. As he drove, he thought, *We could really use a break in this case.*

Chapter 25

E rik slept well Wednesday night. He felt good—he had a plan. To make things appear normal, he needed to go to work Thursday. He went in an hour early, supposedly to make up for being out the day before, but he was really just avoiding people coming and going.

Mid-morning, his cell rang. When he looked at it and saw a St. Paul Police ID, he let it go to voice mail. After waiting a few moments, he listened to it, and immediately recognized the voice as Detective Jack Wright. *Damn. I knew they'd be calling.* And he knew he had no choice but to call them back, but he decided to wait until he was home. He would have time before he needed to go to Andropov's house. Trying to put the call out of his mind, he spent most of the day rehearsing how to carry out his plan. The day dragged on, with the stress building by the hour. By the time he left for the day, he was a mess.

He went home and called Detective Wright just after six o'clock.

"This is Detective Jack Wright."

"Hello Detective, this is Erik Foster. I received your voice mail this morning. Sorry I couldn't answer when you called, but we're not allowed to take personal phone calls at work."

"Thanks for returning my call. I am, of course, here investigating the murder of Jennifer Morris, with the aid of the St. Paul Police Department. I need you to come in for some additional questioning. Can you come tomorrow during the day?"

"Sure, whatever I can do to help. I could take a longer lunch break. Would eleven work?"

"That would be fine. We'll see you at eleven tomorrow. Thanks."

"No problem. Bye."

Erik was relieved that he did not have to answer any questions over the phone. He was on edge worrying about tonight's work, afraid he would somehow slip up and reveal something. By late tomorrow morning, his Mikhail problem would be over, and he could steel himself for an interview.

Too stressed out to eat anything, Erik started his final preparation. He wished he had an extra day to get ready, but knew he had to act tonight. The money was due tomorrow, and he did not have it. He could only assume that Andropov's threat was real, and that he would indeed go to the police. The thought of actually going to prison for the rest of his life was too much to bear. He would just have to take his chances and move forward with his plan.

Erik waited a bit later than he had the night before, hoping that neighborhood people would move inside for the night. First, he drove to Ray's Pub, which he frequented often, and ordered a beer at the bar. To have an alibi, he needed to be seen. He drank it down, hoping it would help to keep his nerves under control. Leaving the bar, he waved obviously to the bartender, and then drove to Andropov's neighborhood. He took a lap around the block, and then parked his car just one block north of Andropov's house, figuring he could run that far, even with the rifle, through the back yard, then down the alley, and back to his car. Earlier, he had practiced walking stiff-legged with the rifle, and with a loose-fitting jacket, he figured he could make it work. He would have to chance it.

On TV, the bad guys always used stolen plates, or a stolen car, but he was not sure how he would do that, so he did not try to hide his car. Again, he would just have to take his chances.

There was one thing that worried him. *What if Mikhail's not home?* Not much he could do about it. With the money due tomorrow, he had to go forward and hope for the best. *Just stay calm.*

It was time to move. Pulling a small rag out of his pocket, he wiped down the Fedex package one more time to remove prints. He got out of his car and put on the jacket. Using the rag, he picked up the dummy Fedex package and tucked it under his jacket. He then picked up the rifle, with a magazine of four rounds already loaded, as well as one round in the chamber. He checked that the safety was on. He closed the car door, leaving it unlocked, and stepped onto the sidewalk and started walking, hoping he would not meet anyone. It looked clear at this point. If he did meet someone, he would have to come up with something, though he was not sure what it would be.

He walked to the corner, then turned right to continue around the block. *So far, so good.* At the next corner, he turned right again, and continued to Andropov's lot. He stepped onto the grass and walked right up to the oak tree he had checked out beforehand. There was some small shrubbery around the base of the tree, and it provided at least a bit of cover. Leaning the rifle against the tree, he took out his rag, and used it to pull the Fedex package out from under his jacket. He quietly walked up to the stoop, put the package on the front lip, stepped up to ring the doorbell, and ran back to the tree. He pocketed the rag, picked up the rifle, and clicked off the safety. Within a couple seconds, the front stoop light came on, and Andropov opened the inside door. He looked out through the screen door, turning his head to look first right, then left. He hesitated when he saw the package. Erik was trying to coax him on, *Come on, open the door . . .* After a few moments, Andropov clicked the handle of the screen door, and pushed it open. He took two steps out onto the stoop, glanced around, and started to reach down for the package. Erik raised the rifle, sighted in on Andropov just fifteen yards away, and pulled the trigger.

There was a tremendous *crack*! The noise was much louder than Erik had thought it would be, but no matter. Andropov's body bucked up, then over. Erik chambered another round, raised the rifle up, and fired again. Another loud crack. The second round hit Andropov fully in the torso. Erik saw a spray of blood fly out the back of his body and hit the wall of the house behind him. *Done. Time to get out of here!*

Every second counted now. He took time to bend over and pick up the first spent shell casing, but he did not waste time ejecting the second one. He turned and started running along the right side of the house, into the back yard, and into the alley. Turning to his right, he looked straight into the headlights of an oncoming car. *Shit!*

He turned back to the direction he had been going. He had taken just four more steps before he ran straight into a chain-link fence. *Damn it!* He looked both ways. The car was still coming toward him. The fence was not that high, so he decided to jump it. He threw the rifle over first, figuring it would not go off with a spent round still in the chamber. Grabbing the chain-link near the top of the fence, he swung his legs up and over. He picked up the rifle and started running through the back yard. Nearing the front yard, he heard a fierce growl on his right, and then a loud bark just ten yards away. *Damn it!* Just as he braced for the dog to attack him, it was stopped by the fence—the dog was in the next yard over. *Thank God!*

Erik continued to the front of the yard. At the fence, he threw the rifle over first, then jumped over, just as he had done in the back yard. A light came on behind him and he heard the click of a door latch. A guy shouted, "Is somebody out there?" Erik ignored him, picked up the rifle, and started running toward his car. It seemed to take forever to get there, and he was winded from running with the rifle, but he made it to the driver-side door and flung it open. He threw the rifle in, barrel first, all the way over to the passenger side door. As he hopped in, he started the engine and hit the gas. He left his lights off, and at the stop sign at the end of the block, he just sped straight through it, praying that no one was coming. Expecting to be side swiped at any moment, his body tensed up, but he made it through.

Halfway up the next block, he turned on the lights and slowed down to stay under the speed limit and not draw attention to himself. After two blocks, he turned left onto the escape route he had planned and allowed himself a small breath of relief.

His next task was to get rid of the rifle and ammo. He knew that much from watching TV police shows. If he was stopped for any reason with the rifle in the car, it was game over. He figured he would either throw them in the Mississippi River or in Lake Como. In thinking it through, he recalled that Lake Como was rather shallow, so swimmers or even waders might find it. Also, people walked around the lake late summer evenings, so he decided on the river.

When he had scouted his escape route, he saw that the Lake Street–Marshall Bridge crossed the river about two miles from Andropov's house. He had driven over and around the bridge and had found a place to park quite close to a walking path underneath the bridge. There was a short fence on the river side of the path, but it would be quite easy to hop over it and go down the short slope to the riverbank. From there, relatively unseen, he could toss the rifle and the ammo into the river, and they would be gone forever.

Driving just under the speed limit, following his planned route, he carefully signaled his turns and obeyed the traffic laws. He pulled into the parking area, but there were two other cars already there. *Crap.* Both cars were empty. Obviously, the drivers were out walking on the path. He had no way to know which way they may have gone. One could have gone left and the other right. No way to know. He waited three minutes but saw nothing. He was getting anxious. *What if the park patrol comes along and finds me?*

He decided to chance it. With his jacket still on, he got out of the car. After checking both directions one last time, he pulled out the rifle and ammo, including the first spent shell, and headed for the fence. He hopped over easily, and was starting to slide down the slope, when someone called out, "Hey buddy, whadda you want?"

Erik was so startled, he fell on his butt and started sliding toward the river. With the rifle in his left hand, he dropped the box of ammo from his right, as he tried to slow his slide. The voice again, now closer, "Get the fuck outta here man, we're a bit busy here!"

Erik blurted out, "Sorry, my bad, didn't know you were here." As he continued to slide, he thought, *Jeez, man, you picked here to get laid?*

He slid another fifteen feet and hit the riverbank. Holding the rifle above his head, he was able to stand up, but immediately started sinking into the mud. *Shit!* He knew if he threw the rifle in at that point, the guy and whoever was with him would hear it for sure. He got one foot unstuck, then the other, and retreated a few feet up the bank. Finding solid footing, he continued along the river's edge for roughly twenty yards, which he figured would be enough. Now nearly under the bridge, he was afraid that someone might see him from up above, but it did not matter. He had to get rid of the rifle *now*. Holding the rifle with both hands, he twisted his body around like a discus thrower and threw it as far out as he could. It hit the water with a loud *kerplunk* sound, which he was not expecting. Still, it was gone.

He turned and tried to make his way up the slope, but the area was densely covered with bushes and weeds. His shoes were wet from the riverbank, and they made the climb slippery. He tried to use some of the larger bushes to pull himself up, but they cut his hands, which were now bleeding. *Damn it.* Finally, he made it to the top. Before hopping the fence, he checked both ways. The coast looked clear. Up and over he went. Walking quickly to his car, he popped open the door and got in.

His shoes were covered in mud, and now it was in the carpet of the car. There was nothing he could do about it at this point. There was blood on his hands, and now it was on the steering wheel, but he could not do anything about that either. He started the car and backed up before turning on the lights. He checked traffic, which was still clear, then turned left onto East River Parkway and went along the river, winding his way north and east through a residential area, then through the city. At an empty gas station, he pulled in and threw his jacket in the trash. As he continued on toward his apartment, he thought about the box of ammo he had dropped, and cursed aloud, "Damn it."

Erik finally made it home. He still had a lot to do. *I need to get rid of all the evidence.*

At the door, he took off his muddy shoes and left them outside. Once inside, he stripped off his pants, shirt, socks, and underwear, leaving them all in a heap on the floor. He walked naked into the kitchen to get a trash bag, then went back and threw all the clothes into the bag. Opening the door just a crack, he peeked outside to make sure no one was around and retrieved his shoes. He threw them into the trash bag as well, pulled the drawstring closed, and knotted it tight.

Next, he got the bottle of Dawn Dish Soap from under the kitchen sink and headed for the shower. He figured the grease-cutting Dawn would help get rid of the gunshot residue on him from shooting the rifle. On TV police shows, he had seen where suspects were tested for that immediately. In the shower, he vigorously scrubbed his hands, arms, face, and hair. Then he washed again using his regular shower soap. Satisfied there was nothing left. *That ought to do it.*

Out of the shower, he toweled off and put on clean clothes. Once again, he opened the door of his apartment and made sure no one was around. He picked up the trash bag and threw it in the trunk of his car. Erik knew there were some dumpsters in an alleyway behind several businesses in a strip mall just a couple of miles away. He had dumped extra garbage there before and it had not been a problem. It was late now, and the businesses were all closed, except for a pizza joint at the far end. He pulled into the alleyway and stopped in front of three dumpsters, figuring one had to have room. He got out of his car and lifted the lid on the first dumpster. It was only half full. Checking once more to make sure no one was around, he popped the trunk open, pulled the bag out, hauled it over to the dumpster, and hoisted it in. He closed the lid, got back in his car, and drove away, congratulating himself. *Good riddance.*

Next, he drove to a 24-hour self-serve car wash. He washed the outside of the car first, then pulled to the vacuuming station, and vacuumed out not only the front carpet, but the entire interior. He bought a pack of paper wash towels from the vending machine and used them to clean the steering wheel and gearshift lever. Pleased with the results, he drove home. It was after midnight. He flipped on the TV to see if there was anything on the late news, but there was nothing.

Knowing he had to go to work in the morning to make everything appear normal, he headed to bed to try and get some sleep. At first his mind was still whirling from the night's activities—the shooting, his escape on foot, then in the car, dumping the rifle, and all the cleaning up. Eventually, he calmed down and was able to sleep a few hours.

In the morning, he checked the TV news first thing. Channel 7 had a brief report, "A man was shot dead last night in front of his house in the Highland Park neighborhood of St. Paul. Police are investigating."

I bet they are! he chuckled. There was no mention of the Stonehenge Murder Case.

After a quick breakfast, he showered again, shaved, and got dressed. He headed to work and was actually on time for a change.

In the office, he could feel people were still watching him, just as they had since he had returned from England. He just focused on his work and ignored them as best he could. Mid-morning, his boss came to talk with him briefly about an upcoming network project, but that was it. A little before ten thirty he started to shut down his PC. Just before logging out, he checked the website of *The Pioneer Press*, the major St. Paul newspaper. *Holy crap!* There was a video at the top of the home page:

> *In breaking news, St. Paul Police have announced that last night's shooting in the Highland Park neighborhood appears to be related to the Stonehenge Murder Case, which has sensationalized the Twin Cities over the past week. The victim's name was Mikhail Andropov, who was a member of the Stonehenge travel group. The police did not release any further details. We'll pass along new information as it becomes available.*

Well, that didn't take long. He finished shutting down and headed out for the police station. Arriving a few minutes early, he sat in his car, prepping himself mentally. He would have to be calm, no matter what. He would have to feign shock over the news of Andropov. Strangely, he recalled being in the sixth grade and having a role in a class play. His teacher told him afterward that he did a great job and would make a good actor. If ever he needed to do some serious acting, it was right now. He braced himself, got out of his car, and headed into the building.

Chapter 26

Dino was about to turn in for the night when his cell phone rang. The caller ID showed Paula Dunn. At this late hour, Dino instinctively thought, *Uh oh*, but he answered promptly. "This is Dino."

"Hi, it's Paula. We've had a fatal shooting over in the Highland Park neighborhood. Tim Baker was next up for a case, so I initially assigned it to him. He's on the scene now. But someone there figured out that the victim is Mikhail Andropov." She paused for effect, "Yup, the one and only."

"Really?" was all that Dino could muster.

"I'm reassigning the case to you, since you're already on the Stonehenge case. Just so you know, the mayor was already miffed before he found out it was related to the Stonehenge case. The case was sensational enough before—now it'll get even worse. The address is 1847 Mortimer Street, just east of Cleveland Avenue."

"I'm on my way!" said Dino, and he hung up. He took half a minute to call Jack, who answered in two rings.

"Hello, this is Jack"

"Hey Jack, it's Dino. I just found out that Mikhail Andropov won't be keeping his nine o'clock appointment in the morning."

"Why's that?"

"Because he was found murdered at his home just over an hour ago. I'm headed there now. I'll have a squad car come pick you up and get you over to the scene."

"Damn. I can't believe it. I'm gobsmacked."

"Isn't everybody?"

"You know what I mean! OK, I'll be ready and out in front of the lobby in three minutes. See you there."

Dino hung up. He jumped into the Alfa and covered the four miles from his house to the scene in just over six minutes. As he turned the corner off Cleveland onto Mortimer, he could see at least four squads and two emergency medical vehicles with their lights flashing brightly in the night. The street was blocked off, and the obligatory yellow perimeter tape was set up around the yard of Andropov's house. On the front lawn, there were tri-pod pole lamps pointed at the front door and stoop of the house. Several neighbors and other onlookers stood across the street, gawking at the spectacle.

Dino pulled up as close as he could get and jumped out. He knew at least two of the uniforms assigned to the perimeter. "Hey Dino," said one of them, "Tim's over there near the front door if you're looking for him."

"Thanks Bruce. FYI, Jack Wright, the detective from England, will be showing up shortly in a squad. Please send him over when he gets here."

"Sure thing."

Dino found Tim and asked, "Hello Tim, what've we got here?"

"Hey Dino, you lucky guy, Paula says you get this one. Breaks my heart."

"I'm sure. Shot on the front stoop?"

"Yeah, it looks like he was lured out by somebody that left an empty Fedex package on the stoop, probably pressed the door-bell, then ran to that tree there. That appears to be where the shooter fired from. The guy used a rifle."

"A rifle? Really?"

"That's what the ME thinks, based on his initial examina-tion of the wounds. Two shots, probably hollow points, both in the chest. He's not sure about the caliber. We haven't found any spent casings. The victim was single and lived here alone, according to the neighbors. That's where we sit as of right now."

"Thanks Tim. Go ahead and take off. At least one of us should get some sleep tonight."

"Works for me. Good luck!"

Dino checked in with Greg Paulson, the medical examiner. He confirmed the details from Tim. The body was still slumped on the front stoop, with a large pool of blood dripping down the steps and onto the sidewalk. *Lovely.*

"You sure about the rifle, and the hollow points?" Dino asked.

"About eighty percent. We'll confirm later. I should be able to get you a caliber as well."

"Thanks Greg."

Just then, Jack arrived. "Good Lord Dino, I can hardly believe it."

"I know. Ya can't make this stuff up."

"I would guess there's going to be a feeding frenzy by the media. I'm surprised they aren't here swarming all over us already."

"It won't be long. I would think this will make a big splash back home in England as well?"

"Oh, for sure."

"One thing, it would imply that the Druids are off the hook for now?"

"Yes, it would seem so."

Dino paused for a few moments while looking over at the ME guys and medical techs working the body, then added, "You know, Jack, to this point, I've just been assisting you. It was your baby. But this now makes it my case as well. And to be honest, it pisses me off. We supposedly have a limited list of suspects, and now this happens right under our noses. Crap. I can tell you that my pucker factor just went way up on this case. And by the way, the mayor is on the warpath about it."

"I figured."

"OK, let's get to work."

The lead crime scene investigator was Terry Bailey. Dino had heard of him but had not worked with him directly. He had a reputation as a pragmatic, matter-of-fact, attention-to-detail kind of investigator. Dino was pleased with his assignment to the case.

Dino asked him, "Looks like the guy used a rifle?"

"That's what the ME says," replied Terry.

"Who called it in?"

"The neighbor directly across the street. Let's see," Terry said, taking a moment to check his notebook. "Mr. Joblinski. He called 911. He's the guy standing across the street in the Minnesota Vikings windbreaker if you want to talk with him."

"Thanks." Dino and Jack walked across the street. "Mr. Joblinski?"

"That's me."

Dino and Jack introduced themselves. "We understand you called 911?"

"I did. I was watching TV in the front room and heard a loud rifle shot. I thought, 'That was odd,' and then six or seven seconds later, I heard a second shot."

"How did you know it was a rifle shot?"

"I've gone deer hunting up north every fall for over thirty years. A rifle sounds a lot different from the pop of your typical handgun."

"True. Did you go over to Mr. Andropov's house after calling?"

"At first, I wasn't sure where the shot had come from. I knew it was close, but not exactly where. I walked out onto the sidewalk and looked up and down the street. Then I saw the porch light on and the front door open at Mikhail's house straight across here. I walked out into the street, and from there, I could see somebody lying slumped over on the stoop. I called out but got no response. The guy didn't move at all. That's when I ran back into our house and called 911."

"Well, you did the right thing, Mr. Joblinski. Thank you. Did you hear or see anything unusual before you heard the shots?"

"Nope. I was watching TV, like I said."

"How about afterward? Speeding car, that sort of thing?"

"No, but I did hear a dog barking loudly behind Mikhail's house just as I stepped out to see what was going on."

"OK. Well, thanks again. We may need to talk with you again

later."

"No problem."

Dino and Terry then met with several of the uniformed officers on the scene, directing them to canvass the neighbors within a two-block radius. They learned that several other neighbors had heard the shots but had decided to just stay inside. Two neighbors behind Andropov's house corroborated the barking dog story. The neighbor directly behind the back alley added that somebody had gone through his yard and set off his motion-sensitive yard light. He had opened his back screen door, but did not see anyone, and no one responded when he called out.

That was about all they learned from the neighbors. No one had noticed any strange cars parked on nearby streets, or anyone suspicious looking. No one had a home-video security system that recorded.

Several TV trucks and reporters had gathered at the west end of the perimeter tape. Dino knew they wouldn't go away until they got some kind of story. He walked over and talked with them as a group, giving them only minimal information, promising a full statement in the early morning. He did confirm the name of the victim as Mikhail Andropov, who was a member of the Stonehenge travel group.

"Sorry guys, that's all I can give you right now."

Dino and Jack walked back to talk with Terry again. Several tarps had been set up as a canopy over the body and adjacent area.

Terry explained, "It's supposed to rain within an hour or so. Photo guy will be done in about fifteen to twenty minutes, but the rest of the team will need more time, so we're taking the precaution." After a moment, he continued, "By the way, we were able to get plaster casts of several footprints just behind the tree where we think the shooter fired from, as well as a couple of faint footprints from the back yard."

"Anything interesting?" asked Dino.

"It's been fairly dry the last few days, so the prints aren't really great. They appear to be athletic shoes, Nike brand."

"OK."

"We also got a couple of prints off the Fedex box. The sides of the box had been wiped clean, but the two ends had at least a few partial prints. Doesn't mean they were from the shooter, so I wouldn't get your hopes up."

"Hey, ya gotta have hope!" replied Dino, trying to add some levity. "Or maybe just a bit of good luck?"

"Sure."

Dino paused, then asked one last question. "How about inside the house? I don't think we need a warrant to look in there."

"We plan to work in there as soon as we're done outside. But you can't go in yet," replied Terry.

"Understand, but we'd love to take a look at his PC, in particular, recent email traffic."

"We'll look."

"Thanks Terry. We need to catch this guy quickly. We'll look for the case file in the morning."

"No problem. I'll let you know if we can confirm a caliber on that rifle."

"That'd be great."

Dino and Jack turned, went back to the Alfa, and got in. Slowly, they made their way out of the maze of vehicles and headed out. Dino dropped Jack at the Hilton just after three a.m.

"I plan to get in a bit early, say seven?" said Dino.

"Works for me. I need to report back home what happened tonight. I'll be ready," said Jack.

Chapter 27

Dino picked up Jack promptly at seven, and they went straight to the station.

Paula met them just as they got to Dino's desk. "The mayor is pissed. Is that a surprise? The media are all over him on this one. He wants an update at nine sharp, from both of you."

"We'll be ready," replied Dino.

Dino started taking off his sport coat, and said to Jack, "Sometimes we need to remind the mayor that we don't *commit* these murders. We're the good guys trying to solve them. Whenever he's out looking for somebody's ass to fry, I think he gets confused on that." He forced a bit of a smile, then added, "Oh well, we'll be ready."

Dino saw Suzie was in early as well. He and Jack went over to ask if she had been able to do any research on markings at Stonehenge.

"I was able to find out quite a bit," she said with a grin. "I've gotta admit, it was fun working on something different for a change. Anyway, I found that there are indeed markings on some of the sarsen stones—those are the bigger stones. There are images of flanged axes and daggers, although they are all but invisible to the naked eye. They were found by 3D laser scans of the stones back in 2002. The markings are actually tool markings thought to be from the Bronze Age, nearly a thousand years after the initial work at Stonehenge." She paused to look at her notes, then continued, "However, some of the faint markings that were long thought to be carvings were actually just natural cracks. And some of the visible markings are graffiti from only a few hundred years ago. So, yes, there are markings, but they would be difficult to see, especially at night."

"Thanks Suzette, for your usual thorough work!"

"You're welcome Dino, as usual," she replied with a smirk.

As they left her desk, Jack told Dino quietly, "She's good. I wish I had an assistant like her back home."

"You can only hope, my friend," replied Dino.

Once back at his desk, Dino said, "We'll see what Mr. Foster has to say about the markings when he comes in. We better get our shit together for the mayor."

About fifteen minutes before the meeting was to start, Paula came over to Dino's desk with an update. "The lab just confirmed the caliber of the weapon used to kill Andropov, ready for it?" she teased.

"Let's have it."

"30-06!"

"Damn, that's just odd." Dino still had trouble believing it. He explained to Jack that a 30-06 was a hunting rifle used by many deer hunters in Minnesota, mostly in the northern parts of the state. For Andropov to be shot with a 30-06 in the *city*, is definitely strange. "It's a clue Jack. Not quite sure how, but it's got to be a clue."

"Thanks Paula. We're almost ready for the nine o'clock."

"See you then."

The meeting with the mayor went much as expected. The mayor let off steam, explaining why "we simply can't have this kind of thing happening in our city," and then eventually asking, "So where are we Dino?"

Dino reviewed the details of the case from last night, and the updates from this morning. He confirmed the lab report of the 30-06. "We interviewed two of our top priority suspects yesterday, Mr. Murphy and Mr. Miller. We were supposed to interview Mr. Andropov this morning. Obviously, that won't happen. We have the last of our priority suspects, Mr. Foster, due in at eleven this morning. After that, we'll go on to the secondary priority suspects—all members of the travel group."

"Well, you've got to catch him, Dino. These media hounds are all over me. We need to show some progress. Paula, you're responsible for feeding them info as best you can. Keep them placated. I want to be updated as soon as anything significant happens." Then after a pause, "Well, get out of here and catch the bastard!"

"Will do," returned Dino.

As they left the meeting, Dino whispered to Paula, "Wow, *placated?* Pretty big word for an elected official."

Paula snickered just a bit, but then mildly scolded Dino with, "Careful there, Mr. Roselli. If it's placated he wants, it's placated he'll get."

Dino and Jack went back and finished their interview preparations. Erik Foster checked in at the front desk right at eleven. Dino went and greeted him, "Thank you for coming in Mr. Foster."

Erik replied, "Sure, no problem. Happy to help."

Dino thought Erik seemed rather flippant in his reply, but he let it go, and escorted him to the conference room. Dino pointed him to a seat in between Jack and his own, closed the door, and sat down. With the Andropov case the direct responsibility of SPPD, Dino now took the lead in the questioning.

"I assume you've heard the most recent news, Mr. Foster?" Dino watched Erik to observe his reaction. "Mikhail Andropov was murdered last night in front of his home in Highland Park."

"Oh my God, that's terrible. How did it happen?"

"He was shot twice on his own front doorstep. Died almost instantly."

"That's too bad."

"Too bad? Where were you last night, Mr. Foster?"

"What the hell, are you accusing me of his murder?"

"Not at all, Mr. Foster, this is a voluntary, informational interview. You are not under arrest, nor are you being detained. There's no need to read you your rights, unless you would prefer that?"

"No, I have nothing to hide. I feel bad for Mikhail."

"Can you kindly tell us then where you were last night?"

"Sure. I went home after work, had some supper, and then went over to Ray's Pub for a beer. I go there quite often. You can ask the bartender. He'll vouch for me."

"We'll do that. So, then what?"

"After that I went home, checked emails, then went to bed. I'm still trying to catch up from the jet lag of the trip."

"OK. How long have you been in the SIG group, Mr. Foster?"

"You can call me Erik. Let's see, a little over two years."

"Some of the others in the travel group mentioned you seem to have a strong interest in Stonehenge?"

"Oh, they did? Well, there's nothing wrong with that. In fact, that's the point of SIG, it seems to me. Who said that? Did they accuse me?"

"No, Mr. Foster. Why would you think that?"

"I can imagine whoever committed these murders would try to cover it up by accusing someone else."

"Do you think someone from the group killed Jennifer? Do you think both Jennifer's and Mikhail's murders were committed by the same person, Mr. Foster?"

"How the hell would I know? I have no idea!"

"OK. Back to your interest in Stonehenge, Mr. Foster. Some of the other members in the group mentioned you had brought up something about a book called Chariots of the Gods?"

"Yes, I've brought it up several times in our discussions at the monthly meetings. It's a book by Erich von Däniken. He lays out strong proof that the people who built Stonehenge, and other ancient monuments, such as the pyramids, had help from alien astronauts who traveled here and gave the ancient peoples the technology to build the monuments. Those people surely did not have the knowledge to do it themselves."

"Really?"

"Yes. Besides SIG, I'm also a member of the Ancient Astronauts Society."

"I've never heard of it."

"It's another group of people who, like me, believe that extraterrestrial beings were responsible for building many of the ancient monuments here on earth. I'm also interested in SETI research. Are you familiar with that? The Search for Extraterrestrial Intelligence?"

"OK."

"Are you making fun of me?"

"Not at all Mr. Foster."

"There is well-documented scientific proof of the ancient astronauts. But you have to have an open mind when considering it, and quite frankly, many of the members of SIG do not have open minds. I've taken a bunch of shit for my views at the meetings, including some from Tom Morris."

"Does that make you mad, Mr. Foster?"

"I'll admit it's a bit frustrating, but it's not a reason for me to kill anyone."

"We never suggested you did, Mr. Foster. Let's move on. Several of the travel group members said you were quite interested in some markings on the stones at Stonehenge. What markings, Mr. Foster?"

"Most people think Stonehenge is unique among the ancient monuments because it has no markings, but that's not true. Markings were discovered just recently on several of the sarsens."

"Sarsens?"

"The big stones at Stonehenge. When we arrived at Stonehenge, I looked for them myself, and it seemed some were visible. I was merely discussing it with some of the other members of the group. They were all supposedly there because of their interest in Stonehenge, so I was interested in finding out what they thought about them. Nothing wrong with that!"

"No, there isn't."

"You're a systems programmer, Mr. Foster?"

Happy to move on to another topic, Erik replied, "Yes, I work at Superior Technical Services here in St. Paul."

"Do you have a girlfriend, Mr. Foster?"

The question clearly threw Erik. It was as if his consciousness had suddenly left the room. He just sat there for some time, with a blind expression on his face. Eventually, Dino prompted him, "Ah . . . Mr. Foster?"

After a few awkward moments, Erik seemed to come to. He refocused himself, and responded solemnly, "I had a girl-friend once, but that was a very long time ago. She's dead." After another pause, he looked up. "Why do you ask?"

"Just routine questions Mr. Foster." Dino made a point of looking through his papers, then stopping on one in particular, he asked Erik, "Do you own a rifle, Mr. Foster?"

"No."

"Any other firearms? A handgun?"

"No. Why would you ask that?"

"Routine questions Mr. Foster. How well do you know Tom Morris?"

"I know him from the meetings. He always runs the meetings."

"How about Jennifer Morris? How well did you know her?"

"I would occasionally see her at the meetings, and of course I talked with her on the trip."

"OK. How about the Druids. Did you interact with any of the Druids?"

"A few. There were a lot of them, spread all over. They're a bit wacky as far as I'm concerned. They don't specifically claim to have built Stonehenge, but informally, they promote the notion. Of course, it's been proven long ago that they could not possibly have built it. Like I said, I did chat with a few of them, but that was it."

Dino asked several other minor questions, mostly just to observe Erik's demeanor in answering them. Eventually, he felt they had learned all they were going to learn for the day and told Erik he was free to go. Dino escorted him back to the front desk and signed him out. He watched as Erik walked to his car. *That is one weird duck.*

He went back to the conference room, sat down, and asked Jack, "Well, what do you think? I confess I tried to provoke him a bit, to see how he would react."

"So far, I think he's the closest match to our profile. He's a bit odd but that doesn't make him guilty."

"You're right," admitted Dino. "Did you notice he had scratches on both hands?"

"I did, and they looked fresh."

"I think we need to have a chat with Paula."

Chapter 28

After the interview, Erik walked to his car, got in, and closed the door. He sat for a few moments, collecting his thoughts and reviewing how the interview had gone. Satisfied that he had performed well enough, he felt confident that he was OK. He was concerned they might be onto him, but even if they were, with Andropov out of the way, they had no proof.

Calling his boss, he told him he needed to take the afternoon off. Too much on his mind, and besides, he was sick of the judgmental stares from his co-workers. *They're all idiots anyway.*

Back at his apartment, he made a plate of mac and cheese for himself. He popped a Diet Coke and sat down to watch the news on TV as he ate. The Andropov murder was still the lead story on nearly every local news channel. He smiled to himself, feeling more confident now, even smug. When finished with his lunch, he turned off the TV and went into the Stonehenge Room. Sitting at his PC, he waded through several junk emails, but then stopped cold—there was a new email from *eyewitness0621@gmail.com,* with a subject line of *"Nice Try"* it said, *"You idiot— you killed the wrong guy. The price is now $20,000."*

What the fuck? Erik was dumbfounded. In less than thirty seconds, he had gone from feeling confident to being in complete shock. Now he was beside himself. *I risked all that for nothing?*

Taking some deep breaths, he forced himself to calm down.

I need to get smarter. After several moments, he arrived at, *I'm a tech guy. How about something techie?*

Thinking about the blackmailer, he envisioned the guy sitting at his PC typing away. He then hit on an idea. *A keylogger! Of course!* He could find a keystroke capture program on the web, send it to the blackmailer, and have it record all his keystrokes, as well as screenshots of every website visited, which he could then retrieve via VPN. The guy would never know. *Perfect!*

He did some initial research, and within ten minutes had found several freeware programs that would work. There was one called "evileyes4you" that he found on the dark web. The program would report itself as, Service Host: Network Statistics on a task manager screen, in case the user should look. It could be installed remotely via email, with no access to the target PC required. The only catch was that the user of the target PC had to click and open an attachment with the program embedded within it, so that the code had a chance to execute. It could be inserted into a simple JPEG, with some benign file name. Erik thought it would be ironic to embed the script in a dummied-up screenshot confirming funds waiting to be transferred. *How could anybody resist clicking on that?*

It took Erik just half an hour to dummy up an official-looking JPEG image appearing to show a bank account with a balance of over $2,300. He modified the program's executable program slightly, to change its virus pattern and help it get by any virus checker. He prepared a reply to the blackmailer's most recent email, saying, "OK. I am ready to send a down payment of $2,000. That is all I can do for now. I can try to get more later. See the attached confirmation screenshot." He sent the email, crossed his fingers, and waited.

Just over an hour later, he was able to access the program. *Yes!* The user had indeed clicked on and opened the attachment, which had installed the code. It was now recording keystrokes and web page screenshots. He let the program run for about thirty minutes, then checked to see what had been captured.

Initially, he just saw several Google searches, a Facebook access, a local news site, but then, there it was: the login page for the largest bank in town. He noted the date-timestamp, then opened the keystrokes file, went to the same date-timestamp, and there was the user ID of 'TammyC3' and a password of 'Lucky57$.' *Tammy? Tammy Anderson? It can't be!* He saw a screen showing an account balance of just over three thousand dollars.

On his own PC, Erik quickly navigated to the same login page. He entered the captured user ID and password, and *voila!* He was in. All of this in less than three hours. He scolded himself for not thinking of it before, and for taking a gigantic risk in getting rid of Andropov. *Oh well, spilt milk. I think it's time to send Tammy an email.*

Five minutes later, he sent:

> Hello *eyewitness0620@gmail.com*, or should I say, Tammy! Yes, I know it's you.
>
> I'm now watching everything you do. I see you have a balance of $3,726.78 at the bank. You know, I think I might just help myself to say . . . $3,500 of that? Yes, that would be nice.
>
> By the way, I just changed the password on your account.
>
> And I'm sorry to tell you Tammy that I will *not* be paying you $10,000, or $20,000, or *even a penny.* I *will* however, be paying you a *visit*, and *soon!*
>
> You shouldn't have fucked with me!

Chapter 29

Dino and Jack met briefly with Paula, updating her on the Erik interview. "I think he's our most promising suspect so far," Dino told her. "Jack has a lot of confidence in the profile from Charlie Evans at Scotland Yard."

"I do," said Jack. "Charlie's been spot on with profiles in the past. He's good. And Erik is the closest to the profile yet."

"I agree," said Paula.

"Still, I think we need to move forward with the Group B interviews," continued Dino.

"Oh definitely," confirmed Paula.

"Then we'll get started," said Dino, heading for the door. He turned back to Paula, smiled and asked, "You'll take care of the mayor for us?"

"Sure, but you owe me."

"Works for me," said Dino with a smirk.

Jack and Dino left Paula's office and headed back to Dino's area to set up the appointments and prepare.

They called the Kellys first.

"Hello."

"Hello, is this Mr. Kelly?

"Yes."

"This is Detective Dino Roselli of the St. Paul Police Department, along with Detective Superintendent Jack Wright, who you spoke with in England."

"Yes?"

"Mr. Kelly, we know you answered a lot of questions back in London following the murder of Jennifer Morris, and we appreciate your time and responses then, but now in light of the murder of Mikhail Andropov, we have additional questions we'd like to ask both you and your wife Isabelle."

"OK. I just got home. I gave my last lecture of the day this morning. My wife should be home in just a few minutes. She works half days on Fridays. I can check with her and call you back. When were you thinking?"

"Yet today, if at all possible."

"Well, I don't think we have anything planned. How long do you think this will take?"

"I would estimate an hour or less. Can you come here to the St. Paul station?"

"Sure. I'll call you back in a few minutes."

"Thank you very much Mr. Kelly."

Richard called back fifteen minutes later and told Dino, "We could be there by three. Will that work?"

"That would be excellent. See you then."

Dino called the Andersons next.

"Hello, this is Tammy," said a rather timid voice.

Dino explained his call.

"I'm afraid Bob called about an hour ago and said he would be working late. Could we do it tomorrow morning, say eleven?"

"That'll work. We'll see you then, Mrs. Anderson."

Finally, Dino called the Halvorsens.

"Hello?" said a quiet female voice.

"Hello, is this Karen Halvorsen?" asked Dino.

"Yes, who's calling?"

"Mrs. Halvorsen, this is Detective Dino Roselli of the St. Paul Police Department, Detective Superintendent Jack Wright, who you spoke with in London concerning the murder of Jennifer Morris, is here as well. We'd like to ask you and your husband several follow-up questions, as well as questions concerning Mikhail Andropov, who, you may have heard, was murdered last night. Would you be able to come to the St. Paul station sometime soon?"

"Oh my, we live in St. Cloud, so it takes a while for us to get to the Cities. Is tomorrow OK?"

"Tomorrow morning would work best. Could you be here as early as nine?"

"Um, I think nine thirty would be better. Traffic can be a problem, even on weekends."

"I understand Mrs. Halvorsen. Nine thirty will be fine. We appreciate your taking the time. We'll see you then."

"OK. Goodbye."

Dino hung up, then said to Jack, "She sounded nervous."

"Really?"

"Not nervous like 'I'm guilty and hiding something.' More like 'small town fish out of water' nervous."

"I think I recall this was their first trip out of the US, and Karen in particular seemed horrified by Jennifer's murder."

"Well, that's understandable. OK, we're setup. Let's get ready for our three o'clock with the Kellys."

"Sounds good."

The Kellys showed up ten minutes early at the front desk. Both Dino and Jack went to greet them. Dino introduced himself and thanked them for coming in. They walked toward a conference room, but paused before going in. Dino explained, "We would like to interview each of you individually. Either of you can be first, but we've found that individual interviews help to keep the responses more spontaneous."

"OK. I can go first," said Richard.

"Let me explain further, for both of you, this is a voluntary, informational interview. You are not being arrested, nor are you in police custody. There is no need to read you your rights. We simply want to ask you several questions about the murder of Jennifer Morris, and now, Mikhail Andropov."

"Alright."

"Mrs. Kelly, you can wait here. Would you like coffee?" offered Dino.

"No, thanks."

As Dino suspected, the actual interviews were unfruitful. When asked about any recollections since the London interviews, they both replied they had none. When asked about Mikhail Andropov, they responded they had only met Mikhail on the trip, and even then, had spent very little time with him. They had no idea who might have killed him and did not appear to be hiding anything. They simply did not know, or at least it appeared that way. The interviews were completed in less than thirty minutes.

Still, Dino thanked them. "We appreciate your coming in. Please contact me if anything further comes to mind." Dino escorted them out of the building and returned to Jack.

"I'm afraid that was a bust. Hopefully, we'll learn more from tomorrow's interviews. I think that's about all we can do for today. Looks like we have a free evening."

"That actually works for me, Dino. I have a lot of correspondence and work to catch up on back home, and my wife always appreciates a phone call. And it's almost bedtime in England. I appreciate your entertaining me these past evenings, but I'm sure you could use some catch up time yourself. It was a short night last night."

"That's for sure. OK, that'll work. I'll drop you off at your hotel, but before heading home, I want to follow up with the bartender at Ray's Pub about Erik being there last night. Does eight tomorrow morning work?"

"I'll be ready!"

Dino dropped Jack off, then drove to Ray's Pub. The Friday crowd was already starting to grow. Dino worked his way up to the bar, identified himself, and asked to see the manager. A heavy set, but pleasant talking guy came over and said, "Hello Detective, what can I do for you?"

Dino asked if he knew Erik Foster.

"I do. He comes in maybe a couple of times a week. What about him?"

"Was he here last night?"

"Let's see, um . . . yeah. He was here earlier in the evening. Had one or two at the bar, then left."

"Do you recall the time?"

"Oh boy, not really. It's always busy, and I lose track of time. It was earlier though, I think. Maybe seven o'clock? Seven thirty maybe?"

"OK. Well, thanks."

"No problem. Anytime."

Dino left and walked to the Alfa. He got in, but before driving away, pulled out his cell phone and looked for messages from Amy Williams. Amy had called several times in the last few days, but he had been too busy to get back to her. He punched her number and waited.

"Well, hello stranger!"

"Hello, sorry I haven't gotten back to you."

"I figured you were busy. The Stonehenge case has been all over the news. Now it's two murders!"

"As if one wasn't enough. But actually, I've had enough of playing detective for one day. Are you interested in dinner tonight?"

"I would love dinner! Just say when and where."

"My place, about seven thirty? I'll pick up some groceries on the way home here and fix us something kinda quick."

"I'm sure it will be fantastic. I'm still savoring the last dinner you prepared."

"Just to let you know, I have a splurge bottle of wine in the cellar that I've been looking forward to for over a year, and I think tonight would be a great time to open it up."

"Sounds lovely. Can't wait!"

"Great! See you tonight. Come hungry!"

"That's never a problem. I'm looking forward to seeing you."

"See you soon."

Dino had decided to make *Pappardella ai Funghi* for dinner. It was a flavorful dish that did not take that long to make. After jotting down a list of the ingredients needed, he headed for the grocery store. When he got home, he went to the basement and brought up a seventeen-year-old bottle of Brunello di Montalcino that he had tucked away several years ago. He picked out a bottle of prosecco as well. The Brunello was a big wine that needed time to open up, so he decanted the entire bottle right away. The prosecco went into the fridge for later. Next, he went to his bedroom, changed clothes, and then headed back to the kitchen to start making the Pappardella.

Preparing nice dinners was relaxing for Dino. He enjoyed working in the kitchen. And he always enjoyed great wine. It was one of his passions in life. He especially loved the great variety of Italian wines. There were endless choices. And he had enjoyed Amy's company at their last dinner, so altogether, it should be just the kind of evening Dino needed, after what had turned out to be a very long day.

The Pappardella was just filling the kitchen with the fragrant smells of garlic, mushrooms, and pasta, when the doorbell rang. Prompt at seven thirty he noted. *Gotta love a girl who is punctual.* He opened the door, and she literally stunned him— she looked just wonderful. And he told her so.

"Something new I bought just a while ago. I thought you might like it."

"You look great. Come on in."

"Oh, it smells wonderful in here. What are you preparing?"

"Pappardella ai Funghi," he replied. "Fancy name for pasta with wild mushrooms. And maybe a few other things thrown in there as well. Come on in, have a glass of wine while I finish preparing." He poured her a glass of the Brunello from the decanter and waited for her to try it. She smelled it in the glass, took a sip, and her eyes nearly rolled back into her head.

"Oh, my goodness, this is just magnificent. What is it?"

"Brunello di Montalcino, from Tuscany. It's made with 100% Sangiovese. I've had this bottle in my cellar for over twelve years, just waiting for a special occasion. No time like the present!"

"What a treat. Thank you for sharing it with me."

"Wine is always best shared. Thank you for coming. Have a seat."

Amy sat down at the near end of the island and took another sip of wine. While Dino worked on the finishing touches of their dinner. Amy asked, "Any chance of talking about the Stonehenge case?"

"None at all," replied Dino, matter-of-factly.

"It's the hottest topic in town, you know."

"I'm sure."

"Any chance at all?"

"Nope. Off-limits."

"OK, I get it."

Changing the topic, Dino asked, "How did that big real estate deal you were working on turn out?"

"Ugh. I was afraid you'd ask. It fell through at the last minute. Another realtor lowered the price on a competing property, and the buyer went for it." After a pause, she added, "But there will be others. I have a couple of things in the works."

Dino had the meal ready within ten minutes. He plated their food, topping it with freshly grated Parmigiano-Reggiano. He lit two candles on the table, and they sat down to enjoy it all.

Amy took her first bite of the pasta, savoring the flavors. "Wow! This is fantastic. The mushrooms are so earthy."

"I think porcini mushrooms work well in this dish, but you can use cremini, or even shiitake."

"And this wine pairs perfectly. I don't think I've ever had anything quite like it. It's very complex. Just lovely."

"Brunello can be challenging. I think most people would say you need to cellar Brunello for at least fifteen years—twenty would be better. Depends on the vintage. It's a flat-out mistake to open a Brunello before ten years. That's way too young. Like many things in life, it takes a while to develop. You must know when it, and perhaps more importantly, you, are ready."

"That sounds profound."

"Profound? Well, for sure it's true, but I'm not sure if it's profound. I guess, if you make enough mistakes in life, after a while, you get smarter. Maybe that's it?"

They continued eating and chatting, until Dino looked over at the bottle of Brunello, and said, "I'm afraid it's nearly done."

"Very sad!"

He poured the rest evenly into their glasses, then raised his and toasted, "Here's to you!"

"And to you!"

They clinked glasses and drank the last of the Brunello down in one gulp. They sat for a few seconds, savoring the moment.

Then Dino said, "Let's leave these dishes. I'll take care of them later. I have a bottle of prosecco chilling in the fridge. Let's grab it and head to the sitting room."

As he heard himself say the words "sitting room," for some reason, it sounded a bit awkward, so he added, "The sitting room is where we . . . ah . . . sit."

"Really?"

"Oh yes. Remember it? The room with the magic fireplace?"

"I do. It's the place I remember from last time, where I couldn't recall ever feeling so warm and cozy with so few clothes on."

"You do remember!"

In spite of the chilled prosecco, they managed to stay warm and cozy for several hours.

Later, as Dino got ready to turn in for the night, he thought, *A nearly perfect evening.* He thought about the food and the wine, but mostly he thought about Amy. *I like Amy a lot . . . I wonder . . . maybe there's hope yet, Momma.*

Chapter 30

It did not take long for Erik to decide he had to get rid of Tammy. *If she squeals to the police, I'm finished. But with her gone, the police have nothing.* It had to be done.

But how? He regretted throwing the rifle into the river, but he knew he could not afford to get caught with it. Maybe I could retrieve it? *No, that's stupid.*

How about a knife? You have to get really close, and she'll probably be on guard and fight back. Could get real messy. He ruled that out as well.

Maybe I could hit her with my car? But I have no idea when or where she goes anywhere. And I'd have to hit her at high speed to be sure of killing her. It would damage my car, leave permanent evidence, and there could be witnesses. Nix that one.

Gun? He had the same problems as before with trying to procure a gun. He could not buy a new one or even a used one, without leaving a traceable sale.

He recalled his dad had an old pistol as well as the rifle. When he went to get the rifle before, he had seen the old handgun there, but had instantly dismissed using it. It was rusty, there was no ammo, and he had never fired it himself. For that matter, he had never actually fired any handgun. His dad carried it when they were hunting, to finish a wounded deer, if need be, but he could not recall his dad ever actually using it. Erik knew handguns were notoriously inaccurate and typically had a short range. He was quite sure that it was a .22 caliber, a revolver, and with a hammer you cocked back manually each time. So, it would be slow to fire. *I'm not sure a .22 can even kill a person.* He researched it online, and quickly determined a .22 could indeed kill a person, but a shot would have to be well-placed, so it might take multiple shots. He thought about it some more. *I can clean it up, and it'll probably work just fine.*

He could not go get it today. Being Saturday, his folks would almost certainly be home. But they always went to church on Sunday morning. He could get it tomorrow.

What about ammo? He researched and discovered he did not need a permit or license to buy ammo in Minnesota. And typically, simple .22 ammo is sold off an open shelf, not from behind a secured counter like higher caliber ammo.

He decided to try it.

Cabela's is one of the largest local retailers of guns and ammo. He was familiar with a nearby store in the suburb of Woodbury but decided to drive an hour south on Interstate 35 to Owatonna, where he would most likely never be recognized or remembered.

As he drove along, Erik thought, *Wait a minute, what if I have a tail on me?* It would not be out of the question after the interview at the police station. He quickly became paranoid and started watching in his rearview mirror. He sped up and slowed down, watching to see if anyone was following. Once, he exited the freeway, but did not see anyone behind him. Satisfied he was not being followed, he continued on to Cabela's.

Inside the store, he found the ammo department and picked out a box of one hundred Remington .22 Long Rifle bullets for less than five dollars. He also picked out a Hoppe's gun-cleaning kit for twenty dollars. As his purchases were being rung up at the checkout, the cashier asked, "Are you going to do some plinking?"

Erik was startled. "Pardon me?"

"Plinking. Are you going to do some plinking?" he repeated as he put the items in a plastic bag.

"Ah, sure," Erik responded awkwardly.

"Well, have fun," the cashier said, and then added, "Thanks for shopping at Cabela's!"

"Sure. Thank you."

Erik walked back to his car. *Damn small-town people are always so frickin' friendly. Why can't they be assholes like everyone in the big city?*

He started for home, checking in his rearview mirror every so often, but did not see anyone following him. The entire trip took him just over three hours.

Once back home, he went to his Stonehenge Room and looked up Bob and Tammy Anderson. Within a couple of minutes, he had an address for them. They lived on Newton Street in South St. Paul. He plugged the address into Google Maps, then switched to Street View. Their house was on a rectangular city block in a well-kept residential area, with straight streets and an alley behind. There was a driveway at the front that went into a two-car garage on the left. The house was L-shaped with two stories, with the garage extending out from the longer length of the L. The house faced straight east.

It was now early evening. He decided he still had time to go scope out the house and neighborhood in person. Putting on dark jogging clothes, he drove to within three blocks of the house, parking due west. Sliding out of the car, he put up the hood of his sweatshirt to partially cover his face and started jogging. Erik would jog occasionally, but not very far, so he went slowly, wanting to check out the house itself and the area immediately around it. Looking around for any cops that might be watching, he did not see any. He went a couple of blocks south, east a few, then turned and went north along Newton Street toward Tammy's house.

As he jogged past, he saw a narrow strip of trees that ran along the left side of the garage, all the way back to the alley, separating Tammy's house from the one south of it. *Maybe I could sneak in there?* But he saw no doors or windows on that side of the house. He could see this was going to be tricky. He continued jogging for about a half mile, then turned around and went back along the same route. As he passed the house again, he looked at the door and windows on the right side but did not see anything that looked promising.

How will I even know Tammy is in there? Or where? What about Bob? He was going to have to think carefully about how he could do this.

He made it back to his car, and still had not seen anyone that looked like a cop. He got in and started toward home. Stopping at Burger King, he picked up a burger, fries, and a Coke. Once home, he changed out of his jogging clothes and went to the Stonehenge Room. He ate while looking at the Google Street and Google Earth Views of the Anderson house. He looked at the front, then the rear. *Any access from the rear?* There was a deck that came out from what must be the kitchen, but the surrounding yard was wide open. He would be seen easily going across the yard or waiting outside near the deck.

He was nearly finished with his burger when he noticed there was a balcony on the second floor, with a patio-style sliding door that had to go into a bedroom, probably the master bedroom. The line of trees he had noticed earlier while jogging, went quite close to the garage. *Could I make it up one of the nearest trees, then get over to the roof of the garage, onto the balcony, and into the house itself? Maybe?*

Feeling tired, he leaned back from the monitor, and his mind drifted back . . . 4,500 years back to Stonehenge. He thought of his beloved Rayla and cursed the High Priest and elders who had taken her from him. *If they hadn't done that, I wouldn't be in this mess right now.* His heart ached as he grieved over the life that had been taken from him. Bowing his head, he soon fell asleep, exhausted by the day.

Chapter 31

Dino picked up Jack, Saturday morning at eight sharp, and they headed straight for the office.

"Did you get caught up on things back home, Jack?"

"I did. Amazing how things pile up while you're gone."

"Wife still talking to you?"

"She is! She appreciated the call, especially since it wasn't in the middle of the night. I'm afraid that this trip is going to cost me an expensive dinner out when I get home, but she's fine."

"I talked with the manager of Ray's Pub last night before heading home. He was bartending the night before and confirmed that Erik had been at the bar, had one or two beers, and then left. He wasn't sure of the time, but guessed Erik left around seven or seven-thirty."

"Hmm, that would be at least an hour, maybe two, before Andropov was shot. Not a very solid alibi."

"That's what I thought. Well, we'll see."

Even on a Saturday, people were in the office. On a high-profile case like this one, people routinely put in a fair amount of overtime. Especially since the mayor was pressing for an arrest in the case, something he could offer to the media as evidence of his personal vigilance for justice. Or in his words, "I want it solved now!"

Paula was in already. She saw Dino and Jack and went over to get an update. Dino told her about the Ray's Pub alibi, and the two couples due in for interviews this morning.

"I hope we get something from at least one of them. We need a break in this case."

"You've got that right," replied Dino.

Don and Karen Halvorsen showed up right on time. Dino thanked them for coming all the way from St. Cloud on a Saturday. He went on to explain the voluntary, informational nature of the interview, and that they would be interviewed separately. They decided Karen would go first, then Don.

It took only twenty minutes to conclude both interviews. They both expressed sympathy for Tom Morris on the death of his wife, and they were both appalled at the murder of Mikhail Andropov. "He was such a nice man. Why would anyone want to murder him?" remarked Karen. It quickly became clear that they honestly did not know anything about either of the murders and had no suspicions about who the murderer or murderers might be. Still, Dino thanked them again for coming in, and escorted them back out of the building.

Dino was becoming frustrated. "Swing and a miss," he told Jack.

"Pardon?"

"I suppose that's an Americanism. It refers to our game of baseball, where you're the batter and you take a big swing at the ball and miss."

"I get it," Jack replied. "Maybe we'll have better luck with the Andersons."

"I sure hope so. We're running out of suspects!"

The Andersons showed up a few minutes late, both of them looking a little haggard. Dino explained the ground rules for the interviews, and that they would be done individually.

Bob went first. He was forthright in his responses but maintained he simply did not know anything. The night of Jennifer's murder, he had spent the evening helping Tom shepherd the members of their group among the stones and the base camp. As far as the Andropov murder was concerned, he was dumbfounded. He had no suspicions or theories about who, or why, anyone would murder Mikhail.

Another swing and a miss. Dino was about to conclude the interview, when Bob offered sheepishly, "There is one thing."

"Yes?"

"Ever since we got back from our trip, Tammy has been acting, well . . . strangely."

"How so?"

"Well, at first, she just seemed nervous, anxious about something. I figured it was grief over her friend Jennifer's death. But the last two days, it's become worse. Now she seems genuinely afraid of something. It could be something related to our trip. I asked her yesterday and again this morning what was bothering her, but she just dismissed it. Said she was fine. I'm really worried about her."

"Do you want me to ask her about it, Mr. Anderson?"

"She'll no doubt be mad at me for mentioning it, but yes, I would."

Dino concluded his interview with Bob and had Tammy come in.

"Thank you for coming in Mrs. Anderson."

"Sure."

Dino asked Tammy the same questions he had asked Bob about Jennifer's murder, and then Mikhail's murder. She was tight-lipped in her responses and appeared to be holding something back.

Deciding to force the issue, Dino asked directly, "Mrs. Anderson, your husband is concerned about you."

"Why is that?" she snapped back.

"He feels that you've been acting strangely since your return from England and is worried. Is something bothering you Mrs. Anderson?"

"No, I'm fine," she replied, but there was hesitation in her voice.

"Are you sure?"

"I'm fine," she reiterated.

"Maybe it would help to have Mr. Anderson join us. OK, Mrs. Anderson?"

Dino was afraid she would object, but after a few moments, her tense demeanor fell, and she gave in. "OK."

Bob entered the room and immediately said to Tammy, "I'm worried about you, honey. Please don't be mad at me for bringing it up."

Tammy looked up at Bob, then looked over at Dino, and said, "I saw Erik kill Jennifer."

Chapter 32

"**W**hat?" exclaimed Bob in disbelief.

"Well, I didn't see him actually stab her, but I know he did it."

"I can't believe this!"

"Mrs. Anderson, that's a serious accusation. What did you actually see?" asked Dino.

"I saw Erik and Jennifer walk from the base camp through the large stones, then out to the Slaughter Stone. It was dark, of course, and they were a ways away, with just a few people milling around out there. After a time, I saw Erik leave, but Jennifer wasn't with him. He was walking sort of suspiciously, looking back over his shoulder. I decided to follow him. Then I saw him take off his jacket, wrap something in it, and throw it into one of those big trash barrels."

Dino, Jack, and Bob were silent as they looked first at each other, and then back at Tammy.

"After he walked away, I went and looked in the barrel. I took out the jacket, peeled it back, and there was a knife—*with blood on it*. I threw them back in the barrel and followed him. He went to one of those Porta-Potty toilets, and then back to our base camp."

"My God Tammy! Why didn't you say something?" asked Bob.

"I should have, I know. I guess I just wanted to see what he'd do, what would happen next. It was stupid of me, and hard to explain now, but at that point, I wondered if I might be able to use the information." After a pause, she took a deep breath and continued, "Bob will confirm that I have had problems with gambling in the past."

"Oh, Tammy!" Bob all but wept.

"I kept quiet during all the questioning in London. When we got home, I did something even more stupid. I set up an anonymous Gmail account, and emailed Erik, telling him I had seen him kill Jennifer, and that if I didn't get $10,000, I would go to the police."

"Why would you do that Tammy?"

"I owe money Bob. A lot of money."

"Again? Good Lord. I thought we were through with that. You promised me!"

"I'm sorry."

"Regardless, I would have thought you would have reported him, for Jennifer's sake?"

"Jennifer? Hah, I never did like her."

"What? You went to lunches with her, hung out together, what the hell?"

"I did, but she was forever sticking their money in my face—that fancy house, new cars, clothes. I grew to hate her for it."

Bob just looked at her with amazement, speechless.

"I never said anything about it, because of your friendship with Tom, and your involvement with SIG."

"Do I even know you?" asked Bob, dumbfounded.

Dino had allowed Tammy to tell her story, but he now asked, "Did Erik reply to your email?"

"He did. He didn't admit anything, but he told me he didn't have any money, except a little in his 401K at work. I figured since he replied, and said he might be able to get something, it confirmed he was guilty, and I had a sure bet with him."

"A bet? Good Lord," said Bob, still in disbelief.

"He said it would take a couple of days to get money out of his 401K, but now I think he was stalling. I think he was trying to figure out who it was that was demanding money."

After a pause, she added, "He must have thought it was

Mikhail."

Bob realized the implication and cried out, "Oh no! No!"

"How was I to know he would do that? I felt bad about it, but it was done. So, like any good gambler, I doubled down and sent him another email, saying I now wanted $20,000, or I'd go to the police."

"Oh, what a tangled web we weave . . ." said Bob, now nearly sobbing.

"But somehow, Erik found out who I was. I don't know how he did it, but he's a computer tech guy, so he had some way. He got the login and password for our bank account, and then changed the password, so now I can't get in. He said he was going to take $3,500 from our account. Oh Bob, I was so afraid you'd find out."

"We need to contact the bank immediately!"

Dino had let her continue with her confession, but now interjected, "I'm afraid, Mrs. Anderson, that we need to have you remain here for a time, while we work out the implications of all this."

"That's not the worst of it," she declared. "He sent me an email saying he wasn't going to *pay me any money*, but that he was going to pay me *a visit*. Good God, I think he means to kill me, just like Mikhail!"

Looking at Bob, she said, "I'm so sorry." She then buried her face in her hands, broke down, and sobbed.

Chapter 33

Dino posted a uniformed officer at the door of the conference room, then he and Jack went to see Paula.

"You know that break you said we needed?" he asked her.

"Yes?"

"Well, we've got it. In spades!"

"So let's hear it!"

Dino related Tammy's confession to her, then continued, "Sometimes you just get lucky. But before we pop the champagne and run to tell the mayor what superstars we are, there are several problems with all of it."

"It seems there always are. What're you thinking?" asked Paula.

"First of all, Tammy's blackmail attempt makes her a tainted witness, and it could really just come down to her word against Erik's. Recall that she didn't actually *see* Erik stab Jennifer. If she were to change her mind, and deny she said anything to us, we've got (ticking off his fingers for emphasis): One, no proof; Two, no weapon; Three, no physical evidence; Four, no apparent motive.

"Erik could just say Tammy was doing it for money to pay off her gambling debt. Even Andropov becomes pure supposition. The fact that she didn't report what she saw earlier effectively makes her an accomplice. I doubt any judge would issue a search warrant, or anything else. Plus, we have some jurisdictional issues, which I'm sure you have identified, Jack. Withholding evidence—would that be British jurisdiction? Blackmail—US jurisdiction? even though it's related to a crime committed on British soil? No doubt there are others I haven't thought of yet."

"There are definitely legal issues that we'll need to sort out," added Jack.

"So how do you think we should proceed, Dino?" asked Paula.

"I'm afraid I see only one option."

"And that is?"

"*Catch him in the act!* We'll set a trap, with Tammy as the bait, and nab him right when he goes for her. He's already threatened her."

"Sounds risky, but you might be right."

"It would be definitive proof."

Paula appeared to ponder it for a few moments, then said, "OK. I'll bite. But I need to see a plan ASAP. At least an outline of your basic idea. In the meantime, we need to get a formal statement from Tammy. And we need copies of the emails she sent to and received from Erik." Continuing, she asked, "What's your take on her? Will she cooperate?"

"I think so," replied Dino. "If we had to, we could use a look-alike stand in, but it would be better if she cooperates. My guess is, she will. What's your take Jack?"

"I think you're right Dino. My gut tells me she'll go along, hoping for some leniency on any future charges."

"OK then, let's get moving!" said Paula.

"Um, there's one problem left, perhaps the biggest of all," announced Dino regretfully.

"And what's that?"

"What do we tell the mayor? On the one hand, he has insisted that we update him immediately on any developments. On the other hand, we can't have him blabbing to the media."

"You're right. I'll take care of him." After thinking about it for a moment, she said, "I'll simply explain to him that if he says one word to anyone, I will remove one of his appendages. And I won't let him know which one it will be until I do it!"

"That oughta work."

"I'm sure it will. I've used that tactic on men before, and it's always worked. They don't even want to think about it."

"I believe you."

"So get going on the plan!"

It took Dino and Jack just over an hour to develop the plan. They jotted down a few notes and headed back to Paula's office.

"Let's hear it Dino."

"First, a few assumptions. Based on Andropov, our guy is not a sophisticated killer. He may be a smart guy tech-wise, but he's certainly not street-smart. He simply went to Andropov's house, lured him out and shot him, using what had to be a weapon of convenience, exposing himself to being seen or even captured in a residential neighborhood, got away with it, and has already threatened to do as much again with his 'paying you a visit' remark to Tammy.

"I also suspect he'll make his 'visit' during the same time frame—not during daylight hours, and not in the dead of night. Most likely, he'll try it late evening while Tammy is still up. So we figure, between nine and eleven.

"We think he'll come alone—no accomplice—and make his attempt with a firearm. We're not expecting a bomb or other explosive device. He might just use that 30-06 again. Now, that doesn't mean he won't try something else, but we've geared the plan to those assumptions." After looking at his notes for a moment, Dino added, "A few other points—no tails on him or his vehicle. We're trying to lure him in, so we need to make sure we don't spook him. No SWAT team. This is not a hostage or standoff situation. No high-powered rifles—we're in a residential neighborhood.

"The Andersons live in the city of South St. Paul, so we'll need to coordinate with their PD, let 'em know what we're up to, but insist on complete secrecy. Their house is located on a roughly square block, with streets that run nearly straight north-south, east-west. The house is a two-story, with an attached double garage and driveway on the left. It sits on the east edge of the block, about in the center.

"Initially, I had envisioned setting up a traditional surveillance net, with officers staked out at the four surrounding intersections, each with overlapping lines of sight along two streets. But then I recalled hearing that the Bureau of Criminal Apprehension has a bunch of high-tech gear that is available for use. I called, and they have exactly what we need—live feed video cameras that can be mounted on a utility pole, a house, roof, even a tree if need be. Each camera has a four-day battery pack, with a WAN range of more than a mile. The cameras can all be controlled remotely. They can pan ninety degrees, as well as zoom. And they have good visibility in low light. They're even waterproof. They were made for us! It means we don't have to staff four outposts, and don't have to risk compromise with the neighbors. We just need to coordinate with them for installation, which the SSPPD should be able to help us with. BCA said they can have the units here in an hour and can arrange a utility vehicle to have the cameras installed and running by six if we give them the go ahead.

"Our command center will be in the Andersons' house, 24-7. Jack and I will provide eyeball security, front and back. We'll need one guy to monitor the cameras on a laptop, and one guy to provide relief to the other three of us on a rotational basis. BCA says they can provide a guy who is knowledgeable about the units, to run the laptop.

"We also need to stakeout Erik's house. Again, no tails, I just want to know if and when he leaves his house. We know his vehicle—a red, late model Honda Accord. From a squad car drive-by of his house, we know he parks outside, not in a garage. So, all we need there is an old-fashioned, really boring stakeout. Got anybody you really don't like?" asked Dino, with a smirk.

Regaining himself, he summarized, "So our staffing will be minimal. We'll all have headset communication. Jack and I will have night vision goggles available, given the expected time slot. As far as Jack here, we can't deputize him because he's not a US citizen, and he can't carry a firearm, but he can certainly help with eyeball security, as well as command and control. The other officer and the BCA guy will carry, and that should be enough.

"We'll ask for two squads from SSPPD to be on standby during our likely time slot, ready to close in to a perimeter of two blocks on our command. We can ask them for our fourth officer as well, then we'd have somebody with express jurisdiction.

"Tammy and Bob Anderson are both cooperating. I offered to use a policewoman look-alike, but Tammy wants to help. Jack was right, she's hoping for leniency on any future charges, and maybe feels some self-guilt over the death of Andropov.

"We'll instruct Tammy to move through the house every fifteen minutes or so, but at any sign of trouble, she and Bob will dive into the basement, which has no outside access. If they can't make the basement quickly, I'll have them hit the deck and stay there.

"Bob Anderson provided a photo of the travel group when they were in London. It showed a full shot of Erik. Physically, he looks to be just under six feet tall, 190 pounds, brown hair, medium build.

"So that's about it. Questions?" asked Dino.

"It sounds good, Dino. Nice job," replied Paula. "By the way, I talked with the mayor. He's all excited about the breakthrough, though he wishes we could just go pick him up and be done with it. I explained why that wasn't possible. Oh, and he complained he's getting even more pressure from the media. Channel 12 wants to do an exclusive feature on him. He's freaking out over that. But he's on board with us, he just asks that we 'hurry up and get it over with.'"

"Great," sighed Dino.

"No worries Dino. This sounds good. Let's do it. Keep me updated."

Dino moved quickly to get everything set up. He was pleased that SSPPD had assigned an experienced officer as the fourth member of the team. Cathy Jackson was a fifteen-year veteran of the force who had gained some notoriety among local police departments a few years back for her role in a successful hostage situation. She had received a citation for personal bravery. In person, Cathy immediately impressed Dino as sharp and certainly competent. The utility truck had the cameras in place by five thirty. The guy from the BCA, named Jeff Nelson, had the video surveillance net up and running on his laptop at the Andersons' by 5:45 p.m.

All four team members were wearing soft Kevlar vests, as prescribed for a tactical situation of this type. Before leaving the police station, Dino had both Tammy and Bob fitted for vests as well. "It's important that the vests fit properly," he told them. They complained a bit that they were heavy and uncomfortable.

"They're actually quite light compared to the old ones," he replied. "Wear a loose-fitting shirt, you'll get used to them."

All team members, along with Tammy and Bob, were set in the Andersons' house by six, right on schedule.

The stakeout of Erik's house reported his status as at home at 6:05 p.m.

The trap was set.

Chapter 34

Erik did not see the video cameras, but the cameras saw him.

At 7:05 p.m. Dino heard the officer staked out at Erik's house reporting, "Subject leaving house now in personal vehicle."

"Got it," replied Dino, which all the team members heard through their headsets.

Dino then spoke directly to Jeff, who was monitoring the surveillance cameras on his laptop in a small office the Andersons had on the main floor. "Google says it takes just over twenty minutes to get from his house to South St. Paul. Heads up for either his red Accord, or Erik himself."

"Got it," Jeff confirmed.

"You get that, Jack?" Jack was positioned at the window of a ground floor bedroom at the back of the house.

"I did. Understood."

"Cathy?"

"I'm good."

Dino setup a rotating schedule so that all of them would get some relief through the night.

Dino figured it was a bit early for Erik to show up, but they'd be ready, regardless. Since setting up their surveillance net, they had seen a pretty steady stream of neighborhood people going by the front of the house, out for after-dinner walks or runs, some with pets, some with small children in strollers or on bikes.

It was just after eight when Dino heard Jeff report, "Heads up, we've got a bogey coming north on Newton, a guy in a dark jogging outfit—hood up. Looks to be about the right build for our subject."

Dino positioned himself just to the left side of the living room front window, looking south. He lifted his set of binoculars, waiting for the guy to appear.

"Slowing down now . . ." came from Jeff, then a few seconds later, "looking over to the house . . ."

"I see him," said Dino. "The hood of his sweatshirt obscures his face a bit, but that could be him."

"If he goes any slower, he'll be jogging in place," said Jeff.

"He's sure interested in the house," from Dino, but the jogger continued on, turning his head forward again, and picking up speed. "Can you pick him up with the northeast camera?"

"I think so, hang on . . ." from Jeff. "Acquiring . . . zooming in now . . . got him! I've got a good still frame of him here. Can you verify Dino?"

"I'll be right there." With the guy now well down the street and headed away, Dino left his spot near the front window and went to Jeff.

"Looks like him to me. Jack, you've seen him in person. Can you come take a look?"

"Sure." Jack joined them a moment later and studied the image. "That's him alright."

"OK, back to our posts. Watch for him doubling back." Once back in place, Dino added, "I certainly didn't see him carrying a rifle. Could've had a handgun though."

"Agreed," from Jack.

"OK, stay sharp everybody," warned Dino.

After about ten minutes, "Subject returning," from Jeff.

Dino picked him up in his binoculars. "He's slowing again, looking this way at the house." The guy went past slowly, then sped up and continued south where he had come from originally. "Well, he didn't seem spooked."

"Agreed," from Jeff.

"Stay sharp guys, he may be going to get a weapon and be

back. Heads up everybody."

After thirty minutes or so, Dino said, "Well, I don't think he's coming back right now. He may just be waiting till dark, so we gotta stay sharp."

"Understood," from the other three.

Dino went to the kitchen to talk with Tammy and Bob, "OK, I think you're safe for now."

"Was it him?" asked Bob.

"He had a hooded sweatshirt on that made it tough to see, but we're sure it was him," replied Dino.

"Good God, he really came," said Bob.

"He was jogging by but slowed to look over the house. I'm sure it was him. We think there's a chance he's waiting for dark, so keep on your toes."

Eventually, the number of people out walking on the street dwindled to nothing. Though they stayed vigilant, they did not see anyone like Erik again. At eleven, Dino told Tammy and Bob they could head to bed if they wanted.

"Try to get some sleep. We'll be here watching all night."

"Thanks everyone," said Tammy. "Not sure we'll get much sleep. It's all quite terrifying."

Tammy had made up some sandwiches and set out drinks for them, including fresh coffee. "I'll leave them on the kitchen table. Please help yourselves. Make more coffee if you'd like. It's all right there."

"Thanks."

At one o'clock everything was quiet. Dino asked Cathy to relieve Jack. "Get some sleep Jack."

"Sounds good. Thanks."

"Then your turn in a couple of hours Cathy."

"That'll work," she replied.

As he sat looking out the front window, Dino relaxed a bit. He didn't think Erik would be back now. He ate half a sandwich and popped a Coke, hoping the sugar and caffeine would help him stay alert. His mind started to wander. *This electronic stakeout is pretty cool.* He had been on plenty of stakeouts in the past— every single one of them boring as hell. But it was part of the job, and frankly, it beat the frustrations of his typical gang-murder investigation of late. He admitted to himself that he was enjoying a *real* case again, and he enjoyed working with Jack. A few minutes later, he thought about Johnny Jump Up and his offer. It was certainly appealing—more money, better hours, no more departmental bullshit. It sounded too good to be true. But whenever he thought about leaving the force, he thought about his dad and his commitment. *I promised* . . .. Then he asked, "Are you listening Dad?" Dino paused for a few moments, hoping to hear that familiar voice in his mind, but there was only silence.

Moving on, he thought, *I could use a glass of wine right now. Maybe two.*

Chapter 35

Sunday morning, Erik skipped breakfast, eager to get the pistol from his parents' house. They always went to church at nine thirty on Sunday mornings. He pulled into the driveway at nine forty-five. The garage side door was unlocked. Erik looked in and confirmed their car was gone.

He let himself into the house with his key and went straight to the basement. He quickly found the pistol in a box with some other old hunting stuff. Looking at it carefully, he noted that most of the rust was on the handle, and along the side of the barrel. The revolver mechanism and hammer appeared to be fine. After checking to make sure the gun was empty, he pulled the hammer back to cock it, then pulled the trigger . . . click. The gun grated a bit, but he figured he could clean all that up. He stuffed the gun in his pants and began climbing the stairs out of the basement when he was startled to hear, "Hello Erik, looking for something?"

"Oh, hi Dad. Um . . . ah . . . I was looking for . . . my old tennis racket."

"I think it might be upstairs in the back closet."

"OK. Gee, you scared me there. I thought you were at church."

"We were, but your mother wasn't feeling well, so I brought her home." As they walked up the stairs, "Are you going to play again?"

"Play?"

"Tennis. Are you going to play tennis again?"

"I am. I need to get more exercise. Thought I'd go out and hit some balls."

"Well, that's good."

They walked down the hallway to a large storage closet and Erik's dad opened it. He reached toward the back and pulled out the racket.

"Here it is." He handed it to Erik.

"Thanks, Dad."

"Are you OK, Erik?"

"Me? Oh sure."

"You seem nervous."

"Oh, I'm fine. Really."

"OK. Well, good luck with the tennis. It would be great to see you pick it up again. You used to be pretty good."

"Well, that was a while ago, but I thought, heck, it might be fun."

As Erik started walking to the door, he told his dad, lying, "I gotta get going. I'm meeting somebody to hit some balls. I hope Mom feels better."

"I'm sure she will be fine. And don't be such a stranger."

"I won't. Thanks again." And he left.

On the way home, Erik wondered if perhaps his dad was on to him or was at least questioning what was going on. His dad obviously sensed that something was up, but apparently had not discovered that the old hunting rifle was missing. If he had, Erik knew he definitely would have asked about it. He figured there was nothing he could really do. *I'll just have to deal with it, if and when it comes up.*

At home, he opened his cleaning kit and went to work on the gun. He used the metal brushes to get most of the rust off and used gun solvent to get the rest. After a few minutes, he wiped the gun clean. It looked OK. After putting gun oil on the revolver and trigger mechanisms, he spun the cylinder several times. "Much better." He cocked the hammer back and pulled the trigger. This time, there was a sharp and definite . . . *click!* He congratulated himself. "Ready!"

He fixed himself a sandwich for lunch, then laid down for a

nap. *It might be a long night.*

But he couldn't sleep. He was anxious about his plan. First, he worried the police were now tracking his phone. He thought they had to have a warrant or something to do that, but maybe he was wrong. *Should I turn it off?* After researching phone tracking online, he decided the only sure way of preventing them from tracking him was to turn it off and then pull the battery. He would do that just before he left the house.

Second, he worried they were possibly tracking his car. *Could they have put one of those tracking devices on it?* Erik had no mechanical experience with cars, or anything else really. He had no idea what a tracking device would look like, or where it might be. Still, it frustrated him. Then he had an idea, *Maybe I should rent a car?* He could drive wherever he wanted, without fear of being tracked. Yes, the rental would be traceable if they looked into it, but why would they? Even if they did, it would take them some time. It seemed like a good idea. Plus, he figured that with a rental, he could park closer to the Andersons' house and could get back to it faster for his getaway. He decided to do it. He would leave the house a bit earlier than originally planned and drive out to the airport. For some reason, the airport seemed like the most anonymous place to rent a car. He was pleased with the rental idea. It made him feel more at ease.

The gun was his next worry. He had never shot a handgun. He tried to think of somewhere he could go to fire some practice rounds and get a feel for the gun, but he could not think of any place, so he had to forget it.

Since last night's reconnaissance, he had thought more about the idea of using the trees next to the garage to get close to the house, onto the roof of the garage, and from there over onto the balcony. He would need a way to get up into one of the trees. He thought he could use a rope to pull himself up and swing over to the roof. It would not take that much, and he could carry it in the pouch of his sweatshirt. *But will I be able to get it over a branch and down?* It would need a weight of some kind. The idea of using a metal clasp with a spring clip came to mind. He could tie the clasp to one end of the rope, then throw that over one of the branches. Once over, he could lower it down, put the opposite end of the rope through the clasp and pull it tight. It should cinch up to the branch. He congratulated himself on another good idea. *You're a genius!*

As he continued to plan, the next concern was the sliding door on the deck. *What if it's locked?* He hoped he would get lucky and find it open but could not count on it. He went and looked at the patio door on the back of his own apartment. The latch was really just a flimsy metal hook, and the wooden framework that it slid into was not substantial. A small pry bar, like his dad used for removing nails, would do the trick. Just enough leverage to pry open the latch. A good sturdy flat head screwdriver might help to get it started. *That'll work.* He made a short list of things he needed from the hardware store and took off to get them. Once at the store, he found some suitable rope, a clasp, a seven-inch pry bar, and a screwdriver. On the way to the checkout, he walked by a display of gloves, and decided that a pair of thin gloves would, not only protect his hands from the rope while climbing, but would prevent leaving fingerprints. However, he was not sure if he would be able to fire the gun with the gloves on. *I can always just throw them away at the last moment.* He bought a pair.

He drove to a nearby park. He got out the clasp and tied it to one end of the rope. After finding a tree that was about the same size as those by the garage, he tried throwing the clasp end over a branch. *It works!* He surprised himself. Once over the branch, the clasp, with the rope, fell down to where he could grasp it. Feeding the other end of the rope through the clasp, he pulled it tight, and was pleased that it worked so well. Now, he was left with the chore of pulling himself up to get it loose and down again. He managed it and felt gratified he had done it all successfully.

It was now past four in the afternoon. He needed to get home and complete his preparations.

He put on jeans and a T-shirt. The sweatshirt was too much to wear into Ray's Pub, where he was planning to go for an alibi again, so he stuffed it into a backpack, along with his tools, the rope, and the gun. He had loaded the gun earlier, and though he figured six shots would be the most he would need, he threw the remaining shells in as well. Hungry again, he fixed himself another sandwich. Eating, he powered off his phone and removed the battery.

Erik left his house just after six and headed to the airport. As he approached it, he saw a Hertz lot. He continued on to the long-term parking lot, parked his car, then quickly took the shuttle bus to the Hertz office. Without a reservation it took a while to get the car and was after eight by the time he left the airport.

Driving back to his own neighborhood, he parked down the street from Ray's Pub. He went in and found a seat at the bar. Though he really didn't feel like a beer, he had to go through the motions and be seen. The bar was busy, and it took a while just to get a beer. He was becoming worried about the time. It was now past nine fifteen. The beer finally came, and as he drank it, he made a point of looking around the room and making eye contact with people. By the time he finished it and paid, it was going on ten. He had not planned on it all taking so long, but figured he was still good. It was now dark and maybe that was OK.

He drove straight to Tammy's house, parking just two blocks straight west, right in the middle of the block, since he was planning to run through the back yards like he had with Andropov. He sat in the car for a couple of minutes, calming his nerves. The clock said 10:25 p.m. *Time to go.* He got out of the car, leaving it unlocked with the keys in the ignition, so he could get in and away as quickly as possible. Putting on his sweatshirt, he put the gun, rope, gloves, pry bar, and screwdriver in the pouch. Steeling his nerves, he pulled up his hood and started walking south.

Chapter 36

The stakeout of the Andersons' house dragged on through the night with unending boredom, like all stakeouts. Dino and the rest of the team were thankful to see the early morning sunrise. Tammy and Bob were now up and had made fresh coffee.

It was going on eight when Bob asked Dino, "Would you like me to run and get some donuts?"

At first, Dino thought Bob was joking, poking fun at the old "all cops love donuts" thing. But then he realized Bob was just trying to be nice, *Minnesota Nice*. "Sure," Dino replied, "that's very kind of you." He added, "Maybe some jellies?"

Bob was back within forty minutes with a box full of fresh donuts. Jeff and Cathy had some first, followed by the second shift of Dino and Jack. They sat at the kitchen table and chatted as they ate.

"I could never be a cop," said Bob, a bit out of the blue.

"Why do you say that?" asked Dino, in between chews of a raspberry jelly donut.

"Because I'm too much of a George McFly. You know, the guy in the movie *Back to the Future*? The guy who says, 'I'm afraid I'm just not very good at confrontations.'"

"Ah, well, we do get our share of that," replied Dino.

Eventually, they were all back at their posts, letting the caffeine and sugar rush work toward the inevitable crash. Still, it was good while it lasted.

At mid-morning, Dino called Paula and filled her in on the developments since setting up the night before.

About an hour later, Dino got a text from Amy, who was wondering if he was interested in a run. He had to respond that he was working on a case but told her he appreciated the offer and would get back to her when he could. As he put his phone aside, he realized how much he liked Amy. He decided they made a good couple—they were both independent, liked good food, and enjoyed fine wine—yup, they were good together. *Does Amy feel the same way about me? Is it time to ask the big question?"* The thought of doing that threw him. *Oh boy.* He filed the thoughts away for the time being.

Late morning, Dino said he would buy everyone lunch if Bob was willing to run and get it. Tammy offered, "There's a pretty good Chinese place nearby, if that works?" The others all agreed it did. "We keep a copy of the menu here. You can take a look. The egg rolls are really good." They each looked over the menu, and Tammy wrote down their orders. She called it in on the phone, and Bob took off to pick it up. Eating their lunch, again in shifts, helped to pass away the early afternoon.

Just past two thirty, the stakeout at Erik's house reported "Subject leaving home in personal vehicle."

Dino told the others, "OK guys, I know we expect him later, but if he's out and about, we need to be ready for him. Stay sharp."

Through the afternoon, they watched people passing by the house on the warm summer day, walking, jogging, and biking.

Just after three thirty, Dino got a text from Johnny Jump Up. "Hey guy, I know you're busy, but I'm getting serious pressure from one of my largest clients for an answer on investigations. He says he can't wait much longer, and has given me a deadline of next Friday—just six days from today, otherwise he's going to look elsewhere. We need to talk *now*. Call me!"

Ugh, just what I need right now. Dino knew he needed to think the whole thing through and decide, one way or the other. He responded with a text to Johnny, "Can't talk now. Will contact you when I can." That would buy some time, but he could not put Johnny off much longer. He needed to decide.

At four fifteen, the stakeout reported, "Subject back at home."

"OK guys, we can relax a bit."

Still watching through the front window, Dino leaned back in his chair. He welcomed the change of focus back onto the case. His mind drifted to Erik and his motives. The Andropov murder seemed straightforward enough—a simple cover up. But the killing of Jennifer still baffled him. *Why?* There was no apparent relationship between them, or even between Erik and Tom. *And if you are going to kill her, why go all the way to England and Stonehenge to do it? It just doesn't make any sense.*

The afternoon dragged on. Then just after six, the stakeout at Erik's house reported, "Subject leaving in personal vehicle."

"OK guys, you heard it. This might be it. Heads up!"

Dino instructed Tammy and Bob to position themselves in the kitchen, which had visibility from outside through a window over the kitchen sink, but the window was several feet above ground level. "Use the restroom, if need be, but otherwise stay in the kitchen."

"Will do."

They all remained vigilant, watching the cameras, the front of the house, and the rear. They studied the walkers, joggers, and bikers. Tammy and Bob played cards nervously at the kitchen table. But the time crawled. As sunset approached, it started to get dark. The passersby dwindled. It was now nine o'clock, but there was no sign of Erik. They continued to wait, expecting Erik to show up at any moment. Nine thirty came and went. Dino waited for what seemed like forever, then looked at his watch again. It was now ten o'clock. Still no Erik.

Checking with the spotter at Erik's house, he confirmed Erik had not returned home. "OK, thanks."

He checked with the two squads, making sure they were in place. "Nothing here," from both of them.

It was now dark, though there was a half moon rising in a clear sky. The entire team was getting edgy from trying to stay sharp for so long. Finally, at ten thirty, Dino said out loud, "Damn it! Where the hell is he?"

Chapter 37

Erik walked away from the car quickly, first going south to the corner of the block, then turning and heading east. After one full block, he looked both left and right along the cross street. Seeing nothing, he continued on for a half a block to the alleyway that passed behind the Andersons' house. Then he headed north until he was at the line of the trees. Staying on the near side of them, opposite Andersons' house, he walked east, trying to stay low. When he was almost even with the rear of the garage, he crouched down and looked at the house through the trees. There were lights on, in what he figured was the kitchen, and also in a room beyond that. There were no lights on upstairs, at least on the back side of the house. Tammy must still be up.

He crab walked several feet more until he was even with the front of the garage. The street out front was clear—no cars or foot traffic coming. Staying low, he broke through the line of trees. Once on the other side, he looked up for a branch that was sturdy, as well as close enough and high enough for him to get up. There was a good one right by the edge of the garage.

Putting on his gloves, he pulled the rope out from his pouch, uncoiled it, and grabbed the end with the clasp. Carefully, he tossed it up and over the branch, and got it on the first try. *Perfect.* He lowered the clasp down, fed the other end of the rope through it, pulled it up until it was cinched snuggly to the branch, and then he pulled himself up.

Pausing for a minute after his climb, he checked the street

again. Everything still looked clear. When he had his breath back, he made sure the rope and clasp were secure. Standing on the branch, he stepped back a bit, then half-swung, half-leapt over onto the garage roof. He pounce-landed like a cat, crouched down and stayed still for a moment. He had landed quietly, and still saw no one, so he crawled the few steps over the roof to the railing of the deck. Peering around the corner to look into the door, he saw it was dark. He lifted one leg over the railing, then the other. *So far, so good.* As expected, the door was locked. Getting out his pry bar and screwdriver, he carefully pried back the latch. It seemed to give a bit, but suddenly snapped open. The sound startled him, and he froze, but he decided it was not loud enough that anyone would have heard it downstairs. He slowly slid the door open, stepped inside, and slid it shut again.

Looking across the room, he could make out the bedroom door. Walking slowly around the corner of a bed, he peeked out into the hallway. There was a small night light glowing that allowed him to see the hallway was clear. The head of the stairs was just a few feet to the left. He did not hear anyone downstairs, but they had to be there.

Taking off his gloves, he stuffed them in the left side of the pouch of his sweatshirt. With his right hand, he reached in for the gun and pulled the hammer back with his thumb to cock it, muffling the sound with the pouch. The stairway went down toward the rear of the house and was enclosed all the way to the bottom. The stairs were carpeted. He started to tip-toe down, confident he was not making any sounds. When he was just three steps from the bottom, he craned his neck around to the left, where he thought the kitchen would be. Tammy and Bob were both seated at the kitchen table. Tammy was on the far side, facing him, but looking down. Bob was facing away.

He took the gun out of his pouch, stepped down two more stairs, then raised the gun in front of him in his right hand, pointed it at Tammy, and said calmly, "I told you Tammy."

Tammy looked up. Her look turned to horror. She jumped up. Erik started pulling the trigger but saw a flash of movement to his right and heard a voice. "Drop the gun Erik!" Erik instinctively swung his arm toward the movement and finished pulling the trigger. There was a loud *bang*. Dino went down hard.

Chapter 38

"Damn it, where is he?" Dino asked aloud. "Maybe he's just sitting at Ray's Pub drinking beer?"

He was about to give up on Erik for the night when Jeff shouted into his headset, "Here comes our guy! Same sweatshirt as last night. Heads up!"

"Finally!" from Dino. "What's his position?"

"He's south of us, first cross street, walking east. And fast!"

"Be ready, guys. Tammy? Bob? You set?"

"I think so," Bob replied, noticeably nervous.

"Less than a block away now . . . getting closer . . . Shit! He turned into the alleyway behind us. The cameras can't see him!" from Jeff.

"Jack? Cathy? You see him?" questioned Dino.

"No. Nothing."

"Use the night goggles!"

It took a couple of seconds to get them on and adjusted. "Still nothing."

Dino was tempted to abandon his position at the front of the house to go back and help in the rear but was concerned Erik would loop around and come in the front. He kept looking left and right out the front window. "He's got to be there guys."

A minute passed, then two. Then Dino heard a faint *snap*. "From upstairs?" He listened carefully but heard nothing more. After a few moments, he decided he had to check it out. He took one last look left, then right. Seeing nothing, he moved through the living room to the edge of the stairway to the second floor.

He was about to turn the corner and look up the stairs when he saw the barrel of a gun poke out of the stairway, followed by Erik's voice saying, "I told you, Tammy."

Dino drew his Glock, raised it in front of himself with both hands, and shouted, "Drop the gun Erik!"

Erik's right arm swung toward Dino and from less than six feet away, Dino heard the gun go off. He felt a sharp blow to his upper left chest, which knocked him flat on his ass. His vest had protected him from a puncture wound but his chest had absorbed the entire impact, and he was driven to the floor. Dazed, he looked up and saw Erik step forward, now fully out of the stairway. Erik looked back toward Tammy, who was up out of her chair, screaming. Bob was trying to grab and shield her.

Erik aimed the gun at Tammy and pulled the trigger again, but nothing happened. He pulled it over and over. It was not firing. He had forgotten that the old gun was a single action and had to be cocked manually each time before firing. Totally confused, he started swearing at the gun, "Work you piece of shit!"

Cathy then appeared from behind Dino, with her weapon drawn, in a two-handed shooting stance, shouting, "Drop the weapon! Drop the weapon!" Cathy had Erik dead in her sights. Tammy and Bob were on the opposite side of Erik, in her direct line of fire. She shouted, "Tammy! Bob! Down on the floor! Down on the floor!"

Erik finally remembered he had to cock the gun after each shot. He pulled back the hammer with both of his thumbs, but kept his finger tight on the trigger, so the gun fired immediately and sent a slug straight down into the floor with a *bang*.

Now totally flustered, Erik looked up and saw a door leading out into the back yard. He panicked, rushed for the door, and yanked it open, still carrying the gun. He ran outside. Having managed to cock the gun, he turned to fire back at them, but tripped on something in the grass and fell. The gun went off and fired a round up into the air. The bright muzzle flash in the night startled him. Getting back to his feet, he started running again. By this time, the noise of the shots had roused the neigh-

bors, and lights were coming on in nearby houses. He continued running and crossed the alleyway into the back yard of the
house directly behind the Andersons' house. Just five feet into
that yard, a motion-activated yard light came on, and he was
instantly exposed. Veering to his right, he heard a voice yelling,
"Hey, what're you doing there?"

Back in the house, Cathy had dropped down to tend to Dino.
He had recovered enough to get up, and call into his headset for
the two squad cars that were standing by. "Shots fired! Shots
fired! Squad cars converge. Suspect armed, running on foot,
headed west. Converge on Potter Street." The squads had heard
the commotion earlier, over their headsets and were ready. They
both switched on their flashers and hit their sirens. They closed
in, one from the north, one from the south, still looking for a red
Honda Accord.

Erik ran through the back yard of the house behind and
one over from the Andersons' and broke out into the street. The
northern squad car saw him running. "I see him! Still headed
west on foot, I'm closing."

Jeff confirmed from his camera views, "I see him too, crossing Potter in the middle of the block."

Erik saw the lights and heard the siren on his right. His heart
was pounding, and he ran as fast as he could. He went straight
through the entire block and came out on the other side, a hundred feet from the rental car. The southern squad car was round-
ing the corner and closing in on him from his left. Erik made it to
the car, jumped in, and turned the keys in the ignition. Realizing
he still had the gun in his hand, he stuffed it into his pouch, and
took off with screeching tires.

He left the lights off, hoping to get away in the darkness, but
in his rearview mirror, he could see the lights of the squad car
coming after him.

Back in the house, Dino checked on Tammy and Bob. Tammy
was sobbing, and Bob was holding her. He looked over at Dino
and gave him a look that told him she would be OK.

"Jeff, stay with the cameras. Give the squads whatever you
can see."

"Cathy, Jack, into the car!" Dino had hidden their car in the Andersons' garage, facing out, ready to go. As they ran to the car, Dino decided his shoulder hurt too much to drive, so he tossed Cathy the keys and told her to take the wheel. She jumped in, fired it up, and lit up the tires getting out into the street.

"Where is he?" Dino yelled to the squads.

"He's in a white, late model Toyota, heading north. I'm in pursuit."

"Bastard changed cars!" exclaimed Dino. "Whatever, stay on him." He then turned to Jack in the back seat. "Jack, there should be a small portable flasher in a compartment back there. Yank it out and stick it up on the roof."

Cathy floored the car and headed north. A moment later, the squad in closest pursuit announced, "Suspect just turned west on Wentworth. I think he's trying to get to the freeway."

"Stay on him! I want that guy!"

Chapter 39

Erik drove west on Wentworth, then turned north on the frontage road that runs along the US 52 freeway. He came to a stoplight with several cars queued up, waiting to get to the entrance ramp on the other side of the intersection. Without stopping, he went down onto the right shoulder, around the stopped cars, jumped the red light and flew onto the ramp. Gaining speed down the ramp, he shot out into traffic, cutting off a car in the right lane. The guy swerved to avoid hitting Erik, then laid on his horn. Erik looked in his rearview mirror and said to himself, "Honking your horn in Minnesota? Really? Asshole!"

With the squad car still in pursuit and gaining on him Erik swung into the left lane and accelerated. There were several slowpokes blocking the left lane up ahead. Erik veered right, passed them, then veered back into the left lane. Looking up into his mirror, he flipped off the lead driver. Then he saw the squad car pulling in behind him with lights flashing and siren blaring.

Erik was now going down a long hill to where the freeway crosses the Lafayette Bridge over the Mississippi River. He gained speed going down the hill, still swerving recklessly between lanes. At the bottom of the hill, the road opened from two to three lanes. Erik dove into what he thought was the fast lane, but US 52 intersects Interstate 94 in a 'T' right on the other side of the bridge, and all drivers are forced to take a hard right to continue. There was a line of stalled vehicles waiting to make the turn. Too late, he saw the field of red brake lights. He jerked the steering wheel to the right but was going far too fast to make it. He hit the rear end of a car in the right lane at an oblique angle, and just like hitting a high-speed jump ramp, Erik's car shot up and onto the railing of the bridge. The car teetered on the railing for a brief second, then tipped over the edge and plummeted straight down into the river below, hitting with a *booosh!*

The driver-side air bag blew when the car hit the water, and Erik was knocked out by the impact. The nose of the car went down, but then the car righted itself, bobbing on the surface. After just a few moments, Erik came to, realizing vaguely what had happened. There were several boats sitting in the water near where the car went in. The people in the boats were just drifting near the bridge, enjoying a pleasant summer evening, watching the city lights of downtown St. Paul. Erik had narrowly missed hitting one of them.

"Holy shit! He almost landed on us!" exclaimed Paul, the driver of a larger cuddy cabin boat with *Ship Happens* painted on the transom. Paul called out to a smaller runabout named *Mermaid* that was pulling alongside the still-floating car. "Mark, can you get to him?"

"I'm going in! Get some life preservers ready!" Mark dove into the water, and swam to the car, which was now mostly submerged.

He could see Erik inside, now awake, and signaled for him to roll down the window. Erik looked at him strangely for a moment, then realized what he was telling him to do. Erik remembered that car doors will not open underwater until the car is filled on the inside. He was able to roll the driver-side window down a little, and the cold river water rushed in. The water was rising quickly and was soon at neck level. As the water was about to go over his head, Erik took a big breath and tried to open the door. It did not budge. He was going to try kicking the door, but could not get himself positioned to do that, so he pushed his shoulder against the door as hard as he could, pulling the latch at the same time. The door slowly opened, and the rest of the cabin filled with water. As the car started to sink, Mark reached in, grabbed Erik, and pulled as hard as he could. Erik surfaced and bobbed in the water, clinging to Mark. Behind him, the car slipped under the surface and quickly sank.

Paul maneuvered his cuddy alongside the two men and threw them life preservers. Mark got his life preserver on, then helped Erik into his. Chrissy, Mark's wife, was now driving the runabout and jockeyed the boat near the two men. Mark got back into his boat and dragged Erik up into the boat as well.

Coughing up water, Erik collapsed onto the rear seat. As he sat recovering, he could hear the sirens and see the flashing lights of the police cars above on the bridge deck. Chrissy was helping Mark to towel off. He looked over at Erik and asked, "How do you feel?"

"How do I feel? I feel like getting the hell out of here!" Erik got up, pulled out the gun, which was still in the pouch of his sweatshirt, and pointed it at his rescuer. His wife screamed when she saw the gun.

"Wait a second pal. I just saved your life!"

"And you're going to save it again. Let's go! Head down the river."

"Ain't that gratitude for you."

"Shut up and start driving!"

Up on the bridge deck, Dino, Cathy, and Jack had pulled up to the crash scene. They looked over the railing at the car in the water and watched Erik's rescue. Dino had called for support from SPPD. He directed the first squad car that responded underneath the bridge on the southern shoreline, as close as he could get to where the car had gone into the water. Dino was expecting the boat to come ashore, but while he was talking on the radio, Cathy yelled, "He's getting away! They're heading down the river. Good Lord, he pulled his gun on the guy!"

"Shit!" As Dino looked out over the river, he saw the rescue boat heading downstream. His eyes followed the river to a bend ahead on the right, and he found himself looking straight at the runway lights of the St. Paul Downtown Airport, less than a mile away. A thought instantly came to him. *State Patrol Helicopter!* He knew the State Patrol had three helicopters code-named

Trooper 9, that were stationed in a hangar right at the airport. If they were not otherwise in use by the governor, or the State Patrol itself, they were available to local PDs for assistance with searches and criminal apprehensions. He called Dispatch on the radio and confirmed Trooper 9 was available, with a pilot sitting on duty. In less than three minutes, the pilot was in the chopper, spinning up the engines. Dispatch had patched Dino through to the pilot. Two minutes after that, Dino could see the chopper lifting off the airport tarmac. "Head down the river," Dino told the pilot. "Suspect is in a light-colored, open-topped runabout, with two hostages. We'll stay here for command and control."

"Roger that," from the pilot. He had a copilot with him in the chopper, to aid in the search.

"We're sending cars down Airport Road, as well as Concord Street, along the river. Suspect is about six minutes out from the Lafayette Bridge. He can't be that far away traveling on the river at night."

Erik had no idea where he was going to go, but he knew he could not stay at the crash scene. It made no sense to head upstream toward the St. Paul Waterfront, so he told Mark to head down the river, into the darkness. The boat was going, but slowly. Erik yelled, "Why are you going so slow?"

"Because we're in a no-wake zone, buddy."

"Screw that, go!"

Mark pushed the throttle down all the way, and the pitch of the motor immediately increased. The front end of the boat went up from the torque, but it quickly planed out and gained speed. Once away from the city, it was quite dark on the river, even with a half-moon in the sky. There were very few boats on the water downstream, although at one point, they went around a bend and Erik freaked out. The front end of a large barge was heading right for them in the narrow channel on the left. However, Mark did not seem concerned. He veered to the right and simply went around. Erik let out a sigh of relief.

They continued on toward some lights ahead, which turned out to be the Wakota Bridge, carrying the traffic of Interstate

494 over the Mississippi river. Staying in the channel, they went right underneath, and on the other side, it got dark again.

Then, from behind, Erik could hear the *thump, thump, thump* of the rotors of a helicopter. He looked back, and there it was—with a bright searchlight shining down, coming right after them. The chopper was on them in an instant. Bathed in the bright light, it became difficult for them to see on the water. Erik yelled to Mark, "Lose the helicopter!"

"Are you nuts?" But after thinking for a moment, said, "Duh, of course you're nuts! Ya can't outrun a helicopter, buddy!"

Erik shouted, "Turn around and go back!"

"What? Alright, you're the one with the gun!" He arced a smooth turn back upriver, but the helicopter followed them easily.

Erik realized it was futile and told the driver to turn around and head back downriver again.

"Sure thing!" This time, the driver jerked the steering wheel around as sharply as he could. The front of the boat stood up in the air, and Erik nearly fell overboard. He ended up on the floor, and got up, pissed.

Pointing the gun directly at Mark, he yelled, "Don't do that again!"

"Then hang on. It's a frickin boat dammit."

The boat smoothed out, and Erik regained his balance. He looked out over the nose of the boat and saw a small marina coming up on the right. Just beyond that was a bar and restaurant, brightly lit up. People were sitting on a patio that jutted out over the river, listening to a guy playing guitar and a woman singing next to him. The noise and lights of the helicopter caused everyone to stop and look up. The guitar player stopped playing and shook his fist at the boat flying by on the water, then flipped off the chopper, chasing in the air right above.

The copilot in the chopper barked out through a loudspeaker, "Stop the boat! Put down your weapon!"

The people on the patio scattered as the helicopter passed just a few feet over their heads, spraying them with water and debris.

Erik, pointing the gun right at Mark, yelled, "Keep going!"

He was desperately looking for a way to escape. There was no way to lose the helicopter on the water. He needed to get off the boat. On the far side of the bar was a parking lot, and beyond that, a large growth of trees. Thinking he might lose the chopper in there, he shouted, "Put me on shore by those trees."

"Whatever you want, pal."

The boat turned sharply to the right, then slowed as they approached the shoreline. The bottom started screeching on the rocks and sand underneath. Just a few feet from the shoreline, Erik jumped over the side and into the water. He shouted to Mark, "Head back out, and keep going downriver for at least a mile, got it?"

"Sure, no problem," he shouted as he backed away. After a few feet, he turned downstream and hit the gas. As he sped away, he yelled back over his shoulder, "By the way, thanks for nothing!"

Erik ran into the trees. The chopper came overhead, shining a bright spotlight right on him. From a loudspeaker, "This is the Minnesota State Patrol. You are under arrest. Stay where you are." But there was no place for the chopper to land.

Erik shouted back, "Screw that." And he ran further into the trees. He was afraid they had night vision or some other high-tech gadgets, but he had no choice. Continuing on, he saw some thick bushes up ahead. When he got there, he stopped and lay down on the ground. To his amazement, the chopper continued past him.

"Yes!"

Erik jumped up and ran back toward the bar. He ran to a fence alongside the parking lot, then crouched and waited. He heard the chopper come back and pass near him, heading toward the shoreline. It then turned and headed over to the marina on the other side of the bar.

The pilot of the helicopter broke in on the comm line with Dino. "Suspect has gone ashore on the west bank of the river, just south of the Rock Island Pub, and north of the old Swing Bridge."

"Roger that. Stay on him," from Dino.

"In pursuit."

Dino had Cathy cancel the Newport squad car on the east side of the river, as well as the squad on Airport Road. She called for support from the Inver Grove Heights PD, "Have them head straight for the pub."

After the helicopter had made several passes back and forth over the trees, the pilot radioed in, "We've lost the suspect in the trees."

"Keep looking," said Dino. "He can't be far."

"Will do."

But after a few minutes more, the pilot told Dino, "Sorry guys, but we've lost him."

Dino keyed his microphone off and let out a "Damn it!" He allowed himself a sigh of frustration, then keyed his microphone back on and told the pilot, "OK. Thanks. You might as well head back."

"Sorry Dino."

"No worries. We'll get him."

As Erik waited by the fence, a couple came out from the bar heading toward the parking lot, holding onto each other as they walked. The girl asked nervously, "I wonder why they were chasing that boat?"

"I don't know, but it had to be something big," the guy replied.

They continued walking through the parking lot, stopping at a black pickup truck. As the guy reached into his pocket for the keys, Erik got up and walked toward them. He was within ten feet when the girl asked the guy, "Do you think they caught him?"

"I'm quite sure they didn't," replied Erik.

Startled by the voice, the guy asked, "Hey, what do you want?"

"I'm taking your truck."

The driver turned to confront Erik, saying, "Really, says who?"

"Says me, and my gun." Erik pulled the gun out of the pouch

of his sweatshirt and pointed it at the couple.

The man stopped in his tracks. "OK, fine, here you go." And he threw Erik the keys.

"Now step back."

"No problem, man. Take the truck, just don't shoot."

"Get back and there'll be no problem. Wait a sec. Give me your phones too."

"What?"

"You heard me, get out your phones, both of you. Now set them there on the rear bumper."

"Damn it, man."

"Just do it."

"Fine, there you go. Don't shoot!"

"Now step back." Erik grabbed the phones and stuffed them in his pouch.

"Keep going."

Erik turned, opened the door of the truck, and jumped in. He started the engine, put it in gear, and roared across the parking lot, spraying gravel with the spinning rear tires. As he turned out of the lot, the helicopter appeared, flying right over him, but it kept going, heading back toward downtown St. Paul.

Out on the exit road, Erik had gone just a quarter of a mile when an Inver Grove Heights squad car came speeding around a bend, with lights flashing and siren blaring. Erik nearly panicked but looked straight ahead and just kept driving. The cop drove right by him, never slowing down. He had just let out a sigh of relief and relaxed a bit, when around the corner came another police vehicle, this time a K-9 SUV. Again, Erik just looked straight and kept driving. As the SUV flew by, he saw two German shepherd dogs in the back. With his hands clenching the steering wheel, Erik held his breath again, but after a couple of seconds, he saw the SUV disappear from his rearview mirror. He did not want to even think about having those two dogs after him, or what they would do to him if they caught him. *Whew.*

Dino was considering his next move, when the dispatcher came on, "Inver Grove unit on site at the Rock Island Pub, man reporting theft of his vehicle by gunman. Vehicle is a Ford pickup, F150, black, 2012."

"Crap, he's driving again. Cathy, get the vehicle description out, ask for assistance. Better make it metro-wide."

"Will do."

Erik continued driving on the exit road until he hit the main drag of Concord Street. Sitting at a stop sign, he reached into his pouch, pulled out the two phones, rolled down the window, and threw them out into the street. He sat for a moment, thinking about which way to go and, more importantly, where to go. In his mind, Erik had only one place he could be safe—his Stonehenge Room. His sanctuary. *I can leave them all behind if I can just get there.* To the right, Concord Street headed straight back to where he had come from on US 52. *Can't go that way.* After pausing a moment longer, he turned left and hit the gas.

He went south on Concord until it ran into MN 55, which he took west until Interstate 35E heading north, back toward downtown St. Paul, but on the west side. From there, he continued on home, making it all the way to his apartment without seeing any police cars. He parked the truck, got out, and headed into his apartment.

Across the street, the spotter, still on stakeout, spoke into his headset to Dino. "Subject has returned, now entering his apartment."

Dino, Cathy, and Jack, having thought they had lost Erik, were on their way back to the office when Dino heard, "Subject has returned, now entering his apartment."

"Yes!" from Dino, "Back to being lucky." He asked the spotter, "Suspect arrived in a vehicle?"

"He did. A black Ford pickup."

"Alone?"

"Yes, alone."

"We're on our way. ETA eight minutes. Additional units on the way. Hold your position. Do not attempt to apprehend unless he tries to leave. Suspect is armed. Understood?"

"Understood."

Dino clicked off his microphone, then to Cathy and Jack, he said, "We've got him!"

Chapter 40

E rik parked the pickup and ran into the house. He quickly changed into dry clothes, then went straight to his Stonehenge Room. After the horror of Rayla's death, Erik had gotten a long black ceremonial robe with a hood, as well as a large ornate liturgical candle. Now, each time he entered the room, he first put on the robe, then solemnly raised the hood over his head. He then turned on the special lighting that illuminated the focal point of the room—his scale model of the stones of Stonehenge. Once seated at the table, he lit the candle as he always did for his Rayla, and carefully placed it next to the Slaughter Stone.

For several moments, Erik sat calming himself. He was safe now, knowing he had left them all behind. Closing his eyes, he drifted back . . . *4,500 years*. He was at the sacrificial ceremony, reliving the horror of hearing his beloved Rayla being called out for sacrifice. Pressure was building in his chest, and his face began to contort. He saw the supreme elder raise the ceremonial knife high above his head, then plunge it into her, over and over. Erik's entire body convulsed, and he cried out, "No!"

Dino, Jack, and Cathy arrived at Erik's duplex apartment, just after one a.m. Two squad cars were already on the scene. Dino immediately instructed the officers to surround the house and standby. A third car arrived, and Dino had them set up street barricades, one block out from the apartment in both directions. He then had them notify the adjacent neighbors, instructing them to stay in their homes until otherwise notified.

The spotter from the stakeout across the street joined them near their car, directly in front of Erik's apartment. "He was alone when he arrived, right?" reconfirmed Dino.

"Yes, sir."

"How about the other apartment in the house?" asked Dino.

"It's vacant. No one has gone in or out since I've been here. It's been completely dark the entire time. No vehicle outside."

"OK, good. Thanks."

Dino studied the house, then looked over to Jack and Cathy. "Situation assessment time, guys. First of all, I would really like to avoid any violence. We don't want any shots fired in this residential neighborhood, if at all possible. So, for now, no SWAT, no flashbangs, no tear gas. However, we have to make absolutely sure he doesn't get away again."

After a pause, Cathy asked, "So, what're you thinking?"

"Let's try calling him on his cell," Dino replied. He dialed the number and waited, but to no one's surprise, Erik did not answer. "Kinda figured that."

Dino asked, "You've had experience with situations like this Cathy, what do you think?"

"I'm afraid that situation was different. There were hostages, the guy was armed with a high-powered rifle and two handguns, and had a long history of violence. This guy seems to be a different kind of animal."

"You got that right," Jack agreed.

Dino said, "Erik is definitely an odd duck. He's been baffling from the start. He's psycho for sure, but I really don't think he's a cold-blooded serial killer. I'm convinced there's some strong reason driving him. And I suspect we might just find the reason in that house."

"I think you're right," said Jack, "but I don't think we should take any chances with him. He killed Jennifer Morris and probably killed Mikhail Andropov. And we know he was planning to kill Tammy tonight."

"True. But I would really like to take this guy alive," said

Dino. After a few moments, he continued, "I'd like to try going in and talking with him. But I can't justify risking your lives, or anybody else's. I'll go in alone."

"I don't think that's a good idea," said Cathy. "He's already shot you once today. Isn't that enough?"

"I don't think he was really after me. I just startled him. You make a good point, but I'd like to try."

"Well, we can't let you go in alone. Besides, he's my man too," said Jack. "I'll go with you."

Cathy chimed in, "Hate to miss the party. I'm in."

Dino instructed the spotter and squads about the plan to go in. "Heaven forbid, if this goes all wrong, do not let him get away. Shoot if you have to. We've got more than enough justification for that. Clear?"

"Understood," from all of them.

They each tested their communications gear, checked their protective vests, tested their flashlights, and then started toward the house.

Dino led them to the side door, which appeared to be the entrance most used. The top half of the door had clear glass panes. There was enough outside light to see it was a doorway into the kitchen, but there were no lights visible inside. Dino tried the door, and it was unlocked. He pushed the door open, stepped inside, and called out, "Erik? Erik Foster? This is Detective Roselli. I'd like to talk with you." There was no response. Dino flipped on his flashlight and stepped in further. Jack and Cathy followed. Dino moved to the center of the room, then pointed Jack to the left, Cathy to the right. They each moved up and cleared the rooms on either side. No one.

Dino led them further into the house, into a hallway that went to the left, toward the rear of the house. At the end of the hallway, Dino saw a door, with light shining out underneath it. He shut off his flashlight and moved toward the door. Jack and Cathy were right behind him. Dino stopped about three feet short of the door and then moved to his left, placing his back against the wall. He motioned for Jack and Cathy to do the same.

Again, he called out, "Erik? Are you in there?" No response. "We'd like to talk with you, Erik." Nothing.

Dino moved back to the center of the hallway and stood for a moment, considering his options. Stepping up to the door, he reached down with his left hand and tried the handle—it turned. He paused for a moment and took a deep breath. With his right hand, he pulled out his gun. With his left, he turned the handle all the way, and slowly pushed the door open.

Chapter 41

All three of them looked straight across the room, where Erik was seated on the far side of a large table facing them. He was motionless, eyes closed, and appeared to be asleep or in a trance. His arms were crossed in front of him, clutching a large leather book tightly to his chest. He did not react in any way.

As they entered the room, they looked about in amazement. The windows were all covered. The only light in the room was shining from the ceiling onto the table, focused on a large model of Stonehenge. There was a large white candle burning, sitting to one side of the model. The room was filled with Stonehenge-related artifacts, including pictures and posters on every wall. Erik himself was wearing an ancient-looking robe, with a large hood pulled over his head.

As his eyes adjusted to the darkness, Dino noticed a handgun lying within an arm's reach of Erik. He was about to reach for the gun when Erik's face started to contort. His body began to tremble. His mouth opened and he cried out, "No!"

His head dropped forward, face down on the table. After a moment, he seemed to wake up. Raising his head, he opened his eyes and looked at Dino.

"They killed her! They took her, stabbed her, and killed her. I had to avenge her! I had to do it! And I did. I kept my promise. Now all that's left is for me to join her."

Dino saw Erik's eyes turn toward the gun on the table. As

Erik uncrossed his arms and reached out, Dino realized he was not close enough to get to the gun first, so he grabbed the edge of the table and jerked it up. The gun slid off and onto the floor, along with the entire Stonehenge model and the burning candle.

"No, please let me go to her! Let me finish it." Erik implored. He was about to scramble down onto the floor for the gun when Dino lifted his own gun.

"Stay where you are, Erik!"

While Dino held his gun on Erik, Jack dove around the table and grabbed the gun from the rubble on the floor. The burning candle had rolled to the wall directly behind Erik, where one of the long, heavy cloth drapes covering the windows and walls had caught fire. Cathy had moved to the back side of the table to put cuffs on Erik, but the flames were climbing the wall. The remnants of the Stonehenge model had also caught fire. Smoke and fumes were now filling the room. Dino moved quickly to the drapes hanging to Erik's right and tried to pull them down, but they were anchored securely to the ceiling.

"Everybody out!" shouted Dino.

Cathy and Jack each grabbed an arm and started pulling Erik out of the room. As they did, Erik dropped the large leather book. "No! My book!" But Cathy and Jack kept pulling and managed to drag him out into the hallway.

Smoke and flames now filled the entire room. Dino gave up trying to stop the growing fire. As he turned to leave, he saw Erik's book lying in front of him on the floor. He picked it up, and ran out the door, yelling to Cathy and Jack, "Cuff him and take him outside. Tell the squads to get the fire department here ASAP."

As they moved to put the cuffs on, Erik threw his arms in the air, breaking free, and dove back into the room, slamming the door shut and locking it. He then shoved a large wooden chair against the inside of the door, wedging the back of it under the doorknob. Dino and Jack tried to push the door open with their shoulders—it would not budge. They looked around for something to ram the door. Seeing a wooden coat rack at the end of the hallway, they grabbed it and, using it as a battering ram, smashed it against the door, but with no effect. Smoke was now streaming from under the door.

"Come out of there, Erik!" yelled Dino.

There was no response for several seconds. Then they heard Erik shriek, "I'm coming Rayla!" Moments later there was a terrifying scream and the *thump* of a body hitting the floor, then silence.

"Let's get out of here!" Dino screamed at Jack and Cathy. They ran from the house and stopped at one of the squad cars. They looked back to see flames spreading quickly throughout the old wooden house. The officer had already called the fire department, and the trucks were just arriving. The firemen quickly applied water to the blaze, but it was too late to save the house—or Erik.

As they stood and looked on, Dino said, "Tragic. This whole thing. Just tragic."

Dino instructed the other officers to notify the neighbors the situation had been cleared.

He then called Paula with the news. She was pleased it was all over but was disappointed there would be no chance to interrogate Erik. Still, she congratulated Dino.

"Good job Dino!"

"I had Jack and Cathy's help the whole way. That, and a little luck."

"That always helps!"

"And ah . . . you'll call the mayor?"

"Sure Dino, no problem."

"Thanks."

Back at the office, Dino sat at his desk with a cup of coffee and Erik's leather book. He started reading it. After just a few minutes, he realized, *It's a journal.* Erik had been recording everything. He had logged his 'trips' back to Stonehenge and all that he 'did' there. It was obvious that, at least for Erik, it was all very real. Dino paged forward and read about the sacrificial ceremony. Then it hit him. *Good Lord, it was all for love.*

As he laid the journal down on his desk, Jack stopped by. "It's a pity we didn't get a chance to interrogate Erik."

"For sure," replied Dino. "I had a list of questions I wanted to ask him, but maybe most of them are answered by this." He picked up the journal and handed it to Jack. "It was all for love."

"What?"

"Read it yourself. It's incredible."

Jack sat down and started reading. After a few pages he muttered, "Oh my ..." Then after a few more pages he mused, "Who would have ever guessed?"

As Jack continued to read, Dino continued his own internal reflection on what he had read. *Here's a guy that, to the outside world, appeared to be a classic geek, avoiding any and all contact with women. Yet inside, he's profoundly in love with a woman who, at least to him, was real.* Dino could not help but draw parallels between himself and Erik. *Erik was running to love, and here I am, running from love.* Then half out loud, "Good Lord. Maybe I'm the crazy one here."

Jack looked up from his reading. "What did you say?"

"Oh nothing," replied Dino. "Just thinking out loud."

Chapter 42

It was nearly four a.m. by the time Dino made it home and into bed. Upon hearing the news of breaking the case, Mayor Bennett called a press conference for nine. Dino was sure the mayor would make it a real media event.

Dino rolled out of bed at seven fifteen and hit the shower, trying to wake up after a very short night. Knowing there would be full TV coverage, he dressed in a dark blue suit with a subtle gray pattern, a crisp white shirt, and a light-blue striped tie. He skipped breakfast and headed out in the Alfa.

He had arranged to pick up Jack outside the Hilton at eight fifteen. Jack was ready and waiting at the front door, with all his bags packed. "Good morning, Jack. You checked out?"

"Good morning. I am! I was able to get a flight home at seven o'clock tonight, which should work just great."

They threw his bags in the back of the Alfa and headed for the station.

"I can take you to the airport whenever you want, so just leave your bags in the car."

"Thanks Dino. I must say, you've been the best of hosts."

"My pleasure." After a few moments, Dino added, "This press conference with the mayor could end up being a media show."

"Actually, the show has already started for me. Remember, it's mid-day in England, and as soon as news of our solving the case hit, my phone lit up. I finally had to turn it off to catch at least a couple of hours of sleep."

"Better get used to it guy."

"I suppose you're right. Still, it's a great relief to be heading home with a complete resolution of the case. Makes life much simpler. On the other hand, I'll probably be filling out reports and paperwork until the day I retire."

"Oh geez, don't remind me."

Dino parked the Alfa, and they started toward the office. From the other side of the lot came a shout, "Congrats Dino! You too Jack."

"Thanks," they both said in return.

They made it just another thirty feet when they heard, "Great job big guy!"

"Thanks John," returned Dino. He then mused, "It's going to be a long day, Jack."

"Probably true, but we could have worse problems."

They went in the front door, and as they walked by the plaques on the Wall of Honor, Dino heard a familiar voice in his head. "Good job, son."

Dino smiled and replied mentally, "*Ah, so there you are. Nice to have you back.*"

"Oh, I've been here all along. We'll talk more later."

"I'd like that," said Dino aloud.

"Pardon me?" asked Jack, a bit puzzled.

"Oh nothing, just thinking about an old friend of mine."

Paula caught them just as they arrived at Dino's desk. "Good morning! Are you ready for the nine o'clock circus?"

"Will there be clowns and jugglers?" asked Dino cynically.

"Hey, remember you have to play nice Dino!"

"Fine."

"We should actually head to the Briefing Room in just a couple of minutes. The mayor wants to meet with both of you beforehand."

"Will do."

The press conference came off pretty much as everyone had expected. The mayor was gushing with praise for Dino, Jack, the

Police Department, and perhaps most of all, himself. He pointed to the successful resolution of the case as definitive proof of his anti-crime programs taking effect. Under the watchful eyes of Paula, Dino displayed a respectful demeanor throughout.

After his introductory comments, the mayor introduced Dino and then Jack.

Dino told the press, "I want to thank the large number of people who helped out and supported our work on this case, including Paula Dunn, Head of the Homicide Unit, Chief Kingston, Suzette Hawkins in Homicide, and of course, Mayor Bennett. I would especially like to thank Cathy Jackson of the South St. Paul Police Department, who played a key role in the apprehension of the suspect, as well as her colleagues, for the support they provided, and also Mark Nelson from the Bureau of Criminal Apprehension. And finally, I would like to thank Detective Superintendent Jack Wright of the British police, and all of his support personnel back in the UK."

Jack then took a turn, thanking Dino and the St. Paul Police for their support and for their kind hospitality.

The mayor concluded the press conference by pointing to the success of the joint US and UK cooperative efforts, for which, somehow, he was at least partially responsible and due credit.

After the press conference, Dino and Jack did several individual interviews for local TV stations and newspapers, as well as for national media, and even international media for the UK. It was nearly noon by the time they finished.

They then spent a couple of hours completing some of the obligatory reports and documents of the case. Just after three thirty, Dino went to Paula to tell her he needed to take Jack to the airport.

"No problem, Dino. I'll come say my goodbyes." They walked to the conference room and found Jack packing up.

"It was great working with you, Jack. Definitely one of the most interesting cases I've ever worked on."

"Myself as well, Paula. Thank you for all the support and especially for your kind hospitality. It was fun. It always is when you end up catching the bad guy."

"Agreed."

As Paula was about to leave, Dino asked her, "Ah, any chance of taking tomorrow off?"

"Sounds like a good idea to me. We can cover for you. And get some sleep!"

"Thanks!"

On the way to the airport, Jack repeated, "It's been great working with you Dino."

"Agreed buddy."

"I have something to confess."

"What's that?"

"I would not have had the courage to open the door to Erik's room on blind faith like you did. You're a brave man, my friend."

"Or maybe a stupid one?"

"Well, perhaps you're just better at reading people than I am."

"I know that's not true."

"Well, still."

After pausing a moment, Jack added, "You have to come to England. I'm sure you'd love it. We could tour Stonehenge."

"Sounds like fun. Don't be surprised if you hear from me some day."

"I'll look forward to it."

Dino dropped Jack off on the departures level and helped him with his bags.

"Say goodbye to Momma for me."

"I will. And don't forget that dinner you promised your wife."

"Oh, she'd never allow that to happen." Then finally he said, "See ya mate."

They shook hands, and Jack was gone.

On the drive home, Dino's thoughts turned to Johnny Jump Up and his offer. He owed him a response. After pulling into the garage, he sat thinking for several moments, then picked up his phone and called Johnny.

"Hey Dino, good timing! I just hung up the phone with my

client. He's getting pressure from his higher-ups and has moved the deadline up two days. I have to give him an answer by day after tomorrow."

"OK."

"So what's it going to be, Dino?"

"Still thinking it over, Johnny. I've been consumed by the Stonehenge case, but we're wrapping it up now. I will have an answer for you day after tomorrow."

"OK, but no later! This guy is one of my biggest clients."

"I understand."

Dino hung up, and thought, for the umpteenth time, *What should I do?*

After several moments of contemplation, his mind drifted to how good it was going to be to have a day off. He needed to drive. *It'll give me a chance to think.* Then he had an idea. He picked up his phone and called Amy.

"Hi Dino. You're a celebrity! I saw you on the Channel 7 news."

"Oh, boy."

"No, it was great! The mayor couldn't stop saying what a great job you did."

"Ah, sure. He actually offered to buy me a cape, but I told him I would feel just silly in tights."

"Stop it, funny boy," she scolded him. "And you were shot! Are you OK?"

"Oh yes. A bit bruised but just fine."

"I was worried about you, Dino."

"No really, I'm fine. And I can prove it. What would you think about taking off tomorrow afternoon and going for a drive in the Ferrari?"

"I'd love it."

"Think you can get off?"

"Sure, no problem. Gee, thanks for inviting me, Dino."

"It'll be fun. It's supposed to be a sunny day. Pick you up at one?"

"I'll be ready!"

Chapter 43

Dino tried catching up on sleep in the morning, but after a couple of extra hours, he was eager to get up and going for the day. He went to the garage and prepped the Ferrari—checked the fluids and tire pressures, then gave it a quick wipe down. *All set.*

Back inside, he showered, dressed, and was out the door by eleven. He had an important errand to run before picking up Amy. It was time to visit Dad at the cemetery and have an overdue chat.

He parked the car along one of the winding lanes of Our Lady of Hope Cemetery and started walking toward his dad's plot. The weather was just as predicted—nearly perfect. Warm sunshine, totally blue sky. He spoke aloud as he approached the gravesite.

"Hey Dad, you there?"

"I am Dino."

"It was nice to hear from you yesterday."

"You're welcome."

"It had been a while."

"I know."

"So . . . I've been struggling with a decision."

"I know that too."

"This new opportunity . . . it's certainly appealing—more money, better hours, no more time spent filling out endless reports, some interesting new work. But I can't get past my pledge to you that I would be a cop and follow in your footsteps."

"Dino, you've become a fine cop and made me very proud. However, that promise was made not so much to me, but to yourself. It's all-important to be true to yourself."

"So, how do I do that, Dad? How did *you* do that?"

"I'll tell you straight up. It wasn't so much being a cop as it was doing what made me happy. You should do the same. Do what makes you happy. The hard part is to know what that really is. What makes you happy, son?"

"I'm not sure. How do I figure that out?"

"You have a heart. It's good for more than pumping blood. Use it, listen to it! You'll be fine."

"OK." Then after a few moments. "Thanks Dad."

Dino turned and walked back to the car. A new feeling of calm and confidence was coming over him. He was still not sure what he would end up doing, but he was sure it would all work out for the best. He could finally move forward.

As he continued walking away, Dino said over his shoulder, "By the way, Dad, the Ferrari's running great!"

He gassed up on the way to Amy's and was there at one o'clock sharp. He got out of the car and walked to greet her as she came down the front walkway.

"Hello!" he called out.

"Hi! I'm all excited to go for our drive."

"You look great."

"Thanks."

"Let's do it."

Dino opened the passenger-side door for Amy, but before she got in, she noticed the cabin space was fairly tight. "Is there someplace I can put my bag?"

"Sure, plenty of room in the boot."

"Boot?"

"Ah, trunk! Keep whatever you need with you, and I'll store the bag itself in the . . . trunk."

"Thanks."

"Here, let me help you get in," Dino offered.

"It's smaller than I imagined."

"No worries. Once you make it in, it's very comfortable."

She ended up turning around and simply plopping her butt backwards down into the seat. "Made it."

"Just swing your legs in and you're good to go."

"OK, I'm in!"

Dino got in, fired up the engine, and they took off. He headed south down the west side of the Mississippi toward Lake Pepin, his favorite route. They chatted as he drove along.

"It's sort of bumpy?" she noted.

"Yup. The suspension is stiff to make it corner better."

"I see." After a few more miles, she asked, "Does it have a radio or sound system?"

"Heavens no. It has something much better. It actually makes its own music."

"Really?"

"Absolutely. It's truly a musical instrument all on its own. It makes lots of different sounds, and you control them as you drive: the engine sings, the transmission whines, the exhaust notes resonate, the tires howl, and the brakes squeal. And the fun part is that the sounds all change as you go up or down a hill, go around a corner, accelerate, brake, or change gears. Put them altogether, and you literally play it like a musical instrument. You make music! Fabulous music."

Dino downshifted for a car up ahead, then accelerated and passed it easily. "See what I mean?"

He continued, "So then each road, with its own twists and turns, becomes its own song, with its own melody. Great roads equal great music! Put several of them together, and a day of good driving becomes a concert! So, you see, no need for a radio."

"My goodness, I had no idea."

"And for sure, I do my best thinking when I'm out driving. Many of life's problems can be worked out and solved when driving."

They drove in silence, listening to the car, eventually getting to the Lake Pepin shoreline. Amy said, "Oh, it's so pretty. All the sailboats make it very picturesque. I have to admit that I've never been here before."

"That's not surprising. The Twin Cities metro area has a population of nearly four million people, but I bet seventy-five percent of them have never seen Lake Pepin or even know it's here."

After a few more minutes of driving, Amy said, "You certainly make a drive interesting. People must love it when you give them a ride."

Dino paused, then looked over at Amy and said, "I've never given anyone else a ride in my Ferrari."

"Oh," she said, blushing, "my goodness."

They continued south to Wabasha, where they crossed over the Mississippi and headed north along US 35. As they neared the town of Pepin, Dino said, "There's a pretty good winery just ahead. Would you like to stop for a glass of wine?"

"Sure!"

Dino pulled into Chateau La Fleur Pepin and parked. They walked to the tasting bar and ordered a glass of one of the house wines made from the Marquette grape. They each took a couple of sips, then Dino explained, "The grape used in this wine is a hybrid developed by the University of Minnesota. It was developed from several grape varietals, including the rather delicate Pinot Noir, but can survive our brutal winters."

"It's very good."

They sat at a high-top table, enjoying the wine. Dino noticed that Amy had become a bit quiet. He asked her, "Is anything wrong?"

"Oh no, this is all very lovely."

Dino was not convinced. He asked again, "Are you sure there isn't something wrong?"

Amy said nothing for several moments, but then said, "Actually, there is something I need to talk with you about."

"Go ahead. Shoot."

"Funny you would say that. That's part of the issue."

"I don't understand."

"Well, this is all so lovely—the ride in the Ferrari, the great dinners and wine, our runs together. I really enjoy being with you."

"I enjoy our time together, too."

Amy paused again, but then continued, "Yesterday, when I heard on the news that you had been shot, I couldn't help but think back to the day my husband was killed in a car accident. That has a horrible day for me, and . . ."

"Yes?"

"I don't ever want to repeat it."

Dino was stunned by Amy's confession, and the sincerity with which she expressed it. He tried to recover by saying, "That's certainly understandable, but as you can see, I'm just fine. It was a fluke, really. I've never been shot before. Can't imagine it would ever happen again." As the words left his mouth, he thought back to just a few days before, when he and George had been shot at, near the scene of the Campbell murder. A bullet had whistled right by his left ear. He instantly dismissed the thought.

"But it could happen," said Amy. "Just like it happened to your dad."

"Touché." Dino knew his pain from that day very well. It had defined his life ever since.

Amy added, "I love our time together, but this scares me."

Dino quietly replied, "I can't deny there's a risk, but everyone takes a chance each day they step out into the world. Your husband's death was certainly tragic, but he wasn't a cop, just a regular citizen. So, sure, it can happen, but we all still have to go on living our lives." After pausing for a moment, he continued, "I really like you Amy, and I would very much like to continue seeing you. How about I promise to be safe?"

"Don't make light of it!"

"I don't mean to. Frankly, you've given me a reason to think more about my own safety. I hope we can work this out. Are you willing to try?"

Amy thought for a few moments, then replied, "I'd like to continue seeing you too. So, yes, I'm willing to try."

"Thank you, Amy."

They finished their wine, and since Dino was driving, they limited themselves to one glass and got back on the road.

They continued north along the Wisconsin side of the river, listening to the sounds of the Ferrari. Dino was thinking about Amy's comments. She was clearly serious about her fears. *One more reason to say yes to Johnny's offer.* Regardless, Dino realized that for the first time in his life, he thought, and more importantly felt, that he was willing to take a chance with a woman. If ever there was a woman worth taking a chance on, it was Amy.

As they neared St. Paul, Dino asked, "Got any plans for dinner?"

"Not really. I wasn't sure how long our trip would be."

"Like Italian?"

"You know I love it."

"Great!" He then added, "In that case, I've got someone I'd like you to meet."

Chapter 44

Dino pulled the Ferrari up to the front door of Roselli's and parked. Larry, the long-time evening valet, stepped out to greet them.

"The Ferrari looks as pretty as ever," he said to Dino as he got out of the car. "And my goodness, a passenger this evening." He opened the door to help Amy out.

"Yes indeed. Larry, this is Amy. Amy, meet Larry."

"Welcome to Roselli's, Amy!"

"Thank you."

"OK to leave the Ferrari where it is?" asked Dino.

"Of course. I'll keep an eye on it," Larry said. "Step right in. I'm sure Momma will be thrilled to see you both."

"Thanks Larry."

Dino and Amy headed in the front door and were greeted immediately by Momma from behind the reception stand.

"Dino! Nice to see you, my boy. And who is this?"

"Momma, this is Amy. Amy, this is my mom, Sophia. Everyone calls her Momma."

"It's a pleasure to meet you, Amy. Welcome to Roselli's!"

"Thank you."

"We were out on a drive this afternoon, and we're hungry!"

"Well, I'm sure we can fix you something you'll enjoy." Looking out over the dining room, she said, "Looks like your favorite spot is open."

"Thanks Momma."

She seated them, then motioned for Dino's favorite waitress, Stacy, to come over to their table. Momma left them with a pleasant, "Buon appetito."

Stacy came to their table wearing a big smile. "Hey Dino, you're a celebrity nowadays!"

"Hardly. How've you been?"

"Busy, but that's a good thing. Can I get you some wine?"

Dino ordered a bottle of Barbera, then went over the menu with Amy. They both decided on pasta dishes with side salads.

Stacy returned with the wine, opened it, and poured some in each glass. They were just taking their first sip when Dino's phone vibrated in his pocket. He checked it and saw that it was Johnny. Dino apologized to Amy, explaining, "I'm sorry, but I really need to respond to this text. Please enjoy the wine. I'll be right back."

"No problem."

"We're down to the wire, buddy. I've got to have your decision."

"I know. How about noon tomorrow? Your office?"

"That works. See you then."

Dino put away his phone, returned to the table, and apologized again to Amy. "Sorry, an old friend of mine."

"Male or female?" she said with a grin.

"Oh, definitely a male. His name is Johnny Jump Up."

"Jump Up? That's his name?"

"It is. We've been friends since grade school. His real name is John Johansen, but everybody calls him Johnny Jump Up. Long story, I'm afraid."

"Everything OK?"

"Actually, he's offered me a job."

"Really? What sort of job?"

"Johnny owns a private security company in town called Johansen Security. He wants me to head up a new division for investigations. He's offered to make me a full partner."

"Wow! That sounds pretty cool." After a pause, she added,

"And safe!" She then asked, "Are you going to take it?"

"Honestly, I haven't decided yet. I'm tempted, though. It's lots more money, better hours, no crappy gang murders, and no more boring reports. And yes, safe. But I'm just not sure about leaving the force, and all the great people I have worked with, including Jack on this last case. I'm sure I would miss them, and the camaraderie." He looked at Amy seriously and asked, "What do you think I should do?"

"I'm not sure I'm qualified to hand out professional career advice. I guess, do what makes you happy."

"You sound like my dad."

"Umm, isn't your dad . . ."

"Dead? Yes, he died twenty years ago, but we still chat from time to time."

Not sure how to respond, she offered, "You're certainly an intriguing guy Roselli, that's for sure."

"Intriguing?"

"OK, let's go with unique!"

"You're too kind." Wanting to change the topic, he asked, "More Barbera?"

They finished their meals with espresso and lemon cannoli. As they got up to leave, Amy said, "This is certainly a fabulous restaurant your family has here. And your mom is very sweet."

"Thanks."

On their way out, they said their goodbyes to Momma. As they turned to go out the door, Dino looked back at his mom, who nodded her approval to him, and then broke into a grin.

Emerging from the restaurant, they came out to a warm, pleasant summer evening. They got into the Ferrari. Dino drove straight to Amy's house. He helped her out of the car and walked her to the front door.

"Thanks for a wonderful day, Dino. The drive, the dinner, all of it."

"My pleasure, for sure."

They shared a goodnight kiss, and Dino walked back to the Ferrari, entirely pleased with himself. As he drove home, he admitted, *I really like her.*

Now, if I can just decide on this Johnny Jump Up business, I'll actually have my life in order.

Once home, he went inside and straight to bed. He lay awake for more than an hour, going back and forth over what to tell Johnny.

What to do?

Chapter 45

Dino tossed and turned through the night, finally deciding to just get up and go into the office. Once there, he got busy trying to catch up after his day off, but the big decision, or lack thereof, loomed over everything.

Mid-morning, Paula stopped at his desk, needing to clarify a point about the case. Before leaving, she asked, "You OK, Dino?"

"Sure, why do you ask?"

"You seem preoccupied. Anything you want to talk about?"

"No, I'm good. Really."

"OK." She seemed suspicious that something was wrong but gave up and returned to her office.

At twenty minutes to twelve, Dino posted an "Out to Lunch" status and headed out. It took him less than ten minutes to get to Johnny's office. He parked and sat quietly for a few moments, collecting his thoughts. His heart was racing.

"Dad?"

"Yes Dino?"

"What do I do?" he asked.

"I told you. Do what makes you happy. Listen to your heart. You'll be fine."

"OK Dad. OK."

Time to go. He got out of the car and walked to the office entrance. "Hello, I'm Dino Roselli," he said to the receptionist. "I'm here to meet with Johnny."

"Yes, he's waiting for you Dino. Follow me please." She guided him to Johnny's office and opened the door.

"Hello, Dino!"

"Hey, Johnny."

"Well buddy, nothing like waiting till the last minute. So, what's your decision?"

"First, a few questions?"

"Sure."

Dino asked several questions—confirming salary, profit splits, and a few admin details.

"You know, we can really capitalize on all the publicity of the Stonehenge case," Johnny stated excitedly. "It's all over the local and national news, and it's all worth money." Johnny was a bit surprised by the lack of a reaction from Dino, but he continued. "So what's it going to be, Dino? I've got the paperwork right here. Sign it, and we're in business. Literally!"

Dino was silent for several moments. He thought about Amy. He thought about Adam Baker and his widowed wife. He thought about the department, and the pledge to his dad—and himself. His heart was pounding. Finally, he looked Johnny in the eyes, and in that moment, he knew.

"It's no use Johnny. I appreciate the offer, I really do. But I'm a cop and always will be."

Dino stood up, turned, and walked out the door.

About The Authors

Herb and LindaSue are fiction writers in Saint Paul, Minnesota, USA. Both are members of the Mystery Writers of America.

They have worked together for over twenty years, and their differences are what make them a good team.

Herb is a "plotter" who loves math and computer science, with everything logical and well-organized. LindaSue is a creative "pantser" who loves spontaneity, non-conformity, and a little bit of chaos.

They both love travel, great food, and fine wine.

They can be contacted at: hemenwayandjohnsonbooks.com

One Last Thing . . .

We hope you enjoyed our debut novel. If so, please leave a review on Amazon and/or Goodreads. It would help us greatly.

Thank you!

Made in United States
Orlando, FL
19 August 2023

36249666R00148